I0593593

HOW THE ANGEL GOT HIS WINGS

ALFREDO

A French Mission

ROSEMARY GARREFFA

A Pocket Full Press

First published in Australia in 2023
By A Pocket Full Press
51949 Sturt Highway Euston NSW 2737
ABN: 56 815 473 484
www.apocketfullpress.com.au

Copyright © Rosemary Garreffa 2023
The right of Rosemary Garreffa to be identified as the author of this work
has been asserted by her in accordance with the Copyright Amendment
(Moral Rights) Act 2000.

This work is copyright. Apart from any use as permitted under the
Copyright Act 1968, no part may be reproduced, copied, scanned, stored
in a retrieval system, recorded, or transmitted, in any form or by any means,
without the prior written permission of the publisher.

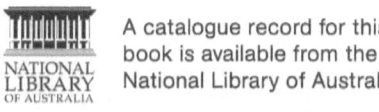 A catalogue record for this
book is available from the
National Library of Australia
www.librariesaustralia.nla.gov.au

ISBN 978 0 6456883 0 6 (paperback)
ISBN 978 0 6456883 1 3 (ebook)

Cover design by Chris Nardo
Printed and bound in Australia by Ingram Spark

Dedicated to

My husband, John – the journey is real.

CHAPTER 1

Alfredo raced down the lush green slope; his golden leaf laurel jammed tight on his head with one hand. Pausing for a moment, he scanned the mass of people below, looking for one particular red headed angel, Gerhard. There. A hand waving above the sea of heads. Alfredo waved back.
He ducked and wove through the crowd, hoping his friends had saved him a place in the best vantage spot in the arena. He wanted a premium view of his hero Gabriel, the Archangel.

Alfredo thought the unusually bright luminosity of the heavens suited the day's importance perfectly. Graduation Day. The shimmer on the clouds and sunlight reflecting on a million diamantes on all the angels' tunics gave off an energy of its own. The Field of Dreams, as the villagers knew it, stretched in a gentle falling slope to the east of the University of Angels. Three hundred angels filled it today, and Alfredo found his place in the centre of this crowd. On the rim of the field, spectator angels gathered, adding even more theatre to the event. Before, Alfredo had been one of them. But today was different and Alfredo felt more alive than ever.
His time had come.

No more poring over books and theorising for him and his fellow angels.

Like everyone around him, he was nervous. Beads of sweat rose on his upper lip, and his armpits smelt of sweet almonds. He lifted his arms a fraction to keep the tunic from absorbing any moisture and adjusted his laurel to an angle that gave some, but not enough, respite from the glare for his baby blue eyes. He strained to hear the surrounding conversations. The whispered questions abounded. Inspirational orchestral melodies filled the air. No less a spectacle would have been expected today.

They awaited Gabriel's arrival. The Archangel was charged with bringing the assignments to today's graduates directly from the Father. To have an assignment meant being present in the earthly realm, something Alfredo relished. Down there, he could finally prove himself and show he was worth more than his teacher's low expectations.

Alfredo recalled the day Yaseem, his teacher, presented the graduate list to his class. As the names were read and the scroll in his teacher's hands tumbled in a pile on the floor, he'd grown increasingly uncomfortable. He'd bent forward, eyes tracing the veins in the marble floor at his feet, listening to the names rattle over and around him. Here and there his fellow students gasped and cheered as Yaseem called their names, and Alfredo wished he might shrink into the ether rather than be the only one not named on the list. The roof of his mouth had dried, and any attempt to swallow proved painful. His mind had closed off. Disappointed, he was already preparing for another year of study when Yaseem hollered the last name. "... and Alfredo."

Hearing his name brought his head up with a jerk. The weight of failure dissipated, and his heart skipped a beat. He lifted his eyes to meet his teacher's, receiving an encouraging smile.

Yaseem had spent the last term rolling his eyes at him and shaking his head. His voice echoed still. "Alfredo, Alfredo, Alfredo, what shall we do with you?"

Alfredo held little store for reading; he preferred to 'do' . And that was his failing, according to his teacher.

"Alfredo, don't rush; there's no point. You'll make a mess of things. Stand still and observe, do your research and then apply your – talent," Yaseem had boomed time and time again.

Well, no more. Yaseem might be happy to see him move on, but Alfredo was even more delighted to go. He suspected Yaseem considered him a once-in-a-generation anomaly that no amount of guidance could correct. It made him grin on the outside; he didn't mind the point of difference, but inwardly, it raised a million what-ifs. He desperately wanted to be a useful angel. Useful angels were rewarded with wings, and it was those wings that spurred him to stay at the university.

Rolling thunder, at first only a distant thrum, became a crescendo of rattling booms. It drowned the orchestra and brought the crowd to a standstill. Every crack sent vibrations up through his feet. Each wave tightened the nerves in his body. An absurd thought occurred to him. They were taut enough to be plucked like the strings of a guitar. He smiled. This was the best day of his existence yet.

The brilliance of the heavens increased, causing Alfredo to close his eyes. He dropped his head and let the heat of the light fall upon him. It wasn't unpleasant, as the light charged him with energy, but there was so much of it he was unsure how long he could bear it. He could only wait for what must come next. When he thought he would surely drop to his knees, the heat diminished to a comfortable glow and the thunderous noise stopped. In its wake came the ringing of silence. Alfredo sighed with relief, opened his eyes, and looked up at the sky as all his companions had done.

A golden chariot behind six magnificent white horses stood on the rise before the crowd. An army of large-winged angels surrounded it. The Archangel Gabriel stood tall on the chariot; in front of him, two smaller angels held a wide scroll between them. When Alfredo saw these two, he hoped his assignment would be something like that. He'd love to hold that scroll and to travel the heavens with, of all angels, the mighty Gabriel. One of the twin angels looked at him, grinned, and shook his head. Immediately, Alfredo's throat closed over and his ears burnt with a flush of heat, engulfing him with embarrassment. How dare he, a minor angel, have such lofty thoughts. There was no time for further reflection.

"My dear charges," Gabriel said in a voice that at once commanded attention, his arms outstretched to the crowd, "your Father sends his warmest greetings to you all. Hear now what he has assigned to each of you. Go forth with the love of his Spirit. Take your place with his children on Earth and bring each one of them home."

Gabriel raised his arms first and then his majestic wings. With one swift flap, he sent out a wave of Grace over the crowd. Every angel collapsed to their knees as this energy reached them, and a scroll appeared in their hands. Alfredo gripped his tightly to his pounding chest.

This was the moment he had been waiting for.

The orchestra played again. In unison, Alfredo and the other angels sang the words of praise with such gusto it caused the clouds above them to shimmer and dissolve into shards of suspended water crystals. The song pitch rose an octave, and the crystals exploded into a million fine droplets in every rainbow colour and floated over them in a perfect storm of heavenly confetti. It settled in Alfredo's hair, on his eyelashes and over his garments. It was as if the Father had bestowed the finest of blessings on them. His heart might burst at the majesty of the moment.

The spell broke as the music ended, replaced with excited chatter and the rustle of scrolls as each graduate tore the seals and shared the details of their earthly assignments.

Gerhard grasped Alfredo's arm and drew in a deep breath. "Oh, I'm going to Switzerland! Look at that little face. His mother is smitten already, and he is only a few hours old." He thrust before Alfredo a vision of a mother and child looking deep into each other's eyes.

Alfredo sensed Gerhard's excitement was more to do with Switzerland than with the child in the vision, but he didn't say as much as he hadn't opened his scroll yet. It made him wonder where on the earth he would be sent. The nagging fear of the unknown returned.

"Gerhard, I'm pleased for you. I wish you the most success, and I hope he has a long and happy life."

Anxious to find a quiet place to open his scroll, Alfredo was about to turn away when Gerhard spoke again.

"The mother's angel has sent a message of greeting already."

Alfredo smiled benignly, wondering how to break away from Gerhard, one of those angels who, once he had your attention, didn't want to relinquish it. In class, Gerhard was the angel who always teased out a point to its nth degree, and that wasn't what Alfredo wanted to experience today. Today was about excitement and adventure.

"And you, Alfredo, have you not opened your scroll yet? Where are you commissioned to?" Gerhard pointed to Alfredo's scroll with the seal intact.

The last thing Alfredo wanted was to have his assignment revealed to someone else. He wanted time to savour the excitement of it and to absorb the feeling of this new beginning by himself.

"No, there is time, I'm sure. I want to wait till I leave here so I can read it. You know how I am."

He tried to sound nonchalant but failed. Gerhard knew he had trouble with scrolls. Everyone did. Reading them didn't come naturally to him, but he'd work out how to decipher the messages in good time.

Gerhard straightened his back and held out a hand to Alfredo. "Good luck, my friend. God speed. And I'm certain I will see you in the village often. We can discuss our charges at length then."

"God speed to you, too." Alfredo shook his hand vigorously, happy that the exchange was ending without him having to be abrupt. Gerhard gave him a brief hug and, in an instant, was gone to his charge.

Alfredo looked about the almost empty field, searching for a secluded place to sit and unravel his scroll in private. Others, he noticed, had done the same. Maybe he was not so different after all.

Without the pressure of Gerhard, his anxiety lessened, and he turned his attention to his scroll. He could take it back to the village and open it, but then he might run into others and face more questions.

He found a tuft of grass and sat with the scroll on his knees. The excitement returned. This was his future. There could be no further delaying the suspense. He took a huge breath, broke the seal and unrolled it. What he saw made him gasp with disappointment. The scroll was blank. His heart sank.

How was this possible? In haste, he rolled the scroll up and looked around, fearful someone close may have seen the blank page. Had Yaseem not said he passed? There must be an error. He knew he'd heard correctly. He unrolled it again and looked for the tiniest mark. He turned it over and searched the reverse side. Nothing. The whole scroll was blank, without even a faint blotch on it. Frustrated, he ran his hands through his hair, knocking his laurel askew. Gerhard's scroll hadn't been blank. Everything should be visible on this scroll, too. In hindsight, had he broken the seal in front of Gerhard, they might have nutted the issue out together. Alfredo sighed and rose.

Gerhard was gone, as were most of the other angels from his class. They were the lucky ones. Alfredo sifted through a list of angels he knew would help him without making him feel like a failure. The problem, he soon realised, lay in the very nature of his predicament. A serving angel, one trained to be a guide, only visited the village briefly. Service meant being in the human realm, where he should be right now. The senior angels he knew in the village, those with experience in the earthly realm, were either assigned teachers or retired. It dawned on Alfredo that he was very much naïve about life outside the university. As much as he hated the idea, the answers lay there, at the university, with Yaseem.

He set out for the village, crestfallen.

The village, with his apartment near the centre, was home to student angels and those not on earthly missions. He lived comfortably but not extravagantly. For a moment, he wished he could return there now; however, Yaseem lived at the university, on the far side of the village. To get there, he would have to walk the length of the main plaza, past the service areas and favourite hangouts of his contemporaries. It never crossed his mind to avoid the crowds until Raffie, a friend still studying under Yaseem, called out to him.

"Alfredo! How are you? Are you coming back to see us all before you go?" Raffie jested, bumping shoulders with a companion.

Everyone knew Alfredo. He was popular among the villagers, but right now, he couldn't bring himself to stop and talk. He waved and smiled back. "Of course, I will miss you all. Good luck with your studies, Raffie."

Alfredo took his laurel from his head and tucked it under his tunic where it was less conspicuous. He didn't want anyone to notice him until he sorted this debacle out. His heart beat faster. What if he failed and had to come back to continue his studies? Reams of scrolls and heavy books flashed before his eyes, and he shuddered. He quickened his pace and found a quieter avenue to walk on.

Yaseem's door stood open. Alfredo slowed at the threshold and wondered if it would surprise his teacher to see him. Music, a rendition of Miserere mei Deus, played from within the home, and Yaseem's voice floated with it. Someone should tell him he could no longer reach the highest notes in tune. The knowledge his teacher was not perfect and, therefore, no different from himself, gave Alfredo the courage he needed to enter Yaseem's domain.

"God willing, Yaseem, may I enter?" Alfredo called through the open door.

The singing stopped.

"Greetings, student. You may."

A golden retriever padded from the depths of the home to greet Alfredo, its tail wagging in delight. Alfredo patted its silky coat and followed the dog to its master.

Yaseem sat at his desk in a sun-filled study. Around him, tomes of books and scrolls filled every corner, cupboard and bench top. Alfredo had been here before, many times. He was at ease those other times, but now there was an anxiousness in his being. His knees shook. Yaseem put his pen down and waited for Alfredo to speak. His high cheekbones and thin lips showed no sign of concern, but Alfredo was tongue-tied. Where should he start?

Seeing his student's hesitancy, the teacher spoke with kindness. "Welcome, Alfredo. I wondered how you fared today. I'm pleased you will get to be of service to the Lord. How may I help you? Are you unsure of the whereabouts of the heavenly ladder? It should be self-explanatory on your scroll."

The mention of the scroll gave Alfredo the opening he needed. "Ah, yes, the scroll." He took it from under his arm, unrolled it and placed it on the desk in front of his teacher. "There might be a problem with it, sir. It's … blank."

The words fell into the surrounding silence.

Alfredo's heart was in his mouth. Yaseem's brow arched over one eye, and his thin lips curled in a half grin. Did his teacher not believe him? Surely, his own eyes could see the problem.

After what seemed an eternity, Yaseem said, "How interesting."

The teacher rose from his seat, clasped his hands behind his back and came around to stand in front of Alfredo. His actions brought back memories of the first day of classes many years ago. Alfredo had forgotten just how tall his teacher was. He looked up, hoping to have the mystery of his scroll explained. Then he could escape from such proximity. He breathed a sigh of relief when Yaseem moved to a pile of books behind them and beckoned Alfredo to follow.

Yaseem scanned the titles and chose a large tome from the bottom.

"Here, this one." He handed the heavy book to Alfredo and pointed to a chair and table. "Chapter three will enlighten you, I think."

Yaseem wouldn't give him the answer. This was going to be a puzzle he needed to solve for himself. He groaned. Yaseem knew how much he struggled with reading. He accepted the book and settled himself reluctantly on the seat, aware he was still under scrutiny from the teacher.

"You know, Alfredo, I'm not surprised this happened to you. Don't see this as punishment. I think you've received a great honour. Fare thee well." The teacher reached for his hat from a hook near the door and whistled for his dog to come.

"Stay for as long as you need. The keeper will give you food when you are hungry. Just call for Anna."

The older angel retreated into the corridor with his dog by his side. The shift in his former teacher's demeanour meant Alfredo was no longer regarded as a pupil. Yaseem hadn't expressed it as such, but the subtle difference in tone was how he spoke to his peers. He hoped he could rise to the new status without disappointing him.

"Come, Rembrandt. Let's take some air." Yaseem patted the dog on his mane and made a measured exit from his study. His companion wagged his tail and padded before him into the evening sun. Yaseem smiled, though the furrows in his brow remained. He dared not linger with his ex-student lest the young angel saw the gravity of the empty scroll written on his face.

Alfredo had what the teachers called latent talent, but they only discussed it among themselves. No angel was treated differently from another; that simply wasn't done. Having said that, not all angels were equal.

He contemplated the student at hand. Short, stocky build – a classic feature for angels – with nondescript features. The usual crisp blue eyes. His auburn locks, worn shoulder-length like all his current contemporaries, reflected sunlight with tinges of corn syrup. Nothing that would spark a comment of rare beauty in a passing moment. Yet the boy had something different in his aura.

Things hadn't come naturally to him from the pages of the scrolls and tomes in class. He had the propensity to want to 'feel' the messages, not read about them.

Yaseem stopped in his tracks. Ah! Why did that fact alone not alert Yaseem to an eventuation such as a blank scroll?

Rembrandt's soft woof urged him to continue his journey.

The situation was not new to Yaseem, but what concerned him was whether his charge was capable of the task ahead. Or that he may have not prepared his student enough to succeed. He would take some time in the coming weeks to pray for them both. Perhaps he could submit a plea for retirement. That idea pleased him, but he conceded that was not for him to choose; the gift would arrive when he least expected it. That was how it worked, and requesting any different would demean himself.

He would not take the usual walk today. Rembrandt had gone ahead towards the lake, and Yaseem whistled for him to return. Instead, he turned onto a narrow path set between two sentinel pines. The path itself was indistinct among the pine needles, but Yaseem had no trouble following it. He knew where he was going.

Rembrandt knew it well too. He stayed steadfastly behind Yaseem, quiet and attentive. He would follow his master even if he did not like their destination.

Little light penetrated the path, and to compensate for the gloom, lamp posts lit up as they walked beneath them and extinguished as they reached the next post.

The path led them to a wrought-iron gate set in a high stone wall. At the entrance, Rembrandt whimpered and sat at heel. Yaseem patted his head to reassure him. Footsteps crunched on leaf litter from within the wall, and Rembrandt let out a soft bark.

"Stay," said Yaseem as the gate swung open without a sound. The dog dropped to the ground and put its head on its paws.

A tall, cloaked figure, shrouded in a pool of light from a small lantern dangling from a staff, appeared at the entrance.

"Greetings, Arthemus."

The figure extended his hand for Yaseem to clasp. Even though the stranger's face remained hidden in the depths of his cloak, his voice revealed a warmth that belied the vision he presented.

"Greetings, Yaseem. You are here late in the day. I trust all is well?"

"Well enough, Artie, well enough." The two angels walked in silence for a short distance. Behind the wall, all sound was muffled. Their voices didn't carry past the air between them. Yaseem was never comfortable here. There was a taste to the air, a bitterness even. Yet he felt compelled to come.

They arrived at a small grove among the gloomy high bushes. There were rows of low stone benches upon which shapeless forms lay covered in what, for a moment, one might think was black snow. It was not snow but a fine layer upon layer of black web. Akin to a spider's web, but too strong to be broken with the brush of a hand. Too sticky to release even the largest of insects. He shuddered and took care not to touch it with his footfall or cloak.

How his friend Arthemus spent his existence among these sleeping ones amazed him. He thanked the Father for his teaching commission and regretted his earlier wish to retire.

"How do they fare?" Yaseem glanced at the forms.

Arthemus turned and swept an extended arm across the grove, surveying his charges. "In this grove, they have not moved at all. We lose many from the older groves; such is the age we are in, down in the earthly realm. But no more this century than the last one."

The men nodded sagely. Yaseem wished Artie's commission did not have to exist, but such was the reality of the ancient battle between the Company of Angels. The Great Fall. There were casualties. Failures.
And he did not want to one day find Alfredo here. In the back of his mind, he wondered how many were here because he'd somehow failed to prepare them for their assignments. He'd had his teaching commission for the past three centuries, and still, he was nervous when he sent his students into what he called battle, but what was, in fact, their destiny.

"War is such a waste, I agree. Still, peace brings its own losses," said Yaseem.

"True, my friend, true. But you did not come to talk about general issues? Who rests heavily on your mind?"

Yaseem smiled. He and Arthemus had a long history of angels they had a special connection to. He would get to the point.

"Felice," he said, "Is she ..."

"Still here." Arthemus finished the sentence for him and pointed to a form three rows away. "But she stirs."

"Really?" Yaseem's smile widened. Could it be that his hunch was right? Was there a connection to Alfredo's scroll? The moment the young angel had stepped into his room this afternoon, thoughts of Felice surfaced. He hadn't dwelt on her in ages.

"That is a good sign, yes?" He looked into Arthemus' eyes. They showed no hint of alarm and Yaseem relaxed, letting go of his trepidation.

"Yes, I would say. Is there something afoot with her charge?" Arthemus sounded surprised. "Don't tell me. She hasn't experienced a change of heart on her own, has she? Felice has been here for a lifetime."

They both knew a human could rediscover God's vision for them without the aid of a guardian angel, but it was not common. A look of realisation crossed Arthemus' face.

"Deathbed? Must be almost there." Arthemus' voice showed his concern.

"I don't know, Artie. But Felice came to my mind this afternoon when a student called on me for advice."

Arthemus grabbed Yaseem's arm, his bony fingers encircling his wrist, which brought their amble to a halt. He let go of Yaseem and pulled his hood back to reveal a balding head with a snowy remnant of hair clinging to the base of his skull. The surprise on his face showed Artie had just remembered the significance of this day.

"I almost forgot, it's graduation day for your class," Arthemus said with excitement flickering in his eyes. "You must be relieved. All went well? Was it Gabriel this time? I love his chariot. Those horses ..."

"Thank you, yes. He was the one. The rapture on the graduates' faces said it all. They all hold him in such high regard." Yaseem steered the conversation back to his problem. "I had a graduate with a blank scroll."

His friend went quiet.

"Hmm. I see." Arthemus looked around at his charges. "And you think it might concern one of these? Felice?"

Both men turned to gaze at the sleeping form that Arthemus had pointed out earlier. As if she knew she was being watched, Felice extended her hand and pushed against the web encasement, fingers spread. It lasted only a moment before she returned to her slumber; her hand once more resting against her petite frame.

Yaseem shrugged. "It's what I feel, but I'm not sure how it will play out yet."

"And your student? He understands what this means for him?"

Yaseem shook his head. "I've left him in my study with a copy of where I expect he might find the answer himself."

"Don't tell me, Yaseem, Free Will and the Unwilling, Chapter three?"

"Of course."

They both laughed knowingly.

Yaseem could laugh with Artie about it, but blank scrolls were not his favourite situation. It meant special forces were at work, and details would come sporadically and need urgent and skilful interpretation and actions. He hoped young Alfredo was up to the challenge. If his charge was the soul originally given to Felice, then his success would determine not only that soul but what became of Felice as well. He prayed he had done enough to prepare Alfredo.

CHAPTER 2

Paris 2000

Camille paid the taxi driver and walked in a daze into the foyer of her apartment building. Her footsteps on the lavish tiled floor sounded hollow. Thankfully, the concierge wasn't there at this time of the day. She had no wish to see or talk to anyone, no matter how banal the conversation. Her head had no room to focus on anything other than getting to the safety of her apartment.

The doctor's words still rang in her ears as the ding from the elevator sounded.

"Camille, my friend, put your house in order. I'm sorry, it is that serious."

Seated behind his standard flat pack desk, his face a pallid grey, he had sought to connect with her eyes. To impart a warped sense of empathy with her, no doubt. Did they teach that at medical school? Camille had wanted to reach over and slap him. She was not his friend. Friends did not charge such exorbitant fees to deliver bad news so blandly.

She entered the elevator only to set eyes on Mr Ying, the insufferable greengrocer, with his loaded trolley of fruit and vegetables. She inwardly groaned. Why today, of all days?

Ying, who she found annoying at his best and irritating at his worst.

She tried in vain to ignore him, but he insisted on striking up a conversation.

"Ah, Miss DuPont, did you enjoy what I left for you last week?" His face shone with expectation. Had she ever not enjoyed his fruit? Did it even matter?

She would keep her response to a minimum, curt but not rude.

"Very adequate, Mr Ying. I would expect nothing less."

Her throat hurt. Involuntarily, she raised her hand to her neck. She coughed, wincing as the pain intensified.

Ying caught her expression. "Miss Camille, you are ill, yes?" He leant over his trolley, closer to her face.

"No," she replied, turning away from him and coughing again. Why couldn't he just mind his own business?

"Hope it's not serious, sounds terrible." He fumbled in the pocket of his apron and pulled out a handful of cellophane-wrapped jubes. "Try one of these. The lemon one will soothe the itch, I'm sure."

Camille waved his hand away in frustration. She wanted none of his remedies. Her brow creased with annoyance, and Ying slowly returned the offerings to his apron pocket, shrugging his defeat.

"Perhaps I pray for you today." His smile widened, pleased with this thought.

This new proposition alarmed Camille and she drew a sharp breath. "No. Thank you. I don't believe in all that nonsense." She snorted. The tickle in her throat became outrageous. She drew a kerchief from her bag and muffled it as best she could, knowing her face would turn bright red with the effort.

"It's just an itch. Nothing more," she gasped and closed her eyes. A tear escaped, and she sniffed to compensate.

"I pray anyway. On my way to church now. Can't hurt."

Ying gave her a quizzical look. One she could hardly ignore unless she closed her eyes, but she worried if she did close her eyes, she wouldn't be able to circumvent any more of his attempts to cure her sore throat. He fiddled with the trolley, adjusting the space it took up between them.

For a moment, Camille worried he might come to her side but was relieved when she realised there was no room for him to do so. Even though he was a small man, the confines of the elevator saved her.

"You really not believe in God?" His head cocked to one side.

Camille fought the temptation to roll her eyes. How could someone be so insufferably cheerful? She drew on years of experience dealing with the half-baked questions thrown at her by gossip writers.

"Not anymore. Not for a long time." The statement fell flat between them. A moment of silence ensued, satisfying Camille that she had won.

"Ah. But you did once. Good. I'll say an extra prayer."

Camille's eyes widened. Did he not realise there were rules and lines you did not cross? Religion was one of them. It was too much for her.

"Really, Mr Ying, who goes to church at three in the afternoon? On a Tuesday! Don't do it especially for me. I'm not worth it."

She eyed the progress of the elevator on the wall panel. It was excruciatingly slow today. She should talk to someone about it.

"Ah, Miss Camille. I go every day to church. Good for Ying and good for business." He crossed his arms and leant back against the wall.

The idea of Mr Ying in church every day made her want to laugh. Did he think her a fool?

"You do not. No one does that except maybe the priests and nuns. And they must. It's their job." She had caught him out in a lie. It pleased her.

"No, no. Every day."

"Which church, then? I don't believe you." The rat was cornered. She narrowed her eyes, watching his face for any sign of a cover-up.

"The big one, on the Île de la Cité. Every day." He gesticulated with his arms as high as he could; ridiculous, as he was no taller than her shoulders and she was not above average.

"Now I know you are lying. Notre-Dame is for tourists."

"Ah yes, Miss Camille. Best place to go. Long line to stand in – with my apron for all those tourists to see. Good advertising, good for business." He held out his apron with 'Ying's Fresh is Best', emblazoned.

"Ah. So, you go to the church but don't go to Mass. There is a difference, you know."

"Oh, I go inside too, every day. I'm too busy for a long Mass, but in there, no one knows I'm not a tourist, so they don't ask me why I don't stay for Mass. I go inside, I sit and I talk with God. Simple. Sometimes on Sunday, I stay for Mass too. Good for the soul."

The elevator reached her floor with a ding and, Camille thought, not before time. Who knows where this conversation might end? She let out an audible sigh of relief.

"Hmm. Interesting thought, Mr Ying. If I ever need God again, I will keep it in mind."

He grinned widely. "I'll pray for you, anyway." He winked and added, "Just in case you have no time to go."

Camille stepped from the elevator with those words echoing in her ears. "No time to go ..."

Her heart lurched, and she quickened her step to her door. He couldn't possibly know how devastating those words were for her. Going to church again was not on her list of things to do with what little time she had left. The mere thought of 'last things' made her tremble with fear.

Camille's hand shook as she turned the key in her door. The coughing made her light-headed. Or was it the knowledge of her illness that had that effect? She didn't want to dwell on it further.

Her secretary had been, judging by the pile of personal letters on the hallstand. Another pile lay opened on her bureau, the contents neatly stacked for her perusal. She glanced at an ornate clock on the bookshelf. Would she bother with business matters today? No, there was always tomorrow.

How long would she be able to say that?

A knot rose in her throat. Already constricted, a sharp stab of pain shouted back. Mercy! Would this wretched throat be all that consumed her? Apparently so. She sighed and drew a cautious, deep breath. Relax. Just breathe through it. Her years of singing training kicked in. She closed her eyes, stuck out her chest and slowly filled her lungs once, twice, and again. The pain eased.

There. She'd won. She gloated at her reflection in the hallway mirror and retrieved the Gucci sunglasses from her hair, folding them with flair. Nothing could break her spirit. She owned her destiny. Not a single man – or disease – had mastered her in the past, and she wasn't prepared to accept a change to the status quo.

Buoyed by this last thought, she tossed her handbag and the sunglasses onto the bureau and headed for the kitchen. She reached for a tall wine glass and opened the cupboard where her favourite liqueurs sat. It was early; she knew this, but today was not a normal day. It had been a horrid day like no other. She corrected herself. Just a recent horrid day. Her life had been littered with such days and she had conquered all of those, and this one would be no different.

She just needed to borrow some strength to regroup. The whiskey, perhaps. She would fight this thing, this throat cancer. What did that young doctor know? He was half her age. She had the money; she would find a specialist. The top one in France, no, all of Europe. Yes, the whiskey would be perfect.

She traded the wine glass for a crystal tumbler. No ice. Neat. One measure? Definitely two. After all, if she didn't beat this monster, who else would drink it? The secretary, Mr Rochet? Possibly, but he would not appreciate it like she would. It really was a tragedy these days. All her friends... she pulled her train of thought up. Friends, no, she had none. Was acquaintances a better word? Contemporaries, even better. All those faces from the past had fallen away over the years. Who was dead or in a nursing home tucked in a woollen lap blanket, or even worse, alive but dead in the mind? So many of them suffered from dementia in their golden years. But not her. She gloated with satisfaction. Not her. She was as sharp as ever. And rightly so. Not for her, the blabbering idiots that eat at one's mind – she'd been smart. No husband, no children to send her crazy.

Glass in hand, she retreated to her study, resisting the temptation to sift through the open letters. Instead, she pushed open the balcony door and slumped into an expensive wicker chair. From her vantage point, she saw office workers in the building opposite hers, engrossed in the normality of the working day. She raised her glass in silent acknowledgment of them. They wouldn't think to look at her balcony; she rarely sat out here, and should they, well, Camille didn't care what they might think of her today.

She sipped on the whiskey. It tasted exquisitely like butterscotch. She let it burn inside her cheeks as she considered her previous thoughts. She could not get around the lie. Cammie, you can tell the world you had no man or child, but you cannot tell that to yourself. There was only one, and he had brought upon her the worst of betrayals. Because of him, she had brought a child into this world. She gulped the liquid down past the offending nodule in her throat.

Immediately, a searing pain gripped her, and she spluttered before wiping some of the liquid from her chin. No. No, no, no, NO! You will not

20

defeat me! She gulped another mouthful of whiskey and swallowed. The pain lessened, and she relaxed. This would NOT be her master, either.

***

Camille woke to a buzz in her ears and a thump behind her eyes. She groaned and put one well-manicured hand to her head. She kept her eyes closed, wanting to block any further assault on them. Two whiskeys had become four. That she could remember. She swallowed thickly. Her throat burned. It had been a while since she'd let herself fall this far into an alcoholic funk. Only now, she remembered her own advice against it.

Her throat itched, and she had no choice but to cough. Straight away, pain akin to razorblades grasped her vice-like, and she cried out between spasms. She dragged her eyelids apart and blinked at the bedside table, where a glass of water sat waiting alongside a foil card with painkillers. She flailed her arm across the pillow, felt for the card and, with practised ease, popped two tablets into her hand. These she swallowed and again reached for the water to wash them down. The tablets stuck to her tongue. She groaned and dragged her body into a sitting position to finish the job. Two gulps and the bitterness faded.

It'd take a while for the headache to recede. In an act of defiance and self-pity, she would remain in her luxurious bedroom until that happened. Would it matter if her secretary, Mr Rochet, arrived and found her still in bed? Camille was always fully dressed, breakfasted, and immaculately made up. No one would recognise her without her signature Serge Lutens lipstick and mascara. She always chose the levres en boite – the red palette was not for the fainthearted. For Camille, it was the mask she wore to face the world. It was who she was.

Years of creating that had been ingrained in her by a strict regimen. Absolutely no one called in person until 11:00 am. Rochet wouldn't dare show up before then. Lunch meetings are at 1:00 pm at the earliest, and the rare dinners she attended are over by 9:00 pm. Any medical appointments thrust upon her out of necessity were always after her midday meal.

She eyed the alarm clock beside her bed. Habit gnawed at her. The digits showed 10:05, and she had an absurd urge to swipe the thing onto the floor. A battle raged within. Get up and keep going as though nothing were amiss or wallow in the outrageous indignity of it all. In the end, drugs having tamed her headache, habit won out and she swung her legs over the edge of the bed.

For all her eighty years, Camille maintained her health despite the excesses of her youth and early midlife. She pointed her toes and studied her legs, from the bright red toenail polish to her wrinkled kneecaps. Years of ballet had kept them in good shape, and no arthritic joints for her, unlike others from her days on the boards. Early retirement came before she wore her joints thin. A blessing that her success allowed.

Perhaps, she mused, her good health had deceived her into thinking she would never fall to the vagaries of old age. Throat cancer. What throw of the dice had given her such a wretched affliction? A spring of anger bubbled up within her, giving her the sting of heartburn. It was just so – inconvenient. She pressed her hands over the pain and glared at the clock, still ticking down the minutes to Rochet's arrival. In an act of defiance, she pulled the plug and the led display disappeared. No. She would fight it. She was a fighter. And she would waste no time wallowing in pity. There was much to do.

When Rochet's key turned in the door forty minutes later, Camille was dressed, had eaten a crumbling croissant, and was sitting at her desk in full make-up with a steaming cup of coffee.

"Ah, Rochet." She greeted him in her usual brisk manner. "Something different today. Clear my agenda for next week, please. I want a list of the top cancer specialists in Paris and any you know from your experience. Anywhere in Europe. I must have an immediate appointment."

She noted his raised eyebrows. He opened his mouth to say something. The last thing she wanted was some pity statement. "Rochet, don't get the idea that I am dying. I refuse." She snapped her diary closed and handed it to him.

He took it from her as though it were a poison chalice.

It occurred to her he might wonder about his future, which was something else she had to contend with. He'd proved loyal in the past. Two decades and still with her, despite her constant barrage of requests, micromanagement, and superiority complex. Camille knew her faults. She was old school. She employed him, and for her, that was the basis of their relationship. None of this modern garbage of raised status to best friend. Rochet understood that. She paid him, and he did as he was bid. Did she care if he thought of her as cold or snobbish? No. Not in the least. His generous wage was enough. Else why did he stay?

Rochet dealt with the mailbox full of invitations to dinners she rarely attended. They were the baggage from her considerable wealth and connection to the dance theatres and the academy. Paris society demanded she be seen at this function or that, for the sole benefit of the hosts, of course. She was over that and found the events boring, and more frequently, she sent him in her place. He enjoyed them, though he would never admit it.

But today, it was about tackling her mortality. Within the hour, Rochet had made Camille's appointments with the top surgeon in Paris and her family solicitor. Tomorrow, her list of necessary and urgent things would grow longer. She still needed him. Would he stay till the end, or would he abandon her to avoid the confronting reality of her death? Time would tell.

As the door closed behind him, Camille let her shoulders slacken. The effort to hold herself erect had been immense. She rested her head on the back of her chair and breathed a deep sigh. So many things to do. More than she had realised. Still, they had achieved a good deal already. She had this beast in her sight now, and she would run it down. Her very life depended on it.

***

Camille sat bolt upright in the modern plastic-moulded chair at the surgeon's office. This morning, her mood was already fouled because not only did this specialist insist she attend his clinic at the ungodly hour of 9:30 in the morning, but he confirmed the findings of her over-priced doctor. There was little he could do for her other than remove the offending nodules and render her speechless, followed by heavy doses of chemotherapy to stop the further spread of the cancer.

Camille couldn't decide whether his sympathetic tone was genuine or whether he saw an opportunity to pick over the bones of her bank balance. All her bravado evaporated.

Until now, she believed there would be a different opinion from this new doctor. That belief was now dashed on the rocks. She struggled to pull the fragments together into some semblance of an acceptable future. Still reeling from the shock, she stirred from her stupor as he rose from his glass-inlaid desk to choose a glossy leaflet on throat cancer from a shelf behind her.

Camille's eyes raked the office for anything she could gain comfort from. A peaceful painting of the sea or a vista of an ancient ruin, anything that would ease the sense of helplessness and panic that sat heavily on her chest. The doctor's office held no distractions apart from the many certificates boasting his prowess, and a full body chart.

He sat down again, flicked through a diary and scribbled her name.

She closed her eyes, focussed on the thump of her heart on her ribcage, and whispered, "How long?"

The doctor cleared his throat, and Camille's eyes snapped open. His eyes met hers, and he offered a genuine smile.

"You do have a choice, Madame DuPont. And your choice will determine the answer." He pushed the glossy information sheet towards her.

Camille fingered the edges of it. Without her glasses, she couldn't read it and didn't even attempt to. She slipped it into her bag.

"A choice?" Camille clung to the promising word.

He leant in towards her.

Camille focussed on his face as if only now noticing the man who held her life in his hands. His eyes were speckled brown and green. They gave him a boyish look, belying the tinges of grey in his auburn hair. Dark circles hinted at long nights. She could only hazard a guess at his age. Late forties, perhaps early fifties.

"I'm not saying we shouldn't operate. I fully urge you to go ahead, as it's your best chance of beating this at stage four. No doubt the tests will show it's already spread elsewhere. I cannot save your voice box. You will lose the ability to speak."

Camille struggled to see the choice in what she had just heard. "You said I have a choice ..." The vein in her neck throbbed.

"We operate, and you have six months. We throw everything at it and pray for a miracle. But you lose your voice immediately. If, by a slim chance, a miracle occurs and we find it contained in that area"—he raised his shoulders and held his palms up— "then you might have a bit longer, say twelve months, but there is no guarantee. The side effects of chemo are well documented, but you will be able to stay in your home longer, under the care of a specialised nurse."

Camille started. "Six months?" She'd hoped for longer than a year. Maybe two, even. Six months was a sobering thought.

He drew a breath.

Why did she feel there was worse to come? She braced herself.

"No operation and we allow things to ... run their course, half that time. You will lose your voice anyway without the operation. We can dose you up with painkillers ..."

A startled cry from Camille interrupted him. She caught her fingers to her lips, too late to stifle it.

"... but without treatment, and as the cancer spreads, there will be a serious deterioration to your other organs more quickly. Hospitalisation and palliative care until ..." He shrugged and shifted uncomfortably in his seat.

She swallowed hard, blinking to stop a tear from forming but his face swam before her, and to avoid him seeing her distress, she fumbled with her handbag in search of a tissue.

He gave her time to regain composure and softened his tone. "Do you have any questions?"

She shook her head, unsure if she could hold back her tears if she spoke. Of course, she had questions; who wouldn't? But her pride would only allow so much of her guard to be let down. She needed to regather her wits.

"It is cruel, but you have the resources to afford the best care, Madame DuPont. Sadly, not everyone is as fortunate."

A familiar hardness returned as his words cut through her distress. How discerning of him. She had money. He was a high-profile surgeon; he also had money. But money wasn't going to buy her a single extra damn day.

"Decide for yourself, Madame DuPont." His voice was more businesslike now. "I've made a temporary opening in my surgical list but can't hold it open past the end of this week. My secretary will give you all the details you need."

He got up, ready to show her out.

Camille stood and left the room with all the dignity she could muster. The door swished behind her with a sharp click of finality, leaving her in the waiting room surrounded by a row of poor unfortunates waiting for their chance to be shocked and brutalised by horrid news. One man looked at her oddly when she stopped in the middle of the room, frozen.

Immediately, she drew her shoulders up and made a beeline for the admin desk. Fortunately, she had recovered from her almost-teary state and was confident no mascara had smudged under her eyes. Money. It got her expensive mascara that held fast under trying circumstances.

Make a choice, the doctor had said. What choice was that? Die muted and ravaged by drugs in her bed or curl up in a hospice ward and wither away. What a waste her life had been. All the accolades were meaningless now. She was going to die, a blatant fact she couldn't change. And with no family to grieve for her.

With a well-practised neutral face, she dealt with the desk nurse, accepted the paperwork and account and left the office, her back as straight as a ramrod.

***

Camille stepped from the specialist's clinic into the midmorning rush and bustle. The harsh sunlight momentarily blinded her. She fumbled with her bag and donned her sunglasses. Relief. The clinic she emerged from was insulated from any outside noise, and now the assault on her ears was unbearable. Each step she took on the busy pavement was less sure than before. Her breathing quickened, and pain rose in her chest. A tourist brushed past her, unaware of his surroundings, and she grabbed an awning pole to steady herself.

"Idiot," she cursed under her breath. "Look where you go. Tourists!"

The man feigned a half-hearted apology and kept walking, his camera in hand, ready to snap another Parisian scene.

Camille held scorn for most tourists these days. Would he be in such a rush if he knew how useless it was? So stupid. Take a photo, race somewhere else and take another. What for? To put in an album and never look at it again?

She held the pole for another moment, glad, in fact, for the distraction. The chest pain subsided, and her breathing calmed. Coffee. She would sit and reread the medical forms. She glanced at her watch. There was time. The solicitor was only two blocks away.

Fate would have it that the awning pole belonged to a café. Perfect. She chose a seat at the rear of the tiny shop, away from the hustle and commotion and prying eyes, and ordered a strong, American-style coffee and a glazed pastry. She'd skipped her breakfast to make the early appointment. Perhaps that explained her light-headedness.

The forms were straightforward. Her details and medical history are not so difficult to supply. The next question, however, brought her to a sharp stop. Next of kin. What did one put when there was no one? The chest pain returned to gnaw at her. Her secretary? No. She would not prevail on Rochet, not for this. Who else in her life could she impose on? Would it matter if this was blank? After all, how many times would it get used? The hospital would only need to contact next of kin if she died on the operating table, wouldn't they? And then it would be her solicitor who was called to arrange her ... disposal.

How shocking it all sounded to her. Gory details she could not ignore. Death. She had never had to deal with burials herself. Her mother died before her papa. And when he died, she'd been a mere child. Eighteen was still a child. An uncle had stepped in and arranged it all. She remembered standing at her father's graveside, dressed in black and angry as all hell at him. Lingering on the memory, the anger was still there.

She touched her cheeks, knowing they burned and made a conscious effort to relax her jaw. Small mercies for make-up.

Well, it didn't matter who came to her funeral. Rochet would come out of duty. As would a few of her contemporaries. All hopeful that she, the famous Camille DuPont, had remembered them in her will. How tragic. She wondered if the society news would celebrate her life as though she were fondly missed. Or had she lived past that honour? The latest 'celebs' were such a shallow bunch. So self-absorbed.

She sighed. Someone from the academy would attend, no doubt. She was a patroness and had donated a scholarship to budding students for the last twenty years. Worth 3,000 lire a year. Not a huge one, but enough to encourage true talent where found.

Would any of those girls attend? She didn't remember the names of the early ones. Not a promising sign, she mused. Ungrateful, or just the way things were these days. Sad, but the former was more likely. The industry thrived on ego, something she knew only too well. The current girl would come, that she knew. Camille smiled with fondness. Asha Villet was a sweetheart and the most talented dancer she had laid eyes on for years. Yes, she would be there.

She ordered another coffee. One thought plagued her. You do have family, Cammie. What if she ... No, Camille forced the thought down. That was no option. That part of her life no longer existed. It was dead. And soon, she would be, too.

As the waiter placed the second coffee at her table, she slipped the form back into its envelope. She would mull over it. It could stay blank for all she cared. If she died on the operating table, who would care anyway?

Having thought that, Camille conceded that bravery was the best option here. Of course, she would have the operation and be damned with the hospice idea. She would spend as much money as she needed to get the most days she could from this wretched situation. Next of kin was a minor detail.

***

Pierre Levin & Son had been her solicitors from the early years. Of course, it was the son part of the duo she dealt with now, Pierre Senior having died years ago. Pierre Junior was very much like his father, which was why she kept her business there.

Her will, made years ago when death was just a shadowy concept, was still relevant as it was, apart from one detail. Back then, she hadn't thought much about who would inherit her considerable estate. Her many interests would have benefited, no one recipient more than the other, but this week gave her cause to reconsider. Inserting an extra line, in the stroke of a pen, should be a simple thing.

Pierre was a pragmatic man and not prone to self-interest. He would carry out her instructions to the letter. Completely at ease while he scrutinised her file, it gave her pride she was worth his time, with such considerable wealth in her name.

Camille smiled to herself. Mistress of her own destiny to the end.

While he read the changes she proposed, she took stock of him. A book man, she decided, with a pasty complexion from years of not enough sun. His hair was thinning on top, and gravity had begun its work on his jowls. The focus on her mortality highlighted it in everyone else around her.

Pierre closed her file with deliberation and removed his spectacles.

"Camille, everything seems in order. I see no problem with Ms Villet being the sole beneficiary, but ... one thing remains. I did some reading of your older files and happened upon a note written by my father." He hesitated. "How can I bring this up without offence? It raises a situation that may affect the execution of your will."

Camille raised an eyebrow. The old fox had made notes on her? Indeed. It intrigued her now. What had he written to throw her will into jeopardy? It was watertight.

"You cannot offend me, Pierre. Speak your mind." She sat back and watched as he struggled to pick his words. A thread of doubt dangled before her eyes. Whatever Pierre Senior wrote had a troubling effect on the man in front of her.

Her stomach muscles clenched. She wished he would just be out with it and made a gesture with her gloved hand to encourage him.

"Alright then. I found a note referring to a child, a daughter." The pasty skin over his cheeks blushed and he blinked as he waited for her reaction.

A stone dropped into the pit of her stomach and her face blanched. She did not recall ever having told Pierre, but evidently, she had. Her eyes averted to the office window and the branches of the street tree outside. She didn't want him to see how it affected her.

Camille nodded. "Yes. It is true. But I've had nothing to do with her. I was young. Extremely young and at the time, had neither the means nor the desire to be a parent."

She faced him again. His form swam before her vision.

"It is of little relevance to me. I had her adopted the day she was born." She hesitated before adding, "I can only hope she's lived a long and happy life. Something I would never have been able to provide."

Pierre was silent. Did he judge her poorly? This generation knew nothing of the hardships that her generation endured. She lowered her head to avoid his gaze. It would be better if she didn't make him more uncomfortable.

"Believe me when I say I understand, Madame DuPont," he spoke in a gentle manner, "and I do not raise the issue to cause you pain."

If she could've left without further conversation, it would've pleased her. But Pierre had raised the issue, and she would see it through.

The nerve was raw. Rawer than she expected. She snapped without meaning to do so. "Then why? Why drag this up?" She instantly regretted the tone of her voice and softened it before asking, "Why does it matter?"

"These days, Camille, it's easy for others to appeal wills. To make claims upon estates, even if it goes against the deceased's wishes. Others may know of your secret and take advantage." He tapped on his desk with his index finger. "An insult to you and the ones you have already generously provided for. Years of court battles with all sorts of stories dredged up. And it grieves me to know that you, an old friend of my father, would have your name dragged in the mud."

Camille noted his honesty and let her shoulders relax. "I'm sorry I snapped. It's not a part of my life I think about, let alone discuss." She folded her hands in her lap. "What do you propose?"

"We find her. Provide for her in a proportionately acceptable way that will not create a wave of lawsuits." A kindly smile flitted on his face.

She cringed at how he thought he had solved the problem so neatly. *Don't patronise me.*

"And you can do this? Find her? I have little time left." Saying the words out loud hurt. The stone in her stomach lurched against her heart. She fumbled in her bag for her painkillers.

Pierre leapt up and poured her a glass of water from a bubbler machine in the corner of his office. Camille accepted it gratefully and swallowed the pills.

"Do you agree?" he asked when she composed herself.

Her heart screamed no; she did not want this. It was too much pain to bear on top of what she must endure with the operation and the disruption of her private world. No, she did not agree. She pursed her lips.

"Yes. Find her if you must. But I won't have this interfere with my wishes."

32

CHAPTER 3

Paris 2000

A stiff breeze followed Asha down the narrow street, catching her hair and tugging it from her hair band. Wisps flew onto her face, across her eyes. She brushed them back with her free hand. She was late, but she would still be home before her mother.

It had been a gruelling session at dance class this afternoon. Her instructor was in one of his moods. Nothing she did was perfect enough, and repeatedly he demanded she retry her steps. Asha knew his temperament and did her best to oblige, leaping higher, lifting her arms in ever so more elegant arcs. Comply, comply, comply. The clock ticked over the end of her session, but still he barked, "Again!"

When he finally whirled and snapped his finger on the off button of the stereo system, she breathed a silent sigh of relief. Nothing she did when he got this worked up would please him, so she did her best to weather the storm. She was his most promising student, and by the next session, he would have forgiven her and forgotten his grievance.

Her teacher was one of Paris' best, and Asha felt privileged to even be here. The scholarship she'd applied for and won made it possible. But now she was late for her next appointment.

The little cafeteria across the street from her flat was opening for the evening crowds. Marco, the bar attendant, waved as she approached, flashing his white-teethed grin. Asha and Marco had known each other forever. His family owned the business and had been there all Asha's life. Like sister and brother, she and Marco had sat with soda and chips at a table in the back, doing homework or playing board games together. He, too, was an only child. Now he works in the business, and tonight he set out the green metal chairs and covered the square tables with their signature cloths – a blue, white and red play on the flag– on the stone pavement in readiness for the evening diners. Marco had cranked up the music as he usually did. His father would turn it down when trade began. It was their own way of testing each other's patience, she guessed.

A thrill tingled Asha's spine. How funny that within the space of a year, they had seen each other through different eyes. Almost like destiny had spoken. She was the first to feel the pull on her heart, watching him as he went about his chores in the restaurant. Little did she understand the effect she had had on him.

She remembered the night the childhood crush burst into a new and tender romance. It was raining, and she'd forgotten her keys to the street door that gave access to the apartment building. Late, dripping wet and shivering from the cold, she had taken comfort under the restaurant eves, waiting for her mother to return.

Marco's father had wanted to close early – the trade fizzling because of the rain. He left his son to lock up, and alone, with the front door closed, Marco had taken her into the kitchen to make them both a hot chocolate.

Marco overcame his sudden shyness in her presence and wrapped his arms around her damp waist. Tentative at first, as though testing how

34

far she would allow him to go, he drew her close and laid a tender kiss on her lips.

Her heart still jumped at the memory, and every kiss since had the same effect on her.

"You're late." Marco's lips curled in a half smile and his grey eyes danced over her curves.

She kissed his cheek, lingering to drink in his muskiness. "Has Mama been up yet?" she asked, and he shook his head.

Good, there was still time. Her mother hated her going to the patroness' place but would never say why.

Asha ducked into the chocolate shop across the street, delving into the pockets of her long jacket for change.

The chocolates were a peace offering. Asha didn't like upsetting her mother, but without knowing why, she had begun to resent the carping every time a meeting came up. Luckily, this was to be the last one. The scholarship ended when she graduated later this year.

"Two of these, please." She pointed to her mother's favourites, strawberry cream with the vanilla bean fondant.

"Hello Asha, late tonight? How's Mama?" Adeline put three into a bag.

"She's well, thank you."

With chocolates safe in her bag, she pushed through their street access door. Closing it blocked all the noise from the street. The only sound was her soft footfall on the concrete walkway as she checked the mailboxes. Number fifteen's box was empty. No bills; always a good thing. She headed for the aged timber stairwell. The familiar cool balustrade under her hand beckoned her upward.

Ever since she was little, the stairwell had been her favourite place. She'd learnt to count, multiply and divide using the number of stairs, floors and homes in the building. Here, she met her neighbours and recognised who to talk with, who to avoid, who could be trusted and who could not.

Tonight, humming the tune in her head, she counted the stairs in time to her latest dance routine, treading the boards as one might play the piano, until she reached the top floor. Her fingers sought the hidden key behind a water pipe, and she let herself into the flat.

Home. Number 15 was once the attic of the five-hundred-year-old building. Converted somewhere in the distant past to a living space, it was the only home she had ever known. Just inside the door, coat hooks lined the wall of a narrow landing. She hung her backpack on one of these and bounded up the last flight of stairs to their living area. It was tiny and too small for them both and she often wondered why Mama hadn't found somewhere larger. Things were financially tight, but her mother insisted they stay here. It made little sense to Asha, but she rarely complained about it anymore.

She and Marco dreamt of a place of their own. It would take one or two lead roles in a big dance company before she had enough savings. The scholarship plus what her mother added were enough for tuition and her dance necessities, not to live on. And to get those roles, she knew she needed to prove herself worthy.

And Marco, well, his family might come round to the idea one day. But not yet. They were more traditional. Wedding and all that. She wasn't ready for that. Maybe further into the future, but not until she'd satisfied the urge to dance. She was grateful Marco understood this.

"We've got forever, Ash," he'd said to her often.

A cooing noise came from an open skylight above her head. Two pigeons were there, waiting for free seed. She laughed at their antics and dragged a stool across to reach up for the tin her mother kept on the roof just outside the skylight.

"You hungry pests," she playfully chided. Asha didn't know if they had adopted her mother or she them, but she'd watched her mother do this every day since she could remember. She would miss them once she left.

Asha looked at her watch. She must hurry. Grabbing a pretty teacup saucer from the buffet, she placed it on the table and arranged the chocolates on it. She scribbled a note for her mother and propped it next to them. Happy with that, she showered, put on a woollen dress and fixed her make-up.

The face that stared back from the mirror pleased her. She had her mother's eyes – two large brown orbs floating in a bright white sea. A little mascara, not too much. Her hair, pulled back into a tight bun, black and shiny, was sufficient and suitable for tonight. She pursed her lips and applied lip balm over her colour of choice, a pale pink, not the stark red used on stage. Her mother often said she had her father's mouth. She'd never met him as he had died when she was an infant, but when she glanced at his photo on the wall, she could see the likeness.

It was his eyes she admired the most. Almond-shaped, not like hers and Mama's, but kind and soft. Eyes that followed her around the flat.

Mama used to say, "Papa is watching over us." And Asha had always believed it to be true. She blew him a kiss.

Footsteps on the stairs broke her daydreaming thoughts. Mama! She had to go. She grabbed her shoes, a coat and bag and let herself out of the flat.

They met on the stairs on the floor below.

"Asha? Where are you going tonight?" her mother's voice sounded strained.

"Meeting, Mama. I told you about it. At the patroness' house, remember? She wants to go over the final term's conditions, I think." Asha gave her mother a quick hug as she slipped past her.

"Oh, yes. I forgot. I'll keep supper warm then."

"No need, Mama. She asked me to stay for supper. I'm sorry, I won't stay out too late. And I'll get a cab home, I promise."

***

By the time Asha reached her destination on Rue Louis Phillipe, it was past three. She fretted that her patroness, Madame DuPont, would be irritated. Hopefully, an apology would stand because there was no avoiding the traffic. She had made it just in time before the concierge who opened the brass-trimmed opaque doors for her, left for the day.
Any later and she might have had to buzz madame from the street, adding to her embarrassment.

Asha headed to the elevator where she pressed the intercom for the DuPont apartment. "It's Asha, Madame."

Madame's voice floated in response. "Sending the elevator now, dear."

As she waited for the doors to slide open, she took in the surroundings of the lobby. Creamy marble floors with plaster columns and strategically placed monstrous plants in oversized, black marble urns completed the dramatic contrast and made for a grand entrance. The stuff of magazines. It reminded her of movie stars and luxurious lifestyles. At her first interview with the academy board, she was unaware of who the benefactress was, hadn't known she sat on the panel alongside the Director of Dance. She'd been nervous that day.

The nerves were there again today, but for a different reason. This was Asha's last term at the academy. The last chance to impress her teachers and be signed up by one of the dance companies. The culmination of four years of hard work. Asha worried that being late today might set a bad mark against her. Strict adherence to rules and deadlines were part and parcel of her chosen career. Had it not been her teacher's foul mood that had caused her lateness? Ironic, she mused.

Asha pressed the elevator button again, tired of waiting and annoyed she'd stood for such a long time. Give her stairs any day. The moment the button light lit up under her finger, the doors yielded.

A heady perfume met her as she stepped into the confined space. Flowers, a trolley full of them. Behind the trolley, a small man with a balding head and grey moustache grinned at her.

"Oh, hello Mr Ying. We meet again."

"Good afternoon, Ms Asha. We do indeed," Ying cheerfully responded.

Every time Asha visited, he was in the elevator, always surrounded by colour and fragrance. She wondered if it was not the happiest elevator in all of Paris.

"Tell me again. This isn't your secret shop front, is it?" They laughed together. It was their private joke.

"You know I'd go out of business very quick if it was. Delivery day today." He winked and chose a stem from within the midst of his trolley. A white lily. "Last one of these, not sold today, so you must have it."

She smiled. There was no other florist in the world as sweet as this man. She would miss their casual meetings. Her smile faded.

Ying noticed, and his face, too, became serious.

"Why the frown? Bad news today?" His eyes lifted towards Madame DuPont's apartment.

Asha drew a breath. He'd taken the wrong meaning from her glum look.

"Oh, no. Not at all. Well, I hope not." She smiled. "I just thought ... I'm going to miss you. That's all."

"Are you not coming back?" He feigned shock.

"I expect I may, but this is my last term under the scholarship, so, no, after this term, I won't be."

Ying's shoulders jiggled as he chuckled. "I will see you after, I'm sure. I sell flowers everywhere. Even outside the theatre companies, after the operas, you know. All those people who will see you dance." His eyes sparkled with his good humour.

Asha laughed. "Of course. I will look for you there, then."

The elevator door chimed, and she took one step into the hallway. She never tired of hearing his uplifting offerings. She would miss this diminutive Chinese flower seller and their conversations. She raised the lily and bid him goodbye.

Asha paused at the door to Madame DuPont's apartment. She smoothed her hair, took a deep breath and pressed the buzzer. The door clicked open, and she entered. Soft orchestral music filtered down the hallway, and she followed it to find Madame DuPont seated at her office bureau. As Asha approached, the older woman looked up from her papers and beamed.

"Ah, finally, you are here, Ms Villet. Traffic? I found it tiresome myself this afternoon." Her voice was smooth, with not a hint of annoyance. Asha's shoulders lost their tension and she relaxed.

"Yes. The traffic seems to be worse these days." She made no mention of the recalcitrant teacher.

"A lily. How sweet of you. There's a vase on the kitchen bench. If you like, pop it in with those."

Asha obliged. A peace offering, thank you, Mr Ying. She smiled to herself.

Madame DuPont followed her into the kitchen and took glasses from her cupboard. "Join me for a drink, yes?" She reached for a bottle of sparkling wine from the fridge.

"Oh, only soda if you have it. Thank you." Is it too early for wine? She didn't enjoy more than an ale on a hot summer's day, and even then, it wasn't her first choice.

"Soda it is. Please pardon me if I prefer a glass of wine. It's been a trying day; I feel I've earned an early reprieve." Her voice held a hint of self-pity. "Come. We will sit in the living room, I think. The view is better there. Although these modern buildings keep growing like weeds around me." She waved a hand across the view. "There was a time when one could see the Eiffel Tower from here. No longer possible, I'm afraid. Still, it may be best if I didn't see it lit up like a neon candle every night."

Asha smiled politely. Her patroness seemed very pensive this afternoon and she wondered what had changed. Every other meeting was a quick lecture on the expectations of the scholarship and a nervous wait in her office for the renewed paperwork. She hoped this time the discussion might turn to her aspirations. To get some timely advice from Madame DuPont, who had been such a tower in the profession.

Truth be told, Asha was in awe of her. She had seen the faded posters plastered around the academy walls. Madame DuPont's reputation far outlived her final curtain. She hadn't performed in a while. In fact, Asha wondered if she had been born before this woman had retired.

Settled on the sofa, Madame Dupont fixed inquisitive eyes on Asha's face, stilled her own body and with a deliberate nod of her head, beckoned her to sit beside her. The blood rushed to Asha's cheeks, and she took a sip of the soda to hide it.

"Well, my dear. We have come to the pointy end of your studies, yes? Are you ready for the exams?"

Asha nodded. "I, I believe so."

"Good. Well done." Madame DuPont carefully placed her drink on the low table in front of them. "It's not why I've invited you here this afternoon. I'm well aware and fully informed of your progress, just so you know." She gave a wry grin.

A knot formed in Asha's throat, and her heart rate lifted. She swallowed to shift it.

"Asha." Her eyes remained focused on Asha's face. "May I call you that?"

Asha nodded again. Every nerve in her body quivered, though she couldn't decide if out of fear or excitement.

"I've had some terrible news." The gaze shifted back to the skyline. "Terrible news."

The unexpected conversation confused Asha and took her completely off guard. She struggled to find words. "Oh," was all she could manage. An urge to find an excuse and leave rose, but she quelled it.

Perhaps this was all Madame DuPont would say. Asha hoped so. Whatever the news, she didn't consider herself close enough to the woman to be the person to share a personal disaster.

Another thought occurred. Perhaps she had no one else to tell. If that were so, it was a minor sacrifice to make. And the conversation would surely shift back to more comfortable ground once she divulged the bad news.

Asha relaxed and listened attentively.

The woman sighed. Every crease on her face showed the toll of worry. "I have cancer."

The words fell into a pool of silence.

Asha gasped. "Oh, Madame DuPont. I am so sorry to hear that."

"Camille, call me Camille." Her voice wavered.

Uncomfortable now, Asha felt she had intruded into the private world of this woman. No, intruded was not the word, for Camille invited her here. The choice to tell her was the older woman's.

"Is it serious? I mean, you can treat cancer, yes? Even at your ..." She didn't like to say the word. Would Camille feel affronted?

"Age? Never fear the obvious, Asha. I'm old. I don't fear age at all. I've lived a long and healthy life until now. That's what I hate about this whole wretched thing, this cancer." She spat the offending word out of her mouth.

"Forgive me, Camille." It felt odd to address her this way. "I am sad about your news, but why tell me? It's a little"—she searched for the word, not wanting to further upset or disappoint her— "overwhelming." It would do, but it didn't accurately describe her feelings.

Camille's smile was full of sadness. Her face had regained its composure.

"I don't mean to make you uncomfortable, dear. I'd rather not face the obvious, but time is of the essence, and I want to ensure I do what I must before"—one hand rose to her throat—"before I lose this."

"I don't understand." Asha faltered. She didn't know of anyone in her life who had suffered from cancer.

"My voice. It's throat cancer. They're operating in a few days. After that, I will have no voice." Camille rose from the sofa and looked through the glass door leading to a marbled patio.

Asha gasped and her hand went instinctively to her own throat. How did anyone cope with not being able to speak? The enormity of it hit her. Madame had been a singer as well as a dancer. It would be devastating for her. There had to be a mistaken diagnosis, as nothing sounded 'wrong' with Camille's voice.

Tears threatened. Still, she had no words that would seem adequate.

Camille turned to stare at her. "There is much I wish to say. I am hopeful you will honour what I'm about to do for you."

Another twist. What did Camille having cancer have to do with Asha? Asha was lost for words. She took another sip of soda, shuffled on the sofa, crossing, and uncrossing her legs and waited for what was to come.

"I have no family." There was no emotion in Camille's statement. "No one. Not a distant relative even." She waved an arm at her surroundings.

Asha's eyes followed the arc of her arm, mesmerised, not by what Camille was pointing out, but by the woman herself. She struggled to know how to respond. Her own family was small, just her mother and herself, so she understood what it would be to suddenly be faced with losing her mother. Or Marco. But to have no one was even worse. Her heart grew heavier with the thought. Any prospect of a conversation about her future had all but evaporated.

Camille continued. "Yes, that is the sad fact. Here I am, at the end of my life, with every conceivable possession one could want. Fame, luxury, holidays to anywhere in the world – if I chose to go. The world at my feet. And not a single, damned person to share it with or give it to."
She gave a half-hearted laugh. The timbre of her voice was clear. The tone of a professional singer.

"Please don't end up like I did, Asha. Live life. Have your success but keep your soul." The last sentence was almost a whisper.

Asha swallowed with difficulty and nodded slowly. She had wanted advice, had she not? It wasn't at all what she expected.

Camille stepped back to the table and picked up her drink. She took a long sip, held the glass in both hands and looked down at Asha.

"I've decided what to do with all that wealth, Asha, and that's where you come in. Come." She marched towards her office again. "Come!"

Asha stood, realising she'd held her breath for most of what Camille had said. Gulping air, she followed as Camille shuffled the papers on her desk and held out an envelope to her.

"It's all in here. My solicitor will lodge it with a notary, so it will stand up in any court of law." Camille beckoned for her to take it.

Asha could not fathom that she was to become wealthy. Wealth was almost a foreign idea to her, something outside all possibility. Mama had always lived pay cheque to pay cheque. This seemed unreal. A joke, even.

Asha took the envelope reluctantly, unsure if she was expected to open it. Would it be rude not to? Sensing her dilemma, Camille waved a hand at her.

"No. Don't open it now. Take your time; it won't matter. I'm not dying yet, God willing." She laughed at her choice of words. "He's not getting his talons into me yet. Heaven doesn't need old show ponies like me right now. With my luck, I'll get knocked back." Her voice betrayed an edge of fear.

"I don't know what to say. Thank you? Why me?" She hugged the envelope to her chest, feeling self-conscious of its size.

Camille came across to her, linked her arm to Asha's and led her back to the kitchen. The envelope, she took back from Asha and dropped it on the sofa as they walked past. "Because, my dear, you remind me of me. Your talent, your looks, your innocence ..."

Asha hadn't noticed before that the table was set for the two of them.

"Come, you can serve us both. I had my chef prepare something suitable for a dancer. Nothing to put weight where it should not be." She let Asha's arm go and placed herself at the end of the table.

The mood lifted as Asha busied herself with the pre-prepared meal – a simple affair of small chicken breasts rolled with prosciutto atop a delicate thin sauce with a serve of steamed greens. The perfect meal to replenish after a gruelling day of dance. All Asha had to do was retrieve the feast from the warming oven. Now, she hoped to steer the conversation back to their common ground.

She plied Camille with questions about her days in the theatre. Camille happily answered them, all talk of cancer forgotten.

Asha loved hearing stories of the backstage dramas that involved some very famous names. Camille truly was a legend. And she felt in awe knowing how comfortably this woman had included her, a fledgling of no account, into the very heart of her life.

Somewhere in Camille's apartment, a clock chimed ten o'clock.

Asha started. "Camille. I am so sorry." She leapt to her feet, scrambling to gather her bag and the envelope. "Mama will be beside herself."

"Go. We will talk soon. And perhaps, I could meet your mother?"

Asha had an image of her mother and Camille together. That would be difficult, she thought, as Mama disapproved of Camille. Would knowing about the inheritance make a difference? It might, or it might make things worse. Only time would tell.

CHAPTER 4

Julia paced the few metres of spare floor in the flat. Asha was still not home.
The clock hands crept past ten fifteen. She would give her another fifteen
then ... Then what? Julia didn't know the woman's address. She poured
another glass of wine and sat on the top stair of the landing inside their flat.

Asha should've known better. She knew how much she worried.
Irrational, she admitted, but it was an ingrained response she developed
once her daughter was old enough to be independent. There were only
the two of them. Had been since Asha was two. The weight of that
responsibility on Julia hadn't diminished with her daughter's maturity but
had grown heavier.

Asha's footsteps echoed on the stairs. Julia, one eye on the clock,
hurried down the landing stairs and opened the door to their flat before
Asha's keys even reached the lock.

"You're late. I was worried." The words sounded harsh, even to her
ears. She softened her face to apologise.

"I'm sorry, Mama. We got talking, and the time got away from me.
I got a cab home; I didn't walk." Asha was still breathless from racing up the
stairs. Julia knew she meant it.

Asha hugged her, took the half-empty glass from her hands and poured the dregs down the sink. Her drinking upset her daughter, but it was the one comfort that got her through the waiting. She wished it wasn't that way, but some things were just too hard to change. No one was perfect, were they?

Julia sat at the table while Asha put the kettle on to boil. "Well, how was it?"

A lump rose in her throat. Asha had been at Camille DuPont's for another meeting. It was more than likely to do with the scholarship, but in the back of her mind, a voice whispered other possibilities.

"How was what, Mama?" Asha's voice sounded guarded, raising Julia's suspicions another notch.

"Your meeting? Why did you need to stay so long? I thought you only had to sign papers and come home. And dinner ... You've never stayed for dinner before. What did she want?" The questions multiplied. She bit her tongue to stop.

Her daughter sighed.

Julia's defences raised against the knowledge she had overstepped the point of reasonableness and now waded through overbearing parenting territory.

"Did you like the chocolates? Adeline put an extra one in." With a smile, Asha handed her a cup of tea.

"Fine. Don't answer me then. None of my business, I know." She pouted but let the anger drain from her. It really was none of her business. Asha was a grown woman. She would soon make her own way. Knowing that made it harder for Julia to accept, but she tried to convince herself it would become easier with time. The ache in her heart told her otherwise.

"I'm sorry Asha," she whispered. "It's just ..." She shook her head. "It's nothing." It wasn't the time to get into why Asha's meetings with

Madame DuPont bothered her. Why she worried when she came in late. One day she would tell her. When the time was right.

She yawned and stretched. Now that Asha was home, fatigue overtook her and dragged her into slow motion.

Asha headed towards the tiny bathroom to brush her teeth and remove her make-up but stopped at the door. "Mama, I'll tell you everything in the morning, I promise. I'll make us crepes for breakfast, yes?"

"Crepes. All right then. I'm too tired to talk more anyway. Goodnight."

She climbed into bed, hoping the darkness would swallow her, knowing what awaited her were the nightmares. Asha's father was killed years ago, caught up in a nuclear power protest. She'd got the news late at night, waiting for him to return. Only he never did.

***

The smell of crepes wafted through the flat. Asha opened her eyes and drew a deep breath. She'd slept later than intended, and now the aroma of coffee teased her senses.

Her mother sat at the table in her pyjamas, one leg resting on the edge of the spare chair. With a crepe stuffed into her mouth, she nodded to Asha. "You said you'd make me crepes. Beat you to it." She grinned. Her hair, caught up in an untidy bun, shone in tones of grey and silver where the morning light streamed in from the skylight above them.

Asha winced. She hadn't slept again, spending most of her night sitting on the edge of her mother's bed, stroking her hand. Only when the nightmares ceased did she crawl into her own bed again. They'd gotten worse lately and more frequent. Asha wondered what would happen when she left home. Who would do this for her mother?

"Sorry, Mama. Yesterday was gruelling. Anton got in a mood and made me work so hard."

"No, I'm sorry. I did it again, didn't I?" Her voice held remorse.

"I'm sorry I was so late. I know you worry." She crawled from her bed and wrapped her arms around her mother. They embraced in silence for a moment, and when her mother's tense body loosened, Asha released her.

"I'm so blessed to have you, Mama." She meant it. Just thinking about how Camille said she had no one brought home how much family mattered.

They sat and ate the crepes in comfortable silence. From where she sat, Asha saw the bulge of the envelope in her backpack hanging on its hook on the landing. Should she open it in front of her mother now or wait for her to go to work?

Asha couldn't understand why her meetings with Camille upset her mother. Last night was fresh in her mind. Whatever the letter held, things would change for them and for the better. She would read it first, alone.

Camille said she would have questions and shouldn't wait too long before asking them – the cancer was serious. They would operate soon, and Camille would lose her voice. Asha couldn't imagine what that would feel like.

"I'll clean up today, Mama. You get yourself ready for work." She cleared the table.

Less than an hour later, as the door closed on her mother, Asha held the envelope, turning it over in her hands. Crisp linen, official and expensive. Now she felt a surge of dread. Could she possibly understand the implications for them both? For a moment, fear paralysed her. What if her mother refused to allow her to accept such a gift? Surely, this was her choice. To accept or not?

She shook the fear off. Excitement took over, and she pried the seal open, careful not to tear the envelope. Inside, an official letter, again written on heavy linen paper. She read the solicitor's details. Pierre Levin & Son. Asha had never heard of them.

The letter was basic. An invitation to attend the office to explain how she would benefit by being named in the Last Will & Testament, as it stood, of Madame Camille DuPont.

After all the build-up, the letter was disappointing. No detail of the inheritance. It raised more questions than answers. She put it back in the envelope, threw it on her bed, and busied herself for the day ahead.

***

Antonio Rochet tidied the papers on Madame DuPont's desk. With one eye on the clock, he swept up the bundle of letters to be mailed. The last of them, he noticed, wasn't sealed. He pursed his lips with an exasperated puff. She'd told him they must all go in the afternoon post. Especially that one. It was her usual practice to seal them herself, and the last thing he wanted was to have her reproach him tomorrow for a job not completed to her exact liking.

He tapped his forefinger on the desk. She'd gone to lie down not five minutes ago. A wave of pity dulled his annoyance. She was sick. Very sick. And if he wanted to keep his job, in whatever capacity that may be, if or when she died, he would need to become indispensable. Or find a new job.

He turned the offending letter addressed to the hospital over. Not just any hospital but the top private cancer clinic in Paris. No, France. It was the top clinic in the country; it just happened to be in Paris. She would've flown anywhere for the best surgeon. Part of him hoped they would successfully rid her of the dreaded disease. Another part, the realist in him, expected she would die from it. No one was indestructible, not even the Iron Lady herself.

He bit his lip and glanced at her closed bedroom door. He could just tap and wave it at her. Ask and be on his way. It was a good chance she meant to seal it, anyway. The urge to check the contents overtook him.

51

He reasoned that if already completed and signed, there was no need to bother her. If not, he would be justified in checking and getting whatever she needed to do sorted there and then. He slid the document from the envelope and read it.

No surprise, it was the admission papers for her operation. What made him catch his breath was who she named as next of kin. The girl. He dropped the form onto the desk as though it had burnt his fingers. Bile rose, the unpleasant sensation making him swallow hard. He was offended, expecting his name to be there. Hadn't he devoted his service for the past two decades? Wasn't he to be trusted with such a thing? The hurt built into an acrid stone in his gut.

Who was the girl? A nobody. No dance company had snapped her up, not yet. He conceded they may because she was talented, but the possibility she meant more to Madame DuPont on a personal level would seal that for her. How had she influenced the cold-hearted queen?

He looked around Camille's office. The walls dripped with her achievements. She had lived for dance, theatre and singing. A true star of her time. But that star had faded. No one out there knew her now. She belonged to the past and, he lamented, so did he. He'd hoped this job would set him up for retirement. A healthy slice of her wealth had been a quiet lamp he had burnt once he realised how remote she was from the world. Almost a recluse, except for her dealings with that wretched scholarship.

A sarcastic voice in his head brought him back to the present. "If it weren't for that scholarship, Antonio, she'd have no need of your services."

Still, he conceded, he felt ill-willed that she had overlooked him.

The voice laughed at him. "If the hospital rang you in the dead of night and said, come quick, your mistress needs you, would you leap out of bed? Or roll over and say, in the morning would be soon enough. Or would you do anything for a few million francs, Antonio?"

Guilty. He cocked an eyebrow.

"Touché, Antonio."

The question burned. It would take one phone call to fix things in his favour. Did he dare? Or was he really such a coward?

He stuffed the form back in the envelope, sealed it and strode out of the apartment without looking backwards. The back of his throat burned, and he worked his jaw to ease the tension. Did she think she was better than him? A voice egged his thoughts on. He was right. She despised him. Bring her down a peg, Antonio, it said. Show her you have more control than she knows. Make yourself indispensable. The girl won't be enough. What does she know of madame's business? Nothing!

Rochet slept uneasily that night. He tossed and turned, grappling with a horror dream where he fell into a pit of vipers. A ladder dangled above him. At the top of the ladder, Camille sat on a swing seat. She looked down on him, swaying to and fro; the ladder beneath her kept out of his reach by her movement.

CHAPTER 5

Yaseem walked past the door to his study. The light was still on.
His student's head lay in his hands above an open book, an empty plate
and mug nearby. He smiled; Anna had fed him. The teacher stood in the
doorway, not wanting to disturb Alfredo's concentration but interested
to see if he'd worked out the complexities of his mission. Rembrandt gave
away his presence with an impatient woof at its master.

"Shh," he gently responded, but it was too late.

Alfredo sat bolt upright at the sound. "Sir. I'm sorry. I was so
immersed in this book. I ... I'll come back in the morning, shall I?"

Yaseem set himself on a stool beside the desk. "I have no plans for
the evening, Alfredo. Come, tell me what you've learnt so far."

Alfredo glared at the book. Yaseem was all too familiar with the
angel's distaste for reading. He lifted an eyebrow and waited.

"Well, for one, it's in French. Everything we've ever done has been
in Latin or Greek ..." His face showed a level of bewilderment.

"And there is some significance to this, you think?"
prompted Yaseem.

"My charge is French? That's the most obvious answer." He beamed at Yaseem. "I find it easier to read. That's a bonus."

"What else?"

"Free Will. You were right, sir. This book is very enlightening. I know I shouldn't question the Father's reasoning, but what a thing to give them. Down there." He waved his hands to emphasise his surprise. "I mean, it's such a gift, but ..." He stalled, lost for words. His brow creased as he tried to explain. "A gift, a curse, a flaw ..."

"Or perfection," Yaseem finished for him. "Yes. All of those things." He stood and walked to his desk, where Alfredo's scroll lay unfurled. "It sets us apart from them, Alfredo. You know that you and I can only do the Father's bidding. If He says to answer this plea, we take it to our charge and offer it. It's up to them to accept. Frustrating for us, and of course, for the Father."

One glance at the scroll made him take a sharp intake of breath. "Alfredo, come. Your scroll beckons."

The angel leapt to his feet, and they both stared at the scroll. Words had appeared where before there were none.

Alfredo jumped with glee. "French! Yes!" He pored over the words, excited.

Yaseem smiled with relief. It seemed the Father had not made it impossible after all.

"And what is it telling you, Alfredo? Do you have a clearer idea of your mission now?"

The young angel, intent on the scroll, paused and sighed. "Do you read Cantonese, sir? It seems there are messages here that require it." His face fell.

"No one said this would be easy, Alfredo. Or straightforward. Had you paid attention to all my classes, you would have known this."

Alfredo hung his head, chastised.

Yaseem softly laughed, enough for his student to relax. "Alfredo, classes may have finished where I stand before you with instruction, but you will never stop learning."

It occurred to Yaseem as he spoke those words that they applied not only to Alfredo but also to himself. He made a mental note to cover blank scrolls with his current students. Just because it was not a usual occurrence didn't mean it should not be addressed. He felt sorry for this angel. In a way, it was his own failure that might mitigate the success of his charge's mission. That was a sobering thought.

"Actual knowledge will come from your interaction with the Father and your charge. Remember to listen well. Sometimes it is in the silence that you will find your answers."

Alfredo still had an expectant look on his face. Perhaps the message wasn't getting through.

"I know your aversion to books, and that leads me to believe that yours is to be a language of the heart."

"Sir?" Alfredo still looked baffled.

Yaseem leant closer, laying a hand on Alfredo's chest. "It won't be what is spoken, so much, but the cries of the heart of your charge that will be important. They say French is the language of love." He pointed back to the book Alfredo had been studying. "The chapter I referred to, chapter three. What was it?"

"The Unwilling." Alfredo's eyes met Yaseem's.

"What does that suggest to you?" He held Alfredo's gaze, compelling him to grasp his meaning. He could almost see the cogs clicking ever so slowly into place.

"That my charge is unwilling? Unwilling to what? To listen, to feel? Why?"

Ah, he has it. The boy was on the right track now. Yaseem broke his hold on Alfredo's attention.

"That is what you must find out." Yaseem pointed to the scroll. "Has your scroll given you the whereabouts of the Angels Ladder? If so, it's time to go. If not, the answer lies with the books still."

***

Alfredo clutched his scroll and dashed across the university concourse. He'd be back at his apartment within minutes. Around him, night birds sang. He never tired of their soulful sound. He hummed in tune to one as it flew from tree to tree beside him. In return, the bird darted and hovered around his head. The exchange lifted his spirit. The row of trees finished, and the bird flew into the night.

He turned his thoughts to the scroll and the new markings on it. His heartbeat increased, and excitement thrilled through him. French, he mused. Now, if all their lessons had been in French, who knows what else he might have grasped better. He could not wait to unfurl the scroll and see what else was revealed.

His apartment lay on the second level of a large complex. A wide staircase led from a central courtyard at street level and branched off in all directions. It was busy, as Alfredo expected, even though the hour was late. Thankful for Anna's delicious offering, he skipped the dining hall and went straight to his room.

Once inside, he laid the scroll on a table and held his breath with excitement and, yes, he had to admit, a modicum of fear. He'd waited his entire existence for this moment, but now it was here he wasn't sure of his readiness.

"I am ready. I am. Just need to remember what Yaseem said. Listen first, act second."

The scroll glowed. Interesting. He hadn't noticed that before. Then again, he'd left it on Yaseem's desk while he read about free will.

Perhaps this was normal. He stood, arms folded, and intently watched the scroll. Before his eyes, words appeared. Soft letters became bold. His excitement grew. Every nerve sang.

The scroll quivered and a photo emerged. Alfredo's eyes widened. It was as if the scroll itself were alive. He leant over the table and studied the image. A woman stared back at him. His charge? He experienced a moment of confusion. Wasn't it usual for a charge to be a newborn? Didn't this woman already have an angel assigned?

He shook his head. He vaguely remembered the class. Yes, it was usual, but as always, there were exceptions. Why had he not paid attention? He knew why. When Yaseem said they assigned exceptions to masterful angels, he immediately dismissed his future appointment would be one of these types. His expectations were never that high. He wasn't a reader. There were more talented angels in his class; ergo, they might be considered masterful. Not him.

He studied the face again. The eyes looked out at him with such deep sorrow, Alfredo had to look away. When he looked back, the sadness had become anger. He started. Panic fleetingly gripped him. Even the sight of such emotion warned him to take a backwards step.

He remembered one important instruction from his last tutorial. The armour. They'd practised it, even.

Yaseem had brought in a serving angel to demonstrate how it all worked. One had to prepare the mind first, empty it of all distractions, then call upon the Father for the armour. It had taken the class many attempts to get it right, but Alfredo had mastered it quicker than most, as no textbooks were needed. It all came down to the thought process. And the timing of the application. A serving angel must always be on guard; therefore, the Armour of God was essentially worn continuously. He had forgotten.

With both arms folded, crossed from shoulder to shoulder, he imagined himself dressed for battle. The new garment weighed heavily across his back and chest. When his limbs moved, he heard the creak of leather. He stared at his reflection – like a roman soldier. Confident he was now prepared correctly, he looked again at the scroll.

A name emerged beneath the photo. Camille DuPont. Age eighty. Native-born French, parents deceased, both Heaven-bound.

Well, that was a relief, he thought. His charge had every chance of getting to Heaven if both parents had succeeded. It still didn't explain why an angel appointment came at eighty years old. Something didn't add up. He must find someone else who'd dealt with this.

The scroll became still again and lost its glow. A sign Alfredo could work with what he knew. He pondered his next move. He had a choice, of course. The major library was open, even at this hour. He'd not been there, as it was for the working angel's use. A thought occurred to him. That was him now. He grinned. A fresh surge of excitement flowed through him. Was it always like this? New revelation after revelation. It was exhilarating. Maybe he should visit the dining hall. He might need to keep his source of energy well fed.

***

Alfredo pushed open the large doors into the dining hall. The noise hit him immediately. The clatter of a spoon on a plate, the conversation and laughter wrapped around him in waves of familiarity. Yet now, there was a sense of awareness he couldn't decipher. Something was different.

He took his place in the line, scanning the hall for a familiar face. There were none. Unusual, as it was a favourite gathering place among students. Of course, he chided. The angels he usually sat with would've left by now. Anyone here was a student still, or, he glanced towards the far end of the hall, one of them. The active angels.

For a moment, he lost his appetite. What was he? He was technically no longer a student but not yet an active angel. Butterflies roiled in his stomach. Then it dawned on him he could use this moment to learn more about what to expect once his task became clear.

Alfredo cast his mind back to his first day of university. His approach back then was to quell any nerves with affable banter. It had worked once, why not again?

He loaded his tray with fruit, bread and the meat offering of the day. It smelt spicy, and already his mouth watered.

He sauntered past the student crowd towards the end of the hall, searching for a table with a spare seat. When he approached, the occupants looked up, smiled, and made room for him. He introduced himself, and they, in turn, did the same. As he ate his food, he intently listened as they talked between themselves about their day. Alfredo was humbled. There was a lot to learn.

One of them turned to him. "How goes your case, friend?"

Alfredo stopped chewing and swallowed. All the charm he'd planned to use had vapourised listening to their conversations. Unsure he wanted to speak but having seen the respect and interest they showed in each other, he decided to share something of his day.

"Thank you for asking. I'm new to all this. I've listened to you all, and I'm not sure my case will be as exciting."

The angel sat silently; expectation written on his face. The others stopped their conversations, and suddenly all eyes were on him. He stammered.

The first angel prompted him. "From the beginning, friend." He grinned. "We have time."

Alfredo explained his day, from the moment he received his blank scroll to his entering the hall and finding himself like a fish out of water. He grinned sheepishly. "See, nothing exciting here."

The angels exchanged silent looks.

The first speaker put his cup down and sat back in his seat. "Alfredo, we are all students till our charge makes Heaven. Or doesn't. Look around you. Even the young among us wear the leather, right through to the old ones." He nodded to an angel down the other end of the table. Alfredo noticed, for the first time, that this angel was indeed older than the others. His face was seasoned – like Yaseem's.

The older angel nodded in agreement. "My charge is on his deathbed. I've been with him since he took his first breath, and I expect to take his last breath to the throne soon. When that's done, I will await the purpose designed for me."

Another spoke. "Your case is just as important. Each soul is on a journey home, and you're there to prompt them onto the way."

The first angel added, "Interesting that you think she should have had a guide before now. Have you heard of the Sleeping Angels?"

Sleeping Angels? Was it bad that Alfredo had no familiarity with this term? Again, he cursed his loathing for book learning.

"The guide may be there," the first angel continued. "I suggest you first go to the library and seek your casebook. It is there. They all are."

They all nodded in agreement. The angel next to Alfredo patted him on the back. "Well done, you. You may find your case so much more interesting than you think, after all."

The others returned to different conversations, leaving Alfredo to ponder who the Sleeping Angels were. And was Camille's first guide one of them?

***

His stomach full, Alfredo returned to his room, where the scroll lay open on the table. He checked in case more instructions had materialised. No glow. No quivering. Relieved, he began to remove the armour, but the Spirit's voice in his head stopped him.

"Meditate," it said. "Let the words on the scroll instruct you."

His eyelids grew heavy as he sat cross-legged on his prayer platform and let the remnant of conversations flow through his mind. Sleeping Angels – who were they? Who are they that need to sleep?

It seemed as if he'd just closed his eyes when a knock on the door broke through his trance. Alfredo's eyes flew open. It was still dark outside. He glanced at the scroll. Was he surprised even in the dark, he could see it clearly? No. The scroll was full of surprises, and he suspected it would continue to amaze him. This was nothing like the reams of rolls he encountered as a student. It even felt different. If he compared it to anything, it resembled skin. Not the hide of an animal. They had those at the university as well. He pinched his arms. Not unlike his skin, but more supple.

The knock came again.

"Enter!"

No one did, which made him curious. He opened the door and peered down the empty hallway. Whoever had knocked was gone, but the air smelt overwhelmingly of heavy blossom and left him with a sense of urgency. Alert now, Alfredo closed his door. The aroma filled his room.

Bewildered by the assault on his senses, he frowned and looked at the scroll for guidance. It glowed again. Hastily, he unrolled it as it quivered under his hands. A rush of energy flowed into him, and on the parchment, three symbols in Cantonese appeared.

"Ah, another language," he cried out in frustration. "What does it mean?"

He had to go to the library. Somewhere there lay the answers to the riddles on his scroll. He gritted his teeth, rolled the scroll up and tucked it under his arm.

CHAPTER 6

The entrance to the Hall of Books was majestic. Impressive in height and columns that ten angels could link hands around and not quite reach. The stairs leading to it were inlaid with pink marble, the colours of salmon and rose, and flowed with seams of black agate.

Alfredo's knees trembled as he climbed. At the top of the stairs, wooden doors of cedar with golden hinges opened as he approached. A faint aroma of sweet almonds and coffee wafted out and drew him in.

Alfredo had never been here before. His aversion to reading had made this a destination for, as he used to say, a time when he had to. After student life. Now, that time had arrived, and the pit of his stomach churned.

The main hall lay before him. As far as he could see, there were angels. All of them wore armour. A glance down confirmed he still wore his, and a moment of relief washed over him. He didn't look as out of place as he imagined. Emboldened, he found the information counter and stood in a line, four or five angels deep, nervous. What should he ask for? Was this the right place? Beads of sweat formed on his upper lip. He overheard an angel in front ask for the Irish section. The questions back and forth between the assistant and angel soon gave Alfredo the start he needed. Then his turn came.

"Name, please. And which section?"

"Camille DuPont. French. Current data and family line." He hoped he sounded confident.

The assistant looked at him with a scrutinising glare, then she smiled. "New?"

He nodded. How had she known? His face reddened.

"Got your scroll with you?" Again, he nodded. She handed him a leather cylinder. "Safekeeping." She winked. "Lots of scrolls in here. You wouldn't like to get yours mixed up with anyone else's."

"Oh, thank you. Has that happened before?" Alfredo's eyes widened with shock. She nodded, winked again and gave him a card with directions. When he looked from it to the hall, she made a squeaking noise, waved him aside and pointed to the western side.

"Follow the blue line, can't miss it." She looked over his shoulder. "Next!"

Alfredo stepped out of the queue and searched for the blue line. It appeared at his feet and stretched only a few metres in front of him. Every step he took extended the line, and when he glanced behind, it vanished. With an overwhelming sense of urgency, he ran. Past tables strewn with books and bent heads, past couches where angels sat in deep conversation with others until he stood before a wall of books. The titles were self-explanatory. Names. And among them was his Camille DuPont.

***

Camille's book lay wedged between two heavy tomes on a high shelf. To get to it, Alfredo dragged a book ladder across the front of the case. Three rungs up, covered in dust and mite webs, it resembled a forgotten diary, its pages pressed together and reluctant to yield to his fingers.

The cover was thick with dust. Where his fingers gripped it, a smudge of colour showed through. It was grimy and uncomfortable to hold. He wished he'd used gloves.

He sat at a table nearby. A brush sat in a groove of the desk. Alfredo understood its purpose. He began gently removing the layers of powder. Each stroke of the brush revealed another glimpse of the cover. Deep emerald-green leather. Her name etched in gold cursive writing. Her birthdate underneath. No death date – a good thing, he thought. Once clean, the book was a wonder to behold.

The scroll quivered. Alfredo unfurled it and stared at the picture. The sadness had returned to the face. With great compassion, he laid an open palm on the green leather and gave thanks for his charge's life. The warmth of it surprised him. A movement in the photo caught his eye. Had the face smiled? Some of the warmth crept into his own heart.

With a deep breath, Alfredo prised open the cover. In perfect handwriting and in fluent French, her story began. How the months in the womb progressed, and how her birthing had gone. Images floated on and off the pages in a dance of colour and soft poetry. Love emanated from the page. She'd been wanted then, he surmised.

There was her angel. Her first appointed angel. His eyes widened. The angel sang. Her voice floated off the page and echoed in his ears. He knew the song well. A Christmas song that made him smile and close his eyes.

But the moment he closed his eyes, the angel wept. Initially, softly, but then in deepening sobs. He opened his eyes. A tear escaped down his cheek. The cherub on the page looked straight at him.

She saw him! He hadn't expected that.

The angel from the dining hall had made a comment. It nudged Alfredo. Of course. The Sleeping Angels, that's where this angel might be. But where? He looked from the book to the great hall. No signs, no directions in view, just rows and rows of bookcases and tables like the one he sat at. A line of glowing chandeliers marched into the distance. It was daunting. He made a mental note to ask the friendly assistant on the way out.

He turned the page. Camille was older now. Her childhood became a movie playing, the years of love, the childish dreams and the aura of her family that surrounded her. But shadows were lurking in the walls of the house. There was distance between father and daughter, and how her mother shielded her from his view saddened him. He sensed innocence and yet, fear. It was expected; he'd been taught to watch for it. He smirked and thought of Yaseem.

See, sir, I paid attention sometimes.

The other angel was still there, too. He observed how she doted over her charge. Her eyes followed Camille in her play. Alfredo went to turn the page when the young angel flew to a window of the house. Whatever was outside forced her to shield her eyes and fall back in pain. Alfredo felt that pain stab at his own heart. It perplexed him. How did he feel things he had not experienced? He couldn't know what she'd seen. Not from outside the world of Camille DuPont.

He turned the page again. Now, a teenage Camille. The smile no longer reached her eyes. At once, the book imparted sadness. Again, the shadows loomed in the background. He searched for the little angel. She was there but meekly following her charge around. Alfredo gasped at the change in her. Had she shrunk? The angel stared out at him with pleading eyes.

"I see you, but where are you now?" he whispered.

He gently touched the page. The angel flew to his hand and touched it from within the book. An electric shock passed between them and forced him to pull away. He sat back from the book in deep thought. When Yaseem mentioned the books in class, Alfredo imagined them as nothing different from the volumes they studied. The description of them being just the unique stories of every human soul on Earth was vastly inadequate. No other book could be described as – he searched for the right word – alive. He wondered if he'd have continued his studies to become a guardian angel had he known their complexity. His whole being trembled.

Now he forced himself to turn the page. At least that was his intention, but the book had decided otherwise. The pages refused to move. It was as if the wrong edges were bound. Alfredo took a closer look and, even though he could see the edges of each page, they couldn't be opened. What lay ahead for Camille was hidden from him.

Alfredo was flummoxed. What now? He'd come to an impasse. The whereabouts of the young angel might have been revealed in the sealed pages, but for now, he had to wait. Or go elsewhere for the answers.

He closed the book and lay both hands on it. A silent prayer was in order. He closed his eyes and began.

"Dearest Father God ..." The book quivered, as did the scroll. "Reveal to me your will; send me forth to my destiny. Alleluia, Amen."

The scroll glowed. Alfredo smiled. He gently took Camille's book and placed it back in its space on the shelf. The leather spine of her book shone as though new. Satisfaction swelled in his heart.

"I will be back," he whispered.

He turned his attention to the scroll. In perfect French, the words Jardin Des Endormis was blazoned across it, along with Demandez Felice and Vitesse De Dieu.

Garden of the Sleeping Ones, Ask for Felice and Godspeed.

A broad grin erupted on Alfredo's face. Finally, some action. And with Felice's help, he would understand his mission better. He just had to find the Garden.

***

Yaseem scanned the faces of his new students, each of them transparent. As his gaze swept the classroom, he saw the fear and excitement in their eyes. Fresh faces that he would transform into wise guardians, all destined for the earthly realm.

It was a familiar scene, repeated over and over, but this year, things were different. No, not things, not the students in front of him. He was different.

One student would not leave the forefront of his mind. He almost expected Alfredo to enter the classroom and slip into his usual seat. But that wasn't to be. His eyes glanced at the spot where Alfredo used to sit. Another angel sat there today.

He was distracted and had been for the past few weeks. He hadn't interfered with Alfredo's research; that would not be proper. Alfredo must do that for himself. Yet all the while, he worried about him.

Yaseem felt partly responsible for his predicament. It had been so long since a blank scroll had arisen that he had brushed over its importance in his curriculum. And now he saw why that was a problem.

He took in the group before him to test his thinking. Was there another future guardian of a blank scroll in their midst, and how did one tell from just looking at them? If the Father had hinted at such a guardian last semester, would he, Yaseem, have chosen Alfredo?

The gravity of his omission weighed heavily on his heart. Alfredo would find Felice because the scroll would lead him there; Yaseem was confident of that. But when he did find her, and together they left for the earthly realm, that was when Yaseem worried for them both.

That was Satan's realm.

A failure would mean a certain return to the Garden of Sleeping Ones for Felice, but only until her charge's death. If Satan won the battle for her soul, Felice would cease to exist and her place in the Garden would be given over to another Sleeping Angel.

For Alfredo, his first failure could be his last.

A shiver ran along Yaseem's spine. He would do better going forward.

He turned to the parchment resting in front of the class and wrote in confident strokes with his quill.

"Blank Scrolls."

***

In the deepest shadows cast by the heating tower on Camille DuPont's apartment rooftop, Satan sat and scratched against the wall. To any living being who may have had the ill fortune to be there at that moment, a bone-deep chill might have warned them away. As it was, the rooftop was unoccupied.

A lesser demon crouched in fear at its master's feet; its eyes, slits of green, watching warily and waiting. It understood the rage brewing was not directed at itself, yet it fully expected to wear the brunt of the master's fury. A clawed foot wrapped around the throat of the lesser demon, rendering it powerless. How long this would continue, it couldn't know.

The angel Felice was about to be set free from the black web. Satan knew that even though the deed had not yet been completed, he could not stop her release. The Greater Power had intervened. Even though the web was his strongest weapon against the angels, it came to nought when God chose to have His way. There was always rage whenever this happened. Someone had to pay. It was the lesser demon's misfortune to be with Satan when the news broke.

Satan's mind raced. He pored over recollections of Felice and the one she used to be attached to, who slept below. Interference started with the new batch of angels sent to Earth. As always, his radar had bristled that day when a new quarry was released from up there. His demons were sent to check the ladder for the fresh ones. None had reported an unusual angel that day. Satan was almost duped into believing nothing out of the ordinary was afoot.

Then, out of nowhere, he sensed a change in the atmosphere and rushed here to see the issue. Paris never disappointed. There was plenty of soul fodder here. But that wasn't what caused his fury.

Nothing annoyed Satan more than a restored soul. Or even the possibility of one. And that was what was happening here. He had all but counted this one as his own. After a lifetime of denying God, she was wavering.

What to do about it?

Deep in thought, he flexed his claw on the demon's neck. The demon's eyes bulged and blinked with every squeeze. Was there time to thwart the outcome? Satan summonsed the demons attached to her. They appeared and hovered just out of reach.

"Report!"

The demons clung to each other in fear. Each pushed the other forward until Satan snarled, tired of their antics. They froze, then one of them cleared his throat and spoke.

"She fights us, master. But we have her surrounded. No opposition. She's almost a recluse. The secretary is a fool. He loves money and is self-inflated over his importance. His guide is weak." They snickered in unison.

"Grr!" Satan snorted. "Then how is it possible we can lose her?"

They could not answer.

Satan rose from his seat. The lesser demons fell back, quivering in fear. He roared in anger, breathing a sulphurous gas over them. "She has cancer. Maybe I can hurry that along ..." He stroked his wiry goatee and, satisfied with his plan, disappeared into thin air.

CHAPTER 7

Paris 2000

Pierre stood at the window. He followed Camille DuPont as she walked along the street below and watched her until she disappeared from his sight. He was restless. It wasn't his usual practice to be personally involved with a client's matters, but she had gotten under his skin. Wills were such sticky things. His father had pressed home their importance.

"That one piece of paper can affect an entire family for generations. A good will can be a blessing to its beneficiaries – make their lives easier. A bad one will destroy even the happiest of families. Take your utmost care when you advise a client."

Wise words, but even his father had conceded a lawyer's part in will-making was minor. If a client so wished to inflict their twisted version of good or bad onto their family, well, he could only suggest alternatives, not make that decision for them.

This case was different. Camille DuPont was his father's client. One of his first. Pierre Senior always considered her special and respected her acumen. When he retired, her file lay open on his desk.

"Son," he'd said, "this woman's heart is stone, but somewhere in there is a brilliant diamond. She's been hurt. Badly. Don't misjudge her."

Back then, Pierre had given it little thought. His years of sitting at the other desk facing the inner courtyard of this building prepared him to wear a mask when in the company of his clientele. He could be invisible, and none of the stains that leaked from the many twisted wills he'd prepared over his long vocation had stuck to his reputation.

This case was different. The scribbled note in Camille DuPont's old file changed everything. He'd almost missed it. Had closed the folder, ready to return it to the archives. But he'd caught his suit sleeve on something and dropped the file, scattering its contents across the floor. The note had caught his eye and his imagination. It was not his father's way to collect newspaper clippings of his clients, but there it was. And the note itself was benign, just his client's name scribbled along the edge of the cutting.

The article ignited his desire to take a fresh approach to this client.

Pierre wasn't a great fan of the arts and knew little of the players in that game, but even he could smell a scandal when it crossed his path. The slip of a girl in the photo looked nothing like the woman who sat in his office this morning. It was difficult to tell if the girl was even the same woman, but he trusted that if his father knew her then, it was in her file for a good reason. He saw only a frightened child with huge eyes staring into the flash of a paparazzi journalist. The magazine itself explained that fear. Les Fichiers De Potins – The Gossip Files. The gossip about his client was outrageous. In today's magazines, it would've brought about a defamation lawsuit. His client's personal life was exposed already in those few short words. And if he had a copy, it still existed for others to see.

Camille DuPont had a reputation for being abrupt. As his father had said, on the outside, one was confronted with stone. But he, like his father, believed actions spoke louder than words. His client's generosity as a benefactress to the arts paralleled none. She gave back to the industry that had carried her to the top. Indeed, she inherited an impressive portfolio from her father, one she'd not touched a hair of. It lay accumulating a massive fortune.

And yet, with no family to speak of, who would thank her for her toil? He knew the vultures would circle the moment she closed her eyes. A heavy burden for her. And for him.

Pierre handed his secretary the file. "Josie, stamp this as urgent. Have it marked confidential and delivered to Jacques Pearson."

"Yes, Mr Levin."

Pierre tapped the file with one bony finger and thought for a moment. His client had only days left with a voice. This was too important to wait.

"Courier it today."

"Yes, Mr Levin, straight away."

***

Camille emerged from the solicitor's office in a daze. The day had gone from bad to worse. She stood on the street outside, paralysed with indecision. Every fibre in her body wanted to burst into tears, the very sentiment she preferred to avoid at all costs.

She could hail a cab and go home, but if that happened, she would succumb to the bottle of whiskey. Too early for that. And besides, today was the day Asha visited. She would not divulge the depth of her misery to her.

Thinking of Asha charged her with new energy. The girl would want for nothing soon. It pleased her that of all the people she had left in her shrinking world, Asha was the most unaffected soul she knew. When she died, that angel would have the means to pursue her happiness. That left Camille with a warm glow.

But somewhere out there, a woman existed who might want to take a piece for herself. If Pierre found her, she might want the lion's share of what was intended for Asha. And, if blood mattered most, she was entitled to claim it. Camille wanted to ensure only a meagre amount went her way from the estate. One tied with so many caveats it would be impossible to unravel in a contested suit without the woman risking every euro.

She hoped it wouldn't come to that. Better still if Pierre never found her. Asha was young and naïve about wealth and what doors it might open for her. A contested will would muddy her life when she could least afford it.

Camille would earmark a tidy sum for the child she brought into the world by mishap to satisfy her conscience and silence the moral objectors. The child had a free slate to live a full life, and Camille owed her nothing more.

She would treat herself to an afternoon at the Louvre. Where better to look at the past than in that glorious treasure trove.

Somewhere close by, above the police sirens and fume-leaking truck noise, a familiar sound floated into her ears. She stopped in her tracks, oblivious to the tutt-tutting of other pedestrians. She checked her watch. Midday. The bells of the Notre-Dame cathedral marked the time. Mr Ying's words came to mind. For a moment, she wondered if he was there today, with his apron and silly grin. She continued to the end of the street, where she faced a red light and waited patiently with a tourist group. Not just any group; a gaggle of photo-snapping Chinese, no doubt on their way to join Ying in the line.

The light turned green. What possessed her, she could not tell, but instead of left, to where the Louvre beckoned, she turned right and followed the bobbing cameras held high on sticks. It gave her a chance to study this curious group. Among them was a woman with a short version of her coat. Camille mused it might be a fake, but without a closer inspection, this was impossible to confirm. For now, any distraction was welcome. She had until three – the time she agreed with Asha to call at the apartment

– and if Mr Ying was at the cathedral, she'd provide him with a modicum of joy at the sight of her herding his fellow citizens towards his advertising. She'd never live it down next time in the elevator, but then, she reasoned, those moments were finite, weren't they? It would give Mr Ying something funny and pleasant to remember her by when she was gone.

The cathedral loomed large ahead. Across the concourse, a plethora of humanity basked in the midday sun. They lounged on every surface, lunch or cameras in their hands, all soaking up the atmosphere.

Memories flooded back from another time. A time of innocence and wonder when the magnificent edifice before her had spoken of fairy tales and magic. It was here her parents came for Christmas service. The crowds then were even greater than the present one. Everyone dressed in their finest and the bells echoed up and down the river, mingling with the sounds of cheerful chatter. But this was not Christmas. A busker further along the street played the saxophone, and interspersed with his tune, the babble of different languages and garish accents washed over Camille.

The memory disappeared, and Camille floundered in its wake. Disillusioned, she made to leave just as the woman with the short fur coat spotted Camille's longer, finer version. As with all tourists, there was little inhibition and before she knew it, five Chinese women stroked her arms and surrounded her with ridiculous grins adorning their faces. There was no escape. In her glory days as part of the social set of Paris, Camille had enjoyed this attention wherever she went. As her career closed and the public memory of her faded, it rarely happened. In fact, she couldn't remember the last time.

The women ordered her into photo after photo, and after a good fifteen minutes, Camille found herself in the cathedral portico with them in tow. Their persistence exhausted her to the point that her only escape was to pay the fee and enter the gloom while the group sorted out the correct currency to use.

She removed her sunglasses and allowed her eyes to adapt to the cavern's darkness. Thankfully, it was also cooler inside. A moment longer out there, she would've shed the coat and risked the tourists whisking it away with them. She shook her head at the thought. Her objective was to move as far from the entrance as possible to avoid being usurped into their midst again.

The walls of the ancient church soaked up the mundane sounds of the city outside, leaving only the muted footsteps of tourists on the stone floor to penetrate to where around Camille chose to sit. The pew felt small. Not how she remembered it from her childhood. Wrapped in her fur coat, she allowed her mind to drift. Upwards, away from the legal jargon of Pierre and the terrifying thing in her throat that she must eventually face. She closed her eyes and took a deep breath, even though it hurt to do so. Tears formed under her eyelids, and she squeezed them tighter. She would not wallow in self-pity. That was not her way.

Instead, she would go back. Go back to the last time she'd been here. It was here she'd felt safe, always. If only she could stay in here, cocooned from the outside world. She opened her eyes and looked around for a familiar landmark. Where was the statue of Madonna? She couldn't see it from where she was sitting. She looked up at the vaulted ceiling and inhaled deeply. A fleeting memory returned of angels floating, and she chuckled under her breath. Oh, to be a child again. The memory crystallised. Five or six? Six. She was sure. Papa carried her, and the snow melted from his jacket all over her dress.

A moment of sadness descended. That was the last time he carried her on his shoulders. It's why she remembered how old she'd been.

"When you are seven, it is proper to walk, Cammie," he'd said. And she'd complied but remembered she didn't enjoy it; lost in the sea of people instead of high on his shoulders, carried among the Christmas lights, the world at her feet.

A wayward pigeon fluttered from one pillar top to the next. Had it been pigeons back then? Probably. Escaping from the winter cold. Camille watched its progress. It homed into what must've been a nest. There were stains down the side of the pillar. Pests. Still, to a child ...

Somewhere from the main body of the church, the sounds of a Mass floated to her. Fools. There is no God. Why bother with him? He did nothing for her when she had the need.

As the words formed in her mind, a clear voice in her head said, "So, why are you here?"

Why indeed? Her eyes burnt again, and she swallowed hard, hurting her throat again. She stifled a cough, worried if she began, she wouldn't stop. She fumbled in her purse for a throat lozenge and put it under her tongue. The soothing lemony liquid eased the itch.

"Why did you forget about me?" she bit back. "Where were you when I needed you?" A tear formed and slowly inched down one side of her cheek. She swiped it away, and angrily crumpled the lozenge wrapper.

Silence. But now that Camille's pain was exposed, she could not stop.

"Maman, Papa." She could not bring herself to add her name. "You took them from me when I needed them." Their images, as she remembered them, swirled in her head. Her maman, who had urged her to pray. Which she had, hadn't she? For what? Those prayers were unanswered. Her papa, locked in his pain, pushed her away. And when she might have returned to him, at the end of school, he was gone. Bloody cancer.

She gripped the back of the ancient wooden bench in front of her, making it creak. A woman in the pews ahead lifted her bowed head at the sound. At that moment, Camille became self-conscious that she wasn't kneeling in prayer. She brushed the guilt aside. To kneel would acknowledge defeat in her inner tussle with God. She was not ready to submit.

Anger rose in the pit of her stomach and latched onto her throat. It burned; the effect of the lozenge not having lasted, and she put her hand to her neck, willing the pain to stop. The skin felt crepey under her fingers. Nothing. He didn't answer her then, and he wouldn't now. The anger faded a notch. What was the point of it all? She had no one to share this pain with.

"I gave you a daughter." The words dropped into the silence.

Camille choked back a fresh wave of tears as the anger flared again. She stamped her foot on the kneeling bar and immediately regretted it. The woman in front of her had stiffened her shoulders at the sound. Camille's indignation would not be calmed easily. She didn't care what anyone else thought right at this moment. "Gave? No! That wasn't a gift. What I went through ..." She squeezed her eyes tight. Tried to block the train of thought. "I was still a child myself. I couldn't be a mother to her. And the war, how would we have coped?" No, she would not feel guilty about that again. She had done the right thing. Right for her and the child. Yet, the emptiness inside would not be dismissed as easily. It started in her gut and clenched at her spine.

"Breathe," the voice said.

Camille breathed slowly, just as she'd learnt in her years of dance. Control. You have control. The pain eased.

"I prayed she would be safe. That she would find someone who loved her like I couldn't. What more could I have done?" Camille whispered to the silence. Grief spilt over the control.

"It's not too late, Camille." The words struck like a dagger into her heart.

How could it not be too late? She was going to die. What could she offer to this child? – who Camille suddenly re-envisioned, as whoever she was, was no longer a child but sixty years old.

Doubt flooded around the stronghold of her resolve to wash her hands of the past. Nothing was clear anymore.

"I'm sorry." Her face quivered. Sorry for the child, for herself, for everything.

"I know."

The pigeon flew down from the pillar and landed a few metres from her. It broke through her thoughts and brought her back to her surroundings. She'd stayed too long. The pew creaked as she rose.

The woman in front of her rose at the same moment, and Camille waited for her to pass. Their eyes met briefly, and Camille saw shock register on the stranger's face.

It could only be Camille's tears that had elicited such a reaction. Camille turned away and dabbed her face with her tissue, embarrassed at her public show of emotions. She allowed distance between them to give herself time to recompose her appearance. This day had left her feeling vulnerable and raw. In hindsight, she should've chosen the Louvre. She doubted God would have found her there.

As Camille approached the cathedral's main door, the bevy of Chinese tourists bore down on her. The very sight of them caused her heart to race. She couldn't bear the thought of being the centre of their attention again, not with her mind in such a fragile state as it was. She spun on her heels and headed to the side alcove, where a row of coin-minting machines stood incongruent to the sacredness of the grand old building. Fumbling in her purse, she wished she hadn't worn the fur coat. It made her so conspicuous. The woman she had followed out was there. She retrieved her souvenir coin from the machine and looked at Camille with pity.

"Here. Let me." The woman handed her a coin. Camille looked at it and back at the stranger. The coin was shiny. One of the new currency coins. A euro. She took it reluctantly and looked at the machine in front of her. She'd never used one of these contraptions.

81

"How?"

The woman smiled warmly. "Like this." She took back the coin, slotted it and pressed the buttons in the correct order. They watched the mechanism spin into life and followed the disc on its way to the press. It clattered out the side into the tray, as shiny as the euro that had gone in.

"There." The woman picked it from the tray and pressed it into Camille's hand. Had she squeezed her hand out of pity? This woman who'd seen her tears.

Camille smiled back. A genuine smile. The stranger gave her a soft grin, let go of her hand and walked away.

"Thank you," Camille called after her. Her eyes darted around for the tourists. They had gone, and she dashed for the door into the afternoon sun. The woman had melted into the crowd, and Mr Ying was nowhere to be seen.

***

Jacques Pearson stepped into the cafeteria and pondered the selection of cakes in the glass display cabinet. Ignoring the protest of his ulcer, he chose a custard pastry, ordered a large coffee and made his way to a maze of tables on the side wall. He glanced at the street before settling for one closer to the front. He needed a clear view of the doors across the street, preferably unimpeded by other diners.

There were days he wished retirement would tap him on the shoulder. An ironic thought. If anyone tapped him on the shoulder, he'd be prone to pulling his small revolver from its pouch beneath his armpit. A reflex he hadn't needed for some time now, thank God. Anyone tapping on his shoulder would stand a good two metres ten.

His height was his best disguise. His hulking frame made discretion difficult, so he learnt early in his detective career to blend into his surroundings in a more homely style. No heavy long jacket and dark shades.

He preferred shock and awe instead. He took inspiration from the plethora of tourists that flooded his city. No locals took account of the garish outfits of a loud American or the beefed German. Today he wore plaid pants and a hunting vest teamed with a white open-collar shirt, slicked-back silver hair and a pair of thin, round rims. The only giveaway for being French, if someone cared enough, was the local French rag he read while he stalked his quarry. He wagered no one would notice such a minor detail. And this job was hardly a high-risk one.

Pierre's request intrigued him. There was little detail. Track down a woman born in Versailles on a particular date – via the adoption trail. It always came with a few hurdles, but not ones he hadn't cleared before. He'd cultivated a perfect contact for that a long time ago. He'd said this was ultra-urgent. And for Pierre to press the point showed it was important. He didn't mind obliging; it meant a quick turnaround of payment. Boring, but sometimes necessary.

Pearson didn't come cheap. Discretion, a thorough job – these things cost money. He lamented his clients these days were rich wives stalking husbands, or vice versa. Not the heady days of business deals and shady contracts of his early commissions. He promised himself this one might be his last. He'd buy his villa on the beach and let them all go to hell.

Settled, he spread the paper on the table and waited. On the flap inside his wallet, he had a photo of a middle-aged woman. Nothing spectacular, this one. Hardly cheating wife material. Widowed. A long time ago. Hmm, he pondered. Mistress of a wealthy businessman? He glanced at the door across the street. These flats in this locale wouldn't impress most business moguls' molls. He shrugged. He hadn't worked out the attraction in most cases he delved into. Whoever she was, she'd made an impression somewhere to warrant tracking down.

He checked his watch. A third coffee sat cold in his cup. No one who remotely fitted the description had come and gone in the past two

83

hours. A forty-year-old male, two boys that had to be twins, a young slip of a thing with a backpack. Student? Pearson sighed. What now? He couldn't sit here much longer. To come back tomorrow and do the same would raise suspicion unless he praised the pastry and coffee and declared the place his new favourite. Possible. But not something he wanted to do. The coffee was lousy, and the young waiter had tired of him. From the corner of his eye, he saw him hover close by, darting impatient looks in his direction. He had clearly overstayed his customer expectations. A good tip would fix that. He dug into his pockets and clattered the coins on the table.

When Jacques stepped onto the narrow street, the woman he was waiting for shuffled towards him. The photo was a mediocre likeness of her. The bone structure stood out; the same curves and brow line, so she was easily recognisable but today she looked tired, if not broken. She wore no make-up, and dark rings under her eyes accentuated her cheekbones. Jacques appraisal of her, as was his usual summing up of a new target, was she would have been striking in her youth, but all he saw now was a jaded shadow of that promise. Her footsteps, one in front of the other, were measured as though she was avoiding an inevitable destination. Pearson feigned interest in the window display of a chocolate shop, convenient for him, right next door to the street entry to the flats.

In the reflection, he watched her dig for her keys and fumble with the lock. Number fifteen. It flashed before him on the tag, and he could not believe his luck. A few more minutes and he'd have missed her altogether. He had to think on his feet.

"Excuse me, ma'am." He feigned desperation. "I've left my key with my wife, and she's gone for a manicure. She won't be back for an hour. We're staying with friends here, and do you mind, could I get in the door with you? They'll be home. I just can't get through this gate. I'm so sorry to bother you ..." His brow creased with exaggerated worry. "I'd wait, but," he whispered, "I really need the bathroom."

The woman stared at him. She struggled to connect with the present, obviously lost in her problems. He hoped he had done enough in his performance to break through the natural wariness of a stranger wanting access to her building. In his head, he counted. Three seconds. If she didn't say yes, he'd have to devise another plan. Do more digging. He would get what he wanted, but now would be convenient.

He must have looked harmless enough. She nodded, entered and held the door wide. Now, he prayed she would ignore him and move on. The woman headed for the stairwell. Pearson fumbled with his wallet, dropped it and stopped to fuss over his shoes. He needn't have bothered. She barely glanced back and was gone into the stair void ahead of him.

As her footsteps faded, he ran his fingers over the post boxes along the entry hall to number fifteen. Bingo! He had what he wanted. It was her. He whispered a breathless thank you up the stairs and let himself out onto the street.

CHAPTER 8

Alfredo left the Hall of Books behind him. The new leather case bounced
on his back as he ran with the blue line ahead of him. It would not stop
at the information counter; instead, it led him out and down the marble
staircase and into the darkness beyond. There was no thought of not
following, just as he would not ignore the urgent message ringing in
his mind.

Find Felice.

The line took him along the path near the university. A breeze
accompanied him. Its gentle force carried him along on its eddy.
Then the line vanished, leaving him between two very tall fir trees.
Darkness swallowed the path behind and in front. Alfredo's heart beat
fast. Without light, he could go nowhere. He turned to search for even a
pinhead of light in the distance. Nothing. From the darkness, footsteps
approached. Soft and irregular steps. An animal? Alfredo pricked his ears
to discern any clues. There were no dangerous animals here, so it wasn't fear
that kept him still. Rather, if he moved in the dark, he might injure himself
or the animal.

The steps reached him, and a low woof told him the culprit.

"Rembrandt? Come." The dog wrapped itself around his legs and licked his hand in recognition.

"Come on, boy. You can take me. The Garden of the Sleeping Ones. Where is it, my friend?"

The dog whimpered and whined. Alfredo patted him.

"Come, Rembrandt. I must go there." The dog woofed in response. Alfredo grasped him by the collar, and he led the way. He would take him where he wanted to go or take him home. It would be better than this darkness.

They moved off together. The path closed in around him. This was not the way he had come. The crunch beneath his sandals smelt of pine, and the track descended an incline. He smiled. Good boy, Rembrandt. They walked for a while until Rembrandt stopped and sat at his feet. Alfredo patted him and waited. The dog whined. He did not enjoy this place.

Alfredo's ears strained for sound. Any sound. As the minutes ticked by, he thought he should give up and get Rembrandt to take him home. A voice in his head said to stay. Patience. Yaseem had stressed that over and over. It was not one of his best attributes.

A light above him flickered on. Alfredo looked about at his surroundings. He had never seen this place before – the high wall or the wrought-iron gate. He looked down at Rembrandt, who lay with his nose on his paws.

"Good work, my friend," he said in a low voice to the dog. "Stay."

He was about to push through the gate when it opened of its own accord, and a cloaked figure appeared.

"Greetings, angel. What brings you here?" He looked at Rembrandt. "Ah, Yaseem's dog. Did he send you?"

"Greetings. I'm Alfredo. Yaseem's student." He should have said ex-student, but he guessed that would come. "No. Rembrandt brought me here as the light guiding me ceased at the roadside, leaving me in complete darkness. I'm searching for the Garden of Sleeping Ones, sir." He bowed to the angel in the dark cloak.

This angel knew Yaseem. Why had Yaseem never spoken of the Garden in his classes?

"Is this it?" he asked.

The angel stepped back to allow Alfredo entry through the gate.

"Yes, but if Yaseem did not send you, what makes you call on me?"

Alfredo wasn't sure how or where to start. Did that mean he shouldn't be here? He stalled. "My scroll. So, I expect it's God's will I come."

This answer pleased the angel, who walked ahead of Alfredo, holding the lamp high. "Your scroll, did it say why?"

Alfredo followed. "No, but I am to ask after a Felice. Is she here?"

He almost said the scroll hardly gave any clues. But that was a whole other conversation he didn't have time for.

He tried to peer past the circle of light. It was impossible. The other angel quickened his step. Alfredo wished it wasn't so dark. The pool of light gave away nothing but where their next step would fall; the whole place made him feel uneasy.

"Felice. Good. Yes, she is here. And you are to speak with her?"

Alfredo hadn't thought about what to do when he met Felice. So, it surprised him when he said, "No. I am to take her with me."

"Even better." The angel started to run.

Alfredo had to run to keep up with him until he came to an abrupt halt. The angel hooked his lantern to a ring on the end of a chain. It dangled at head height between them, swinging gently, making the shadows about them leap and dance.

With one practised yank on the chain, the lantern floated above them, suspended in the branches of a gnarled, ancient tree. As he did this, his hood fell back, revealing an aged angel with a balding head rimmed with

89

snowy hair. He looked even older than Yaseem, though he was not as tall. His face was pale but friendly, and Alfredo's unease evaporated.

His companion turned and addressed him. "I am Arthemus. Keeper of the Sleeping Ones."

Alfredo bowed. Arthemus bowed in return.

"Alfredo, Felice has been here for over sixty years. Of late, she has stirred. For you to call upon her is a sign you've been given a difficult but important calling. For you to request she leave here with you is akin to a miracle being granted. Pay attention to your scroll and have great courage."

A miracle? He was part of a miracle!

Alfredo looked around in awe. Bench after bench lay shrouded in black snow. He had seen nothing like it. He stepped towards a bench, ready to reach out and touch the delicate layer, but Arthemus grabbed his hand and stopped him.

"You cannot enter, Alfredo. It may look harmless, but this is not black snow, as your eyes would have you believe. It is the web of the devil. Even I will not touch it."

Alfredo recoiled with distaste, drawing his hand close into his chest before leaning forward to look at the forms more closely. "Is Felice in here?" Arthemus gravely nodded. "Then how can I see her and have her leave with me?"

Arthemus wisely smiled and knelt on the path. "In all things, prayer." He motioned Alfredo to join him.

Alfredo obediently knelt and bowed his head. Arthemus began praying to the Father for revelation, the prayer he knew by heart as they recited it at the beginning of every lesson Yaseem had taught. Alfredo's voice fell in unison. Within minutes, it began to rain. Hard rain, with drops that stung like bees. They stayed on their knees, chanting the words in a steady rhythm.

The stone benches disappeared from their view, hidden by the intensity of the storm. Yet, amazingly, he and Arthemus remained dry. This was not rain he'd seen before. A sense of wonder began to build. Hearing of miracles and experiencing one were two totally different things.

Footsteps approached, and then two tiny feet appeared in front of him. He looked up at a small angel clothed in a white tunic and dripping wet. She smiled as tears mingled with the rain running down her face.

"Felice?" he whispered.

She nodded.

The rain ceased. Alfredo and Arthemus stood, and Alfredo reached out to touch Felice, but Arthemus warned him.

"Not yet."

Alfredo stopped.

Arthemus pointed to a pathway behind them. "Felice, go first to the Holy Water Well and wash away the bonds put on you by the Dark One." She nodded and left. Arthemus reached into his cloak in search of something. He thrust some empty vials into Alfredo's hand. "Collect water from the well and take it with you. The demons may try to bind Felice again. It seems they want that to be her destiny. Walk behind, but not close to her. Once she does as I have asked, she will be released from here to go with you."

Felice walked; Alfredo followed. A light above them kept the path clear, and he was careful not to get close. Felice said nothing, but he could hear her weeping. Tears of joy, he hoped.

The light brought them to a stone well. Water flowed and bubbled from the well into a pool below. Felice didn't stop at the edge; instead, she stepped into the pool and under the stream from the well itself. She closed her eyes and lifted her face into the water. Alfredo watched as steam rose from her being and changed her skin from torpid grey to rose pink. Clean, she stepped from the pool and onto a large stone nearby.

From nowhere, a strong wind came and whirled around her, and within minutes, she emerged dry .

Satisfied he could approach her, Alfredo dipped the vials in the pool and filled them to the brim. He tucked them into his armour for safekeeping.

The light drew them back to the Garden's main entrance, where Rembrandt still waited. When they appeared, he wagged his tail vigorously, looking very pleased to see them. From there, the darkness fell again, and Alfredo clasped Felice's hand in his and allowed Rembrandt to take them back along the path to the main road.

By the time they reached the road, the sun had risen. Felice blinked at its brightness, yawned and stretched.

"I'm starving," she announced. "Do you think we might eat, Alfredo?"

Heartened by her emerging spirit, Alfredo laughed. "Of course!"

But what really made his heart sing was that he was closer to getting answers. He'd found the Garden and Felice. What lay ahead excited him. The Angels Ladder and the earthly realm. Surely, now the scroll had started to show him his mission, they could go.

***

The dining room was the perfect place for Felice to listen to Alfredo's progress so far. Without clear instructions on the scroll, she realised Alfredo wasn't sure where to start. For Felice, it was simple. The beginning, of course. She listened patiently to his questions, one after the other, while she ate her third apple.

"I'd forgotten how delicious these are!"

Alfredo was impatient with her. He tapped his knuckles on the table opposite, and his sandals jiggled against his chair. In the end, she grinned widely and held up a finger to silence him.

"Forgive me, Alfredo. Have you done this before? Had a charge? Been down there even?" The answers were obvious, as some of his questions gave him away. She took one last bite of the apple and pushed her plate away. "It's been a while since I last went down the ladder, through ... that realm." She shuddered. "But I remember everything as clear as day. The first time, you get attacked from every side. The demons"—she shuddered again— "know you're fresh."

Alfredo fell silent.

"But we have the advantage over them now. Knowledge. Not 'stuff' sort of knowledge, but real knowledge. We won! Jesus did it for all of them down there and us." She laughed,— a tinkling laugh like water bubbling over rocks in a stream. "They know but try to bluff us like they still bluff the ones on Earth. You'd think they'd learn, but no, they won't."

"Who won't learn? 'They' or the ones on Earth?" She had confused him.

"They. The Fallen Angels who've become the demons. Humankind needs us for enlightenment of God's plan for them. Or at least point them in the right direction." Her eyes misted over, and she hung her head. "I failed."

"Failure – I remember some of the lessons – is not our fault; it's Satan's. And the ones he tricked into rejecting the truth." Alfredo stated it verbatim, as she remembered. She smiled at him. He was so young.

"Alfredo, listen to me. I don't understand why I'm not stuck in the web anymore. I expect Camille's been given a Grace. A second chance. And the Father sent you to me for a reason. He needs us both to achieve her saving." She stretched. "I've wanted to do that for so long. Those benches are unforgiving."

Alfredo stood up and looked about the room. She sensed his impatience.

"Where shall we start then?" he asked.

"The Hall of Books first. And have you talked to anyone who guided the people close to Camille? Her parent's guides? Of course, her parents will be dead, so the guides may have been given another assignment ..." Her mind raced.

"Whoa! Stop!" cried Alfredo. "Why don't we just get down there? Find Camille and ..."

Felice looked at him incredulously. So green. "Alfredo, have you even read your scroll?"

"My scroll was blank when I got it," he admitted flatly. "And the messages come and go." He blushed as red as the apple she had just enjoyed.

She'd listened to enough. She took him by the hand, and they ran to the library. She understood why he needed her now.

"Right, let's see who we need to collaborate with. Show me the scroll, and I'll make a few notes. I'm so excited to discover how she turned out. Eighty!"

They worked all that day and into the night. Felice recounted Camille's quirks and told stories of her early years. The scroll changed once; a picture appeared of a cathedral on the banks of a river along with a date. Felice's eyes sparkled, and she clapped with glee.

"Notre-Dame. She's going there! And look, the date is soon. Oh, Alfredo, that was a happy place for her when she was young." She sighed. "She saw me once. There. It's special if they see you. Rarely happens, you know. Most are just children, and they grow up and forget."

***

By the time the sun rose on Felice's second day of freedom from the web, she had a long list of other angels. Most had moved on to other charges, and she explained that getting their attention would be hard. Alfredo offered a solution. The dining hall – where he'd met with the active angels. If they left word there, they might have success. He was learning.

"Why do you suppose her scroll was blank?" Alfredo asked.

She pondered for a few minutes, letting the tip of her quill stroke the edge of her chin. "The original scroll wasn't blank when I got it. And it wasn't blank the last time I saw it either." She put down her quill and leant back in the chair. "Her childhood was splendid until it wasn't," Felice recalled. "Her father was too busy making money to pay her attention. Common," she impressed on him. "But when her mother died, things became difficult." Felice thrummed her fingers on the desk. Alfredo would have learnt in class some of what she was telling him. She didn't want to sound like she knew all the answers.

"All humanity has to face trials," she continued. "Disappointment is absolutely a normal part of the journey. They don't understand the whole death thing. We do; death's the passage to here, but for them, to lose a loved one is excruciating. And she was young when that happened."

Another angel sped by them, and Felice's quill floated towards the edge of their table. She rescued it and scribbled another angel contact on her list, tapping the delicate nib beside the name. Sarah. The household's cook's guardian. Might be useful, she thought.

"If her papa hadn't sent her away, I could've had the family angels' support and done more to keep her safe. But he did send her away. It made my job that much more difficult." The memories flooded back and the emotion with it. "School abroad brought her trouble. The dogs got her there."

Alfredo flinched. "Dogs? Like Rembrandt?"

She laughed. "No. The dogs. Satan's dogs: Fear, Anger, Unforgiveness ..." She shook her head, put her quill down and sighed deeply. The next part for Felice was the worst. "And then ..." she whispered sadly, "he got to Camille." A tear fell onto the desk.

Alfredo reached over and dabbed at the tear. "Who?"

"Her teacher, and because of him, the worst dog of all. Hate."
She shook her head to remove the pain of remembering. Her voice cracked.
Even though the incident happened so long ago, it seemed like yesterday.
For her, encased in the web, time had stood still.

"Something bad happened, and she said she hated God!"
Felice shivered. "Camille hated everyone for a while. Even herself.
And while that happened, Satan's demons spun the black web around me.
I lost my power to get into her dreams, to talk to the angels around us.
It was so heartbreaking." She looked at Alfredo with sad eyes.

"But Felice, I've never heard of the web that held you captive.
How did that come about?" Alfredo asked.

"Ah, the web. Well, neither had I. Satan has a few special deceits he
uses. When he gets a human into an impossible situation, and they declare
they hate God, he binds up their spiritual guide. By the time hate was
declared, we … I … was too weak to fight."

Alfredo cringed.

Felice wondered if any of this was taught at university now. If not, it
should be.

"I found myself on the bench in the Garden of Sleeping Ones."
She looked into Alfredo's eyes, trying to impart a sense of urgency.
She wanted him to understand, so he might never find himself there.
"You don't sleep all the time, mind. There were moments when I heard her
call me, but never strong enough to free me. I despaired because I knew that
when she died, not only was she lost to Satan, but I would no longer exist."
She stirred herself and sat erect in her seat.

"And then, God sent you. Alleluia!"

***

The desk groaned under the weight of the stack of books Alfredo and
Felice collected. Each one belonged to a person connected with Camille.

96

Felice's head was bent in concentration. The feather of her quill swished this way and that . Alfredo glanced at his shorter list and threw his quill onto the desk.

"Do we not have enough names yet?" He flexed his writing hand. Felice looked up, yawned and smiled.

"We'll need to investigate what happened for the last sixty years, Alfredo. If we are to understand how we can help her."

All this book trolling frustrated him. He wanted action. He stood and stretched.

"I've been thinking, why don't we call a Conference of Angels? Yaseem spoke of these often. We have the key players in her life; why not concentrate on them?"

Felice paused in her writing; eyes focussed on her list. Alfredo already decided she was the opposite of him. She lived for books. He lived for action. How might he shift the momentum his way?

"Better still," he stated, "we have a date and a place. We could call on anyone who is in that area to attend."

Felice's eyes brightened. "Good call. Let's do it."

The ease with which she agreed surprised him. He'd never called a conference, or attended one, so he didn't know how. Now Felice sat expectantly in front of him. He grinned sheepishly at her. "Er, how do we do it?"

"Come on. I've attended a few," she said with a chuckle.

She began sliding books back into their spaces on the wall, each one carefully returned to their original place. Alfredo leapt into action and passed them to her as she slotted them away. With each book rehomed, a fresh surge of energy overtook him.

On their way to the entrance, Felice paused at the information counter to lodge the conference. She handed him the card. "Welcome to your first. You can lead, by the way. You're the Convenor."

Alfredo's eyes widened. He'd asked for action, and Felice was making sure he got it. He nervously patted the leather scroll holder. "Felice, you know who leads. And it's not me."

She threw a crumpled note at him. "Just testing."

They'd spent so much time in the library, Alfredo wanted to feel the sun on his face. Felice shielded her eyes. He remembered where she had been and led her to the dappled shade of a tree. They had time before the meeting, and he wanted to go over what they should discuss. It was one thing to have names, but what to do with them?

"Let's recap," he said. "Camille denounced God when she was in her early twenties? So, sixty years of darkness." That sounded awful.

Felice nodded slowly with sadness in her eyes. "I saw you, remember?" she whispered. "You opened Camille's book." Felice picked a flower from a garden bed nearby and twirled it between her fingers.

He met her eyes. "I remember. What was outside the window? I couldn't tell, but you were so afraid and upset." This was painful for Felice, but he had to know.

She sighed sadly. "I knew what was going to happen. Her mother's death, the war. I tried to intercede but failed. There was so much fear – because of the war – no one could get a message to their charges. It was the worst feeling." A tear fell onto the flower she held.

Alfredo could imagine, but that didn't answer one question he had. "I tried to look forward, but the book was sealed. Why is that part locked?"

She shook her head. "The book will stay sealed until the day Camille seeks God."

Something occurred to him. "She's going to ask, Felice. That's why I got the scroll. She's going to ask."

Excitement surged through him and he grabbed Felice's shoulders in his hands, barely able to contain himself. Mindful she was still weak from her confinement, he let her go and rubbed his hands together vigorously.

"I agree," Felice whispered back. "We must make sure she does. It won't be easy for her. They will attack her many times. You do realise Satan thought he had her. I mean, her life is almost over. She is so angry at God, at herself. He will do everything he can to keep it that way." She held the flower up to the sun.

Alfredo thought hard. Perhaps more answers will materialise from the conference. If Camille had not yet asked, how was it things appeared on the scroll?

"Felice, do you understand Chinese?" He turned to face her. "The symbols on the scroll. Do you get what they mean?"

"It's a complicated language. Ancient too." She paused. "I looked at the marks, and I first guessed they were just pictures. Well, not pictures, but I translated them to words like vegetables and flowers." She shrugged. "Don't worry, Alfredo. They are there as clues. What they mean will be revealed, I'm sure."

The card in Alfredo's hand vibrated. It was time to go.

***

When Alfredo pushed open the doors to the conference room, he almost fell at the wave of noise that greeted him. Every language under the sun assaulted his ears and mixed into a cacophony the likes he'd never heard. Felice beside him clapped with glee. She called over the noise.

"Alfredo! You hit the nail on the head. What a response. Now, all we need to do is sort them out." She pointed to a rostrum at the front of the room. "Go on. You've got this." She beamed encouragement at him.

Alfredo strode to the front and, as he did so, the crowd fell silent. Somewhere between the entrance and the front, his nerves disappeared, and a great humbleness overtook him. It was awe inspiring. How could he, a novice, command such a great crowd? Felice fell in behind him and stood at his side at the rostrum. He remained there, dumbfounded for a moment. Row upon row of faces stared back at him. Expectant and attentive.

"Start with a prayer," Felice whispered.

Alfredo bowed his head. "Father God, I bring before the guardians of your children – especially one – Camille DuPont. You deem her worthy of Your Grace, through Your Son, Jesus and Your Spirit, Yahweh. Release those who have other places to be and leave me with those who can aid us in Your work. Amen."

Immediately, there was a flurry of angels. The crescendo of voices rose again and, as the crowd thinned to a few dozen, fell to a murmur. The look on Felice's face told him that was an exceptional move. She nodded towards the smaller crowd for him to continue.

"Friends, I appeal to you. Among you are guides whose charges will be in Paris on this day. Our mission is to facilitate my"—he paused and pointed to Felice— "our charge to go to the Notre-Dame. We know by an act of Grace, she is to be met by God there on this day."

Some angels stepped forward and introduced themselves. They all talked in unison and in Chinese. Alfredo and Felice gasped with delight and exchanged a knowing look. The Chinese connection. Alfredo waved them quiet.

"Pardon, but Chinese is not our strong point. Please." He pointed to one named Chi.

Chi bowed and said in French, "We are already assigned to encourage our charges who are on the holiday of their life to – shall we say – herd someone into the line at Notre-Dame that day. It sounds like it could be your Camille." He motioned to one of the others. "Zi here has a charge who loves fur coats. Notre-Dame is at the top of her list. Tourists – what a wonderful way for us to see it for ourselves in person, before it burns down. My scroll says the person in question hasn't been guided for six decades? If this is the case, Zi must impress her charge emphatically."

Zi nodded enthusiastically in agreement.

Another two stepped forward.

"Our charge is a lawyer. We've already done what we were asked. Callo here, was guide to our charge's father, and now together, we guide the son. It's difficult for them, lawyers, I mean, to stay on the path. Tell them, Callo, what you did."

Callo chuckled. "Just caused a file to drop, that's all. Amazing how easy it is when you know how."

Alfredo nodded but failed to see the connection.

Callo continued. "It's what fell out of the file that concerns your charge, Alfredo."

His companion guide nodded thoughtfully. "We did think your charge was facing a bleak end. I'm thrilled she has a chance now," he added as an afterthought. "Callo and I will pay close attention to Pierre for you. Now that we understand the gravity of your case." He shook Alfredo's hand.

"Well done. God be with you both."

One by one, the remaining angels offered bits of information. None of them had previously understood their contribution to Camille's case. It made Alfredo wonder why not.

Felice reasoned. "Until Camille called on God, nothing was clear."

"Possibly, Felice. Are you hungry again?" All this thinking had whetted his appetite. In its case, the scroll quivered, and something told him he needed to recharge.

CHAPTER 9

Paris 1926

Snow fell in silent waves on the streets. Strings of fairy lights swayed above the flurry of crowds of Parisians busy buying last minute gifts or drinking in the sights and soaking in the atmosphere. Past every shopfront a Christmas carol floated out, each one different to the last. No one bothered about the snow or the icy chill biting faces and feet. After all, it was Christmas Eve and what was a festive season without the promise of a pillow of snow to frolic in.

Camille raised her arms high, gloved hands waving to catch the delicate flakes before they landed on her face. The entire street was in her view from her perch on her beloved papa's shoulders. His breath forged a path for them through the crowd. Camille pretended it was fire from a dragon and those mere mortals in front of her, the trees of a living forest that bowed and fell as Papa and she made haste to the castle. The castle was the Notre-Dame, of course. The fairy lights were especially for her. Diamonds to collect on her victory march.

She turned to her mother. Maman, smaller than her father, always walked a step or two in his shadow. Her head bent, eyes intent on the slippery surface lest she fall. Her boots, smooth underneath, made staying upright in them a challenge. A band of soft fox fur draped over her shoulders, perfectly matching her fur coat and cap, completed the spectacle.

Truth be told, Maman's fur collar frightened Camille a little. She had touched the snout of the mummified fox once. Was it her imagination, or did it stare at her? Camille feared being bitten if she blinked her eyes while her fingers stroked it, so she'd only ever touched it once. And she avoided the cupboard where it slept for the summer months. Even though she had seen the maid box it, wrapped in sheets of crisp white paper for protection, she feared it would escape and eat her. After all, it looked genuine enough, and real foxes were hungry foxes.

She had seen a real fox in their garden just a month ago. Hungry and thin, it had tipped over their trash can, leaving a mess of food scraps and paper. Papa had set a trap for it, vowing to have it stuffed if he caught it before their neighbour Mr Le Roix. Camille felt sorry for it. She imagined it had only come to find its baby, wrapped in the box upstairs.

And now, as Maman tagged behind her fiery dragon, all Camille saw was the magical beast that she and her Papa rode on to the castle ahead. Bells pealed, their melodic tones drawing the crowds closer. She swivelled, facing forward to where the castle came into view at the end of the street. Infected with excitement from the sea of people around her, she wriggled with delight. She heard the songs now. Christmas carols, beautiful music floating in the night air. Her father's steps quickened, and the fresh ice crunched under his feet as they joined the crush to get inside the castle and find an empty seat.

This was, to Camille, the most magical night of her life. On any other day, by now, she would have had her evening meal and be tucked into bed, fast asleep. But on Christmas Eve, she, Maman and even the housemaid drew the curtains and took an afternoon nap so they would stay awake late for Midnight Mass in the castle. A family tradition, Maman said.

"And you, *ma Cherie*, Cammie"—she flicked her daughter playfully on the nose— "have yet to keep awake for the whole thing. You are six now. Maybe this year, yes?"

"This year, Maman. For sure, I will." She beamed back as Maman tied a ribbon in her plait and tucked it under her woollen cap. The cap itched, but Camille knew not to complain. Papa had already warned her to be on her best behaviour, lest she was left at home with the cook. She knew he wouldn't but didn't want to test him in case he came good on his word.

They pushed into the depths of the castle and made themselves comfortable, the cold outside replaced by a heady warmth from her parents, one on each side. The seats filled, and the space between them decreased until not another body fitted. From her sheltered spot, she saw the high-arched ceiling and the angels that danced there.

How was it possible to fly? She wished she could. She would join them and look down on her parents instead of being squashed between them. One of the angels waved to her. She waved back.

"Sit still, ma Cherie." Maman pushed her hand down.

The angels were mesmerising. It was the first time she remembered seeing them. How pretty they were, their sparkling gowns and long, flowing hair. She wished her maman hadn't put her hair into tight plaits; rather, she wanted curls like the angels.

"Look, Maman! Look. So pretty." Her mother ignored her. Camille closed her eyes and wished she could fly like them. When she opened them again and looked up, the angels were gone.

***

March 1933 Paris

Winter had faded. Rain spattered the windowpane and painted the entire garden the one colour, a dismal grey. Here and there, early bulbs pierced the garden beds with bright green tips, but not enough yet to make a difference to the overall pallor. The grey tones perfectly matched Camille's mood. Life was grey. Indeed, life was black.

Camille turned her gaze from the garden back to her bedroom. A pretty room. High ceilings, heavy white drapes, polished floorboards and thick, luxurious carpets that Camille's toes sunk into. Her large bed sat at the centre, decorated with the latest style of bed linen in hues of pink and crimson flowers. She and her mother had pored over the magazines to choose their favourite design. It arrived a week before Christmas, and Maman insisted it be aired, ironed and made up onto her bed immediately.

"I know it's against the rules," she'd whispered, "but I can't resist. I should wrap it for under the tree, but ..."

Camille sank into the sea of carnations and hollyhocks and her fingers traced around each floral motif. A tear escaped as she remembered her mother and herself laughing as they shook the duvet together, smoothing it across the bed. Maman plumped the pillows with matching coverlets. It looked exactly like the picture in the magazine. Now its charm was lost. It was too cheerful.

Two weeks ago, her dearest maman succumbed to her illness. Now the house was quiet. Too quiet. None of the bustles of everyday life returned to pull Camille back into the joy of living. Papa sat alone in his study every night and stared at his paper-filled bureau. She'd tried to join him last night after supper, but he hadn't even looked at her. She'd taken one step into the room and waited for him to beckon her over. He'd not even noticed her arrival. She retreated to her bedroom; heart heavy. Had she lost them both? It appears she had.

Her eyes caught sight of the ballet shoes dangling from the end of her bed. Maman bought her those a month ago. She wanted her to be ready for the new school term. Her first at the dance school. Her best friend Genevieve begged her to join. She and Vivie did everything together.

Camille pleaded with her parents to sign her into the class, and they relented. It was the last thing her mother won over Papa for her. Would she still be allowed to attend the first class tomorrow?

She picked up the buttercream ballet shoes by their ribbons and dangled them before her. What would Maman have said? "Oh Leopold, let her go!" and bat her eyelids at him.

Maman had a way of melting her Papa's stern resolve. Only Maman. Not Camille. Not since she was a little girl. Only now could Camille see how he had drifted away from her, a widening gap she could not cross without her maman.

She knelt at the side of her bed, head bowed and prayed.

Me voici Seigneur,

ma journée est pour Toi,

Je veux la vivre avec Toi.

Beni sois-Tu, Seigneur, au debut de ce jour.

It felt odd not having her mother kneel next to her as she had always done.

Beni sois-Tu pour ceux que je vais rencontrer.

Donne-moi Ton Esprit Saint pour que je fasse ce qu'il Te plait.

Maman's words, before she left her, ran through her mind.

"Always say your prayers, ma Cherie. Do it for me, and I will come and kneel with you. Promise me?"

Donne-moi Ton Esprit Saint pour que je vive dans Ton amour...

"Yes, Maman, I promise," she'd said as she stroked her mother's damp hair from her face. She vowed to bring her favourite breakfast the next morning, poached eggs and weak black tea. Two sugar cubes. Maman had a sweet tooth.

Camille hadn't known those were to be her last words said especially to her. That same night, Maman had breathed her last. Camille had gone to bed and was woken by her Papa's anguished cries.

Too frightened to see for herself, she lay with her duvet held tightly over her head to drown the sound. But she understood. Maman was gone.

A tap on the door brought Camille from her reverie.

"Amen," she whispered and quickly rose from the floor. Cook poked her head around the door, coughing politely to catch her attention.

"Miss, your father wants you to come to the study when you are dressed and ready for school. Be quick, dear; he has early appointments."

Camille quickly donned her pinafore and braided her hair as best she could. Maman would have done this for her, had she still been here. Camille's fingers were clumsy at it still. The fact Papa wanted to see her was enough to lift her spirits. And a good sign that he wanted her to go to school. Perhaps she would get to start the dance class after all. She turned her mind to her old friends she would see for the first time since last year's term ended. She would be thirteen this year, her first year at intermediate school, and she hoped to make many new friends. Her excitement increased.

Her father still wore his smoking jacket. This surprised Camille. Hadn't Cook said he had early appointments? She dismissed the thought. Papa did nothing in the usual way these days.

"Camille." Her father stared at her and said nothing else for a few minutes.

The silent pause made her mouth go dry. It had been weeks since he had spoken to her directly and she had started to wonder if he had forgotten she was still here. Cook had called his mood 'morbid', and said he was not himself. Cammie knew he loved her maman deeply, but she'd never seen her papa so overwhelmed by any emotion. She was at a loss for how to respond and waited nervously, holding her breath till she could no longer manage without another. His eyes were fixated on her and bored into her and yet she felt she was invisible. Like he was looking through her to a point somewhere behind her. Her skin broke out in goosebumps.

"I've made a decision." He sprang to life, swivelled in his chair and faced the window behind him.

The sudden movement startled Camille. Her heart leapt to her throat. She swallowed audibly.

"Yes, Papa?" She wished he would turn and look at her again.

"You will go to school today."

"Yes, Papa."

Had he not seen her in uniform already? She forgave him for the oversight. More than anything, she wanted to rush to him and be enveloped in his strong arms. But he seemed so unapproachable now. She dared not.

"In Switzerland. Not here."

The words slapped her. Cold. Every fibre in her chest hurt. Her cheeks burnt.

"Papa?" Tears ran down her face and splashed off her chin.

"It's done. I will have your things packed by this afternoon." There was a crack in his voice.

She raced to stand before him, willing him to say it was a joke. A bad one. He stiffened when she wrapped her arms around his neck.

"But Papa, I cannot leave you! You would be all alone. Please, say it's not true ..."

He lifted her from his body and held her chin so their eyes were level. Even though hers swam with tears, he also cried. Papa didn't cry. He was a rock. Camille felt weak with fear. It was true, then. She was to be sent away. Away from her papa, her friends, and the house where she had known so much love.

"You will make new friends, Cammie. And have so much adventure." He spoke with forced cheerfulness, trying to convince them both. It didn't work. How could he betray her this way? Her throat closed over as anger replaced her fear. Blood rushed to her head so fast that her ears popped. Did she remind him of Maman so he could not bear to look at her?

Camille took a step back, detached herself from his hands and glared at him.

"You are cruel. I don't want to go." She stamped her feet. "I hate you."

With that declaration, she ran to her room and later, as she listened to her things being packed into cartons from where she lay under her duvet, she vowed she would never forgive him for this, ever.

CHAPTER 10

September 3rd, 1939. Villars-sur-Ollon, Switzerland.

Snow covered the slopes around the hamlet of Villars-sur-Ollon.
Clear skies demanded all who ventured out to wear dark glasses to avoid
the glare. Camille and her friends discarded theirs and sat in a sheltered café
out of the wind. Hot coffee sat on the table in front of them, along with a
jumble of European rag sheets that competed for space.

The mood was charged. Some of her friends wore worried frowns
and spoke in quiet voices, pointing to articles and gasping with disbelief.
They all knew Europe flirted with war, but it had little effect on them until
now. Everyone had their concerns, of course, as the boarders came from all
parts of Europe. Most of Camille's friends were French. They shared the
news from their families whenever it came to hand, and sometimes, one
or two boarders left when their family fortunes dissolved in the struggle
back home. Letters from Papa were rare. She didn't show it bothered her, as
she'd decided long ago that his silence confirmed she was a part of his past
and he'd moved on without her. A by-product of his only love, Louise, her
mother. Maman's death had cut that connection. She preferred not to think
about her past life.

Except that was what she missed the most. Love. And to live this long without it created a veneer of steel resolve around the innermost core of her being. Impervious to any attempt by her friends to thaw her, she gave nothing back if it meant having to unlock that sentiment of love. She loved to dance and sing and was blessed with the talent to do both. Her friends soon learnt to give her the space she needed.

But today was different. Every paper had headlines blazoned across them: France and Britain Declare War on Hitler's Germany.

No matter how she felt about her relationship with Papa, she worried. War meant nothing was certain anymore.

Would Papa bother to send for her? The moment she thought that she felt ashamed. How selfish of her? But even those who left, went home to families. She only had Papa, and yet she didn't, not really.

Still, she mused, Papa was too old to fight in a war, and his company would survive, perhaps even thrive, with the investment business he ran. She didn't imagine him suffering a great deal. He had offices in New York. Perhaps he would go there and to safety.

She worried more for Cook, and Genevieve, her oldest friend who had written to her for many years. She'd kept up her dance classes, despite Camille being whisked away from her. The Nazi party in Germany horrified Vivie's parents, and relatives had brought tales of personal disaster to her home. Many had fled as soon as they were able. She lamented those of her cousins who could not. Vivie's family was Jewish.

Camille received a letter from her friend a week ago, filled with sadness, so much so, she put it down half-read. Vivie had left her studies and was aboard a ship to the Americas. Camille was not to expect any letters until the ship landed in New York. Her friend's heart was broken since the boy she had fallen in love with had no way of making that same journey with her.

That news stabbed at Camille's heart. At once jealous of this boy, that he had a claim to Vivie's heart and might push her out, and then relief that he'd been left behind. Immediately, remorse flooded her. How could she entertain such cruel thoughts?

Aghast, another thought occurred. Here she was, tainted with her papa's sin. Hadn't he been jealous of the bond between mother and daughter? So much so that he couldn't bear being pushed out of Louise's heart? Did his feelings not rake him with guilt for not loving her, Camille, despite his loss? Well, she had lost something back then, too. He was wrong to abandon her. She had needed him. Then, but not now. She wished her friend well. And prayed her love might ride the war out in safety.

She pushed aside her thoughts when a man entered the café and joined their table. It was her dance and vocal teacher, Mr Roach. He beamed at her, brushed snow from his coat and edged onto the seat next to her. Camille obligingly moved along the bench to allow him room.

A boy, one of the other students on residence, who sat across the opposite table from them called for his attention. "Sir, look! We are at war. You are British, yes? Will you go to fight?"

Camille cringed at the excitement in his voice. What possessed boys to treat war as an adventure? Mr Roach had noticed her reaction, and without taking his eyes off her said, "Yes, I see we are indeed at war, but I will not be a part of it. British or no, I'm here doing an important job, and unless I'm forced otherwise, I'll stay here."

The boy snorted. "Oh, sir, I would go in a heartbeat. Beat them back where they came from. No, beat them to death. They don't deserve to live."

His comments drew gasps of horror from the girls at the table, Camille included.

"Come now, Rowan," Mr Roach chided, "that's not the way to talk in front of these ladies. How crude of you. Save it for your dormitory."

The boy hung his head sheepishly and apologised, but there was a glint in his eyes, and Camille's heart sank. She prayed Papa was on that ship to New York, too.

***

The dance hall lay nestled at the end of the west wing. It was typical of most school halls, used for school assemblies, Christmas pageants and, at the end of every school term, a place for examinations to be conducted.

Camille passed the staff amenities room and the teacher's dormitory to get to it. Familiar posters of dance academies with which the college had partnerships lined the walls. The notable ones were academies in Paris, Berne and London.

It's where her dreams led her. To the stage as a lead dancer. Paris? That would be the first preference, but sometimes she dreamed larger. Why not here in Switzerland? Would Papa come and watch her? To have that dream come true, the resident teacher must suspect exceptional talent and write recommendations for the student to the relevant academy. Everyone knew a recommendation meant the future was 'assured' on graduation.

Camille knew she was one such pupil. Her teacher, Howard Roach, had hinted at it many times. Said her dance and voice were 'like jewels in a crown'.

Of course, it flattered her. He favoured her, and she eagerly poured her energy into her studies and practised her routines, often in the evenings after classes had long finished. For a time, it filled the void left by her papa. But as she got older, she continued for her own self-satisfaction. Being in control meant the world to her.

Ever since the café gathering, her inner peace was disturbed. For so long, she'd intentionally blocked thoughts of Papa. War changed that. Now he consumed her for days. The war raged within.

She was still angry at his rejection, but the yearning for his approval and love spilled from the darkest crevice and flooded her being. If the war put him in danger, the chance of reaching and receiving love from him might be dashed. Part of her craved that chance so badly, yet another sentiment scorned it. He had missed his chance. Thrown it away. When she danced, she found peace. It had brought her here tonight.

She flicked the light switch on and set her music on the gramophone. The orchestra scratched into life and wobbled as the needle set into its groove. Camille positioned herself for her first steps, engrossed in the music. As her cue arrived, she moved gracefully in sync with the violins. Her eyes closed, and she immersed herself deeper and deeper into the steps and lunges, the pirouettes and leaps. It was a long dance, one Camille loved for that exact reason. The longer the dance, the better she felt. At the last strands of the song, she fell to the finale position and let her arms glide to rest over her extended legs. Slowly, she brought her mind back to the room. A deep breath and she stood, her arms stretched in the air, leaning back, face to the sky.

The clapping started, slow and deliberate. She whirled around, her heart in her mouth. Nobody should be in here. She wasn't supposed to be here either, but the teachers turned a blind eye to her. She peered into the side-stage shadows where the sound came from.

"Who is it? Show yourself!" She tried to keep the fear out of her voice despite the prickling hair on the back of her neck. Footsteps, faint but measured, gave her a direction to focus on. From the shadows, her teacher appeared. She relaxed and breathed a sigh of relief.

"Sir. You frightened me!"

"Did I? Forgive me, Camille. That was so beautiful. I recommend you do it with your eyes open next time. You wobbled coming out of the coupé-jeté en tournant. You know it's a male routine, yes? It requires much strength. Although you executed it admirably."

Camille blushed. This routine was not composed for ballerinas, but it mattered little. What she wanted was to dance. And to be the best at it. So, away from class, she added little routines the male dancers attempted.

She curtsied.

He came towards her. Close enough that she could smell the fug of tobacco on his body. A shiver ran up her spine, and she took a step away to create more space between them.

In class, there were many times he had come and stood close to her, touching even. He would lift her arm to show the correct elevation or put his strong hands around her waist and lift her high to show her dance partner the right way. But tonight was different. Camille sensed his closeness had nothing to do with him being her teacher. She reached for her jacket and covered her leotard, suddenly self-conscious.

"Thank you for the advice. And encouragement." She wrapped her arms around her body. It wasn't that the room was cold. Something else awakened in her. An awareness of his maleness, perhaps. The nape of her neck tingled uncomfortably again, and gooseflesh rippled up the inside of her legs. Whatever it was, it disturbed her.

Roach stared at her with such intensity her skin burned. Then, just as suddenly, he broke from the stare and looked over her shoulder.

"Go to bed, Camille. Enough for now." His voice held a huskiness that floated on the air between them, thick and charged with something unexpected and dangerous.

The hair on her arms stood erect. She needed no encouragement to gather her things and leave him behind in the empty hall.

***

The end of the midyear term approached. This year, the usual exodus of students would not happen. War changed the holiday season.

Parents begged the school to remain open, and for those who afforded it, the school obliged.

For Camille, it was a welcome change. She'd never gone home. Holidays were the loneliest time for her. When all her peers went home for holidays, Camille and a handful of other students remained. And only she had stayed for even the long summer breaks.

In the early years, a chaperone from the skeleton staff left at the college took her into the village for excursions, but now she often slipped away on her own and became a local whenever she pleased.

Unlike the other students who shared a common dormitory, Camille had her own permanent room. It set her apart, and she knew most pitied her. They all knew of her circumstance, so they kept discussions of their holiday antics to a minimum on their return. It used to bother her, but now, in her last year, it filled her with dread. This was her home. And soon it would not be so. Every night, she prayed for an academy to accept her before the end of the year.

Camille finished breakfast just as a school receptionist sought her out. A letter had arrived for her. She first thought of Vivie. Had her good friend arrived in New York? Every detail of her new life in America would be in it.

The heavy linen envelope dashed that prospect. Excitement turned to intrigue. Her name was written boldly in a formal script. Vivie addressed her correspondence using her pet name, Cammie. This letter bore only her initials and surname. Camille's hope faded for entertaining news to brighten her day.

It was not Papa's writing either. That would have been cause for excitement to return. No, this letter was from Papa's solicitor, Mr Levin. She slit open the envelope with her butter knife. The contents were written on crisp white sheets, as heavy and expensive as the envelope.

Camille's heart pounded. She opened the folded sheets tentatively and read the small handwritten note attached to the front of the official letter.

My Dear Miss Camille, I congratulate you on your soon-to-be coming of age.

Camille thought it odd, as her eighteenth birthday was months away. She continued reading.

You will find enclosed legal papers that require your attention and a signature where necessary. Please return one copy in the enclosed envelope and keep the other in your safe possession. Your father had these papers drawn up to ensure your continued pecuniary wellbeing. You will note the bank documents; these will become active upon any necessity arising, and you should immediately sign them.

Please note that I am at your service for any matter you may need to address. I have been your father's solid friend and adviser and shall extend that service to you should you feel it appropriate and agreeable.

Warm regards

Pierre Levin, Solicitor

Camille laid the papers on the table and flattened them. Why didn't Papa write for himself? This was an insult, like the birthday cards hand-picked by a secretary, not her papa. Another cold slap. She had no choice but to oblige. To sign the papers and seal the only thread between them. The stone in her stomach ground deeper. How had she wasted her last few weeks with worry for him? This Pierre Levin seemed at least to care for her, albeit out of duty. She tucked Levin's card from the envelope into her jacket pocket, took the offending letters to the front desk, signed them and left them for postage back to their source.

As she turned to leave, the dean's secretary, still on a call, raised a hand to Camille. She covered the receiver and asked her to wait a moment. Camille obliged. There was no hurry to her day. Classes were not due to start for a half hour. The woman continued to nod at the speaker at the other end of the call. From her expression, Camille construed the call as serious. It was awkward being a witness to it. She would leave and return at a more convenient time. Whatever the secretary wanted, it couldn't have been so urgent. She turned towards the door as the woman lay the receiver in its holder.

"Miss DuPont, a moment, please." Her voice was sombre. "Please, step into the dean's office."

Camille felt a moment of dread. Had the call concerned herself? An ominous pall descended on her. First the letter, and now this. She complied and followed the woman towards the dean's office, but she was made to wait at the door while the secretary spoke with the dean. Having to wait made Camille even more worried. What news involved her? Her heart lurched. Her papa? She hoped not.

After what seemed ages, they ushered her into the room. The secretary left, and the door clicked shut behind her.

Dean Schiller was a large man, in his late sixties, she guessed, and well-padded around the waist. Camille had little to do with him, apart from the occasional casual conversation in a hallway on the way to class or the formal moments that every school student suffered through. He was the figurehead of the college, so he had the meritorious duty of handing certificates at graduations and awards events. Polite nods or quick replies to questions were the only conversations she'd had with him in all her years here. Everyone considered him a benign grandfather figure.

For this reason alone, Camille was comfortable as she sat in front of his expansive desk. The dean, however, looked anything but comfortable. He cleared his throat a number of times and shifted his weight in his chair, clearly unsure of where to begin.

"Miss DuPont." He spoke with a nervousness that puzzled Camille. "We've just received terrible news, I'm afraid." He fidgeted with a paperweight, put it aside and twisted a large garnet ring on his finger instead.

Camille swallowed but remained silent. Every nerve in her body strained.

"A Mr Levin. Your father's solicitor."

Camille relaxed. It must concern the letter. "Oh, yes. Mr Levin. I've just now signed the papers he sent." She pointed towards the office. "Was there something wrong with the papers, sir?"

He shook his head. "No, Miss DuPont. Camille."

"What then? You said terrible news? Has something happened to my father?" Camille wanted to shake this man. Out with it. She couldn't bear the wait, the not knowing.

The look on his face confirmed her fear. She closed her eyes and sank back into the leather chair.

"Tell me," she whispered.

"He has succumbed to his illness, I'm afraid. Last night, it seems. My deepest condolences, Miss DuPont. This must cause you great distress." He rose from his chair and came to stand beside her.

The room swam. His words punched her chest like he'd laid a fist on her. She choked on her tears and gasped for breath. Her heart pounded. One word reverberated in her head. Illness.

The dean patted her hand, clearly out of his depth.

"Mr Levin pressed me to tell you he did not suffer too greatly at the last. Small mercies—"

"Illness? Papa wasn't sick; he would've told me." Her mind raced. "What really happened?"

Images of her father flashed before her. That last day in his study. He'd been thin but healthy, as far as she knew, anyway. A cold truth washed over her. That was so long ago. His life was a mystery to her. And he had kept it so.

120

Shock turned to anger. He had cheated her. Robbed her of all that a father was supposed to be. Fathers came to their children's recitals and had them home in the summer holidays. Loved them.

The blood drained from her face as she sat huddled in the dean's office, oblivious to everyone. Her papa was dead. All her chances of reaching him were gone.

Someone led her to her room.

"Have this Camille, dear." The doctor handed her two pills and a glass of water. She swallowed and let them carry her into the blackness.

CHAPTER 11

Switzerland 1939

Daylight had yet to grace the skyline when Camille took her place in the car sent for her by the family lawyer. She peered out the window at the dark façade of the college, her home for the past six years. But no more. Shuttered windows stared back at her, cold and indifferent to her leaving. The trunk slammed shut, and the driver's feet crunched on the gravel. A tendril of icy air followed him into the cab and settled around her feet. She tucked her fur jacket closer and wished she'd chosen her boots for the journey.

Next to her, Howard Roach breathed heavily and yawned. His gloved fingers tapped on his expensive tweed trousers. He was annoyed already at having to wait. The fact he kept consulting his watch confirmed this. In the confined space, his male, musky smell overpowered her senses. She sighed, shifted her body closer to the door and leant back against the seat. The cab sputtered, vibrated and roared into life, and they were away. Camille stared through the side window, entranced by the ghostly white orbs filled with rock face, trees and the occasional early risen farmer.

Their destination was Zurich. After that, a train across the Alps and into the heart of Paris. Mr Levin would meet and take her to the house. Cook would stay there until Papa's affairs were completed and she decided what and where she wanted to be. Camille wondered whether she would recognise Cook. Or vice versa. Six years was a long time.

Mr Roach leant towards the driver's seat. "Do you mind if I smoke?"

It brought Camille back to the present. He wasn't asking her, just the driver. So rude of him. Camille wished he'd be more considerate. When he lit the cheroot, swirls of smoke filled the car. She hated the foul smell. It burnt her lungs and eyes. She coughed and wound the window down a fraction. Roach sat back and closed his eyes to a narrow slit as he drew on the offending cigar. She could feel his eyes on her, and her skin twitched under her coat. She shrank even further into her corner.

The events of the past few days filled her mind. She shifted her understanding of Mr Roach in that short period, now viewing him in a new light. Gone was the veneer of sir, the aloofness between teacher and student. Not that Camille expected or encouraged any different behaviour; no, Mr Roach was altogether a changed person almost overnight. This new insight did nothing to put Camille at ease in his company.

The day after being told of Papa's death, the dean, on instruction from Mr Levin, had arranged for her to travel back to Paris for her father's funeral. Her schooling was over. As was proper, she required a chaperone.

Mr Roach had resigned from his teaching commission immediately. A decision, he said, brought about by the war. He would go home to England and, from there, enlist in the army.

When Camille stepped into the dean's office that day, Roach was already there.

"Now Camille, Mr Roach has offered kindly to be your escort. A wonderful gesture, if I don't say so myself."

A look passed between the two men, and Camille caught the slight nod of her teacher's head. His eyes dropped, and he fiddled with a button on his coat rather than meet her gaze. The dean continued laying out the details, but Camille heard none.

Neither had asked if she was comfortable travelling alone with a man.

Roach sat, legs crossed, in the other chair, giving the dean his full attention.

A warning buzzed in the back of her mind. She could not put her finger on the cause of this alarm, but it was there all the same. She had no alternative except to accept the dean's proposal, and Mr Roach nodded in agreement, a benign smile on his face.

Now, with the journey started, she wondered if she'd had time to think things through, could she have made other arrangements that didn't involve Mr Roach? No, she quickly surmised, despite the polish a private boarding school proclaimed to develop, she had absolutely no idea how to arrange and conduct even the simplest of travel plans. And if she had insisted Levin engage a woman, she might have delayed – or worse – missed her father's funeral. She wished Vivie were here. She would have known how to manage it.

The morning passed quickly. A stop to refuel and a quick bite to eat at a café. They reached the midday train in good time, and with all her luggage stowed in the baggage car, Camille settled herself in her first-class seat. She had a cabin to herself, a great relief after the confined car with Mr Roach.

He had conversed sparingly with her the entire journey; instead, he struck up banal conversations with the driver. She had been rendered invisible, which, if she were honest, she preferred. It gave her time for reflection.

Papa was gone. Part of her suffered enormous grief; she was alone now, an orphan. There was an old uncle, her father's brother, who Camille had never met. Nor did she want to.

Yet, part of her seethed with angry thoughts that burst through the grief and lashed her with sharp questions, the answers to which she did not have. An unopened book lay beside her on the seat as she stared out the window; the rolling countryside lulling her into a daze. It was only when the electric lights flickered on in the cabin and the outside world melded into a canvas of grey shadows, did it register that nothing was ever going to be the same again.

***

A knock on Camille's door jolted her back to the present. With no time to respond, it slid open, and Mr Roach's body filled the doorway. He swayed with the rolling train, paused for a moment to scan the passageway behind him before entering, and sat on the seat facing her.

He had doused himself with a liberal amount of aftershave, shocking her senses with its overpowering smell of bergamot and lavender. Underneath this bouquet the now familiar notes of his preferred cheroot percolated.

Annoyed that he hadn't bothered to ask if he could join her, Camille pursed her lips and said nothing. He took her silence as approval, leant back on the seat and put his arms behind his head.

"Will you join me for supper, Camille?" He kept his eyes fixed on her face.

Since when were they on a first name base? It grated on her. Yes, he was no longer her teacher, but it was rather forward of him to assume he could use such familiar terms with her. Her first inclination was to decline.

"Thank you, sir, but I'm not hungry tonight. I want to go to bed early. Tomorrow will be ..." She didn't want to think about tomorrow.

A tear slid down her cheek and she brushed it aside, annoyed with herself for showing emotion in front of this familiar, but now strange, man.

"Camille, there's no need to be so formal now. I'm not sir anymore." He spoke softly, but his tone did not reassure her. A prickle ran up her spine. She tried to read in his face where this alarming feeling emanated from. The teacher she had always looked up to stared back at her. His eyes held hers.

"Call me Howard. Adult to adult." He patted her knee.

She stiffened. His hand on her knee sent a jolt through her body.

"You must eat. It's too early to turn in for the night, and I will not allow you to wallow here on your own while I enjoy the excellent supper. Tomorrow will come soon enough, and I think you will find a good meal, and maybe a bit of wine, will do you more good than harm."

The mention of wine brought a moment of recognition to Camille. Howard Roach had been drinking already. When he spoke, the sweet, pungent aroma mixed with his aftershave and the cheroot, and she realised this was behind his relaxed manner. Her stomach growled noisily. The sound made her blush.

"See, you are hungry. Freshen up. I've already made our reservation in the dining car." He slapped his hands on his knees with finality, got up and stepped outside her cabin.

"Don't dally; there's a good girl." The old sir was back, if only for a moment.

***

Camille reluctantly made her way along the train as it swayed rhythmically into the night. The dining car was the next carriage, so she had no trouble finding it or the waiting Mr Roach. He studied a menu in his hand, his legs crossed, and his jacket sprawled over the seat's back. As Camille approached, he looked up and smiled at her.

127

"I've taken the liberty of getting you a small beverage. Nothing too strong. I dare say you're not schooled in such things. It will help you sleep later."

Camille looked at the drink with apprehension. She hadn't had alcohol before. It wasn't condoned by the college, and even on her holiday forays to the village, it never occurred to her to drink. She would take a sip and leave the rest. Politeness for his gesture, but no more.

The meal was enjoyable, more than she liked to admit. As a first-class traveller, it had all the trimmings. Hot bread rolls, soup served in a terrine by a waiter, and a steamed chicken breast with fresh garden vegetables.

Alone at the table, Mr Roach became sir again. He talked of the college and how much he would miss it now that he had ceased his tenure. She learnt he was travelling home to see his family; his mother missed him terribly. With talk of war having taken a turn for the worse and Britain joining the fray against Germany, his father wanted him to join. He hadn't made a decision yet. No, he was set on sailing to the Americas and trying his luck there.

"I have no wish to partake in the violence of war," he exclaimed. "Life is too short for such shenanigans. And no more teaching. I want to get my teeth into something more satisfying – stage or theatre, perhaps." He drank a half glass of wine and raised it to catch the eye of the waiter.

Camille counted. Three glasses already. Her first glass was near to the dregs. Whatever he ordered had relaxed her. Gone was the discomfort from earlier in the evening, but she sensed that her dinner companion meant to continue drinking. She looked forward to the meal ending. Tiredness had overtaken her.

The waiter arrived with more wine. Roach pointed to her glass. "Same again, if you please."

The waiter reached over to fill her glass; his face unreadable.

Camille leant forward and covered the rim of her glass. "No, no, thank you. That was more than enough ..."

"Miss Camille, you must indulge me," he hushed. "I've yet to tell you the best news. And it does concern you. Indeed, it is my finest achievement. Not this drink, no. Champagne!" The waiter nodded and left.

Camille's heart pounded. Her head ached, a dull thump at her temples. "Just a few more minutes. Then I really must go."

The drinks arrived, and the waiter popped the cork, spilling froth onto the floor. He poured two flutes, handed them one each and left. Camille sat back and waited. What news involved her? Her schooling was over, her life an uncharted sea before her.

"I have, in my jacket pocket, a letter of recommendation to the Paris School of Music and Dance." He beamed and sat back, his eyes intently watching for her reaction. "With your name etched upon it."

Camille blushed. She hadn't expected this. The news uplifted her. She'd been sure her future in the arts was a lost treasure. It was front and centre again. Unsure how to react, she sat stunned and lost for words.

"I, I don't know what to say," she stammered.

"Thank you would be appropriate, my dear. I pulled every string I had to get this for you. And some."

"Oh, yes. Thank you!" Her cheeks ached from smiling. "Thank you." This time in a whisper. She put her hands over her face to hide her embarrassment. "I'm sorry, Mr Roach. I don't mean to appear ungrateful, but—"

"Howard, remember," he interrupted. "We are adults, both of us. Please, see me as a friend." His hand reached for hers, and he clasped it, drawing it to his lips. His eyes never left her face.

Camille wanted to wrench it back.

"Howard, it ... it's wonderful news. And it means so much to me. Forgive me, but I think the alcohol has gone to my head. I've had such a wretched few days, with Papa dying and—"

He cut her short, her hand still in his clutch. "Say no more. I understand completely." He looked at the still-untouched champagne and nodded to it. "Drink that up, and you will sleep like a baby. A good night's sleep. Your future is assured, Camille dear. I've made sure of it." Howard's words whispered into her fingers. He released his hold and passed the glass to her. "Bottoms up."

Camille, against her better judgement, obliged. The bubbles, tart and cold, fizzed in her throat. She hiccupped, and some of the fizz came out of her nose. Embarrassed, she dabbed it and laughed. It gave her the chance to stand.

Roach fumbled for his jacket and searched for the letter. One pocket, then another. "Ah, blast! I must have left it in my cabin. Never mind, I'll bring it to you."

Camille protested. "In the morning is soon enough, Mr ... Howard." She gave him a tired smile followed by a small, feigned yawn. His response was that of a satisfied cat. He looked thoroughly pleased with himself.

"Not a worry, I'll do it tonight. Tomorrow we may get caught up when I change trains for the coast. You know how mad the crowds are at train stations." He stood aside, letting her pass. "I won't be a minute." His breath, warm on her neck, reeked of alcohol.

An involuntary shiver ran up her spine. The champagne, she thought. She let herself into her cabin and waited.

While they were at supper, the train service had made up her bed. Camille searched for and found her nightgown. She folded it on the edge of the bed and sat. The minutes ticked past, but Mr Roach did not appear. Her head thumped solidly now. She would go to bed after all. It really could wait till the morning.

Her mind had slipped into the edge of deep sleep when she heard his voice.

"Camille. Camille. It's me. Open the door, Camille." His voice was low, pressed into the crack of the door.

"Sir? I'm not dressed. I'll see you in the morning." She sat up in her bunk, swaying to the motion of the train. Her mind fought the webs of sleep and the fog of the champagne. Her head still thumped. She wished she had a powder to take for it.

"I'm here now. It won't take long. Just a minute. See? The letter is in my hands."

There was a rustle of paper against the door. He tapped persistently again.

She sat silently, holding her breath and wishing him to go away. On the other side of the door, his deeper breath told her he was still there. The seconds ticked by. He would not leave her be.

She relented. "One minute. That's all."

She leant over and unlocked the door. He stepped inside, quickly locking it behind him.

Camille regretted her actions the moment the latch disengaged. She fumbled for the light switch in the dark. His hand beat her to it and stopped her.

"Don't," he said.

"Mr Roach ..." she protested.

"Shh!"

He sat beside her on the bunk, his frame taking up what space was left.

"I won't hurt you." His words were thick.

Camille's heart pounded with alarm. She hadn't entertained the thought he meant to harm her ... until now. If she screamed, would anyone hear her over the noise of the train?

131

Almost as if he read her thoughts, he put one clammy hand over her mouth. The other found her bare shoulder. The envelope fell to the floor.

"The letter, as promised. The world is at your feet, my beautiful butterfly that sings like a bird." His breath, strong with wine, stole the last of the fresh air.

Panicked, she struggled to move away. He pushed her against the wall of her bunk and crushed her with his body.

Disbelief quickly turned to revolt at his touch. She had seen lovers in the village before. Had even envied them and the tenderness of their embraces. Nothing was like this beast's behaviour. It was ugly, and she tried to shrink away from him as panic surged through her. Her mind raced for any way she could escape, but he clamped his hand on her mouth even tighter, making it almost impossible to breathe.

She whimpered, and he dug his fingers into the flesh of her shoulder as a warning. Her heart hammered against the wall of her heaving chest.

His hand explored her body, tearing the nightgown where it resisted. His fingers snaked in deliberate arcs over her breasts and beneath them, squeezing her flesh at will. Her body jerked in fear at every new movement. She begged him in her mind to stop, but the words failed to reach her mouth.

"Good girl," he whispered behind her ear. He slowly released the hand over her mouth and fisted it around her hair, pinning her on the bunk.

The other hand reached lower, and his fingers sought what he wanted. Her stomach reacted with violent spasms. She tensed her muscles to refuse him. He bit her ear in response.

"Relax. Or it will hurt."

He pushed his trousers from between them and thrust himself into her. She screamed, but whether or not the sound came from within her, she

132

did not register. He locked his mouth onto hers and forced his tongue deep into her mouth, choking her. She gagged but he refused to stop.

Suddenly a white-hot pain seared between her legs, and he was in her, pushing deeper with each thrust of his body and grunting with the effort. It went on for an unbearable eternity. The throbbing stopped, and he collapsed on top of her. She went limp, unable to breathe under his weight.

Every inch of her trembled and pulsed in pain. Disbelief left her paralysed. She closed her eyes and wished she was anywhere but in this stinking cabin filled with a stinking man.

Calmly, he sat up next to her. Her first breath seared her lungs and she sobbed and scrambled to the corner of the bunk as far from him as possible. No more. She could not bear it.

His voice was casual, as though nothing differed from the banter and chatter of dinner. "Come now, birdie, cheer up. Every charity deed deserves its reward. I've opened doors for you that will see you loved by millions. I won't be the last to make a claim on the ladder to success, you know." He laughed softly. "At least you will remember your first one."

He stood, and his zipper slid closed. The door opened a fraction to check his escape was clear, then a sliver of dull light pierced the cabin, and he was gone. Camille jumped up, locked the door, and dropped to the floor. She sobbed, yet no sound emerged. The train rolled onward towards dawn, oblivious to her pain.

***

Felice struggled for room to move. The back seat of the cab where Camille and the teacher sat reeked of the atmosphere of the in-between realm. Between Heaven and Earth. Felice's stream of Spirit language was constantly broken by the clawing of the man's demons on her arms and thighs. There was no place she could hide from them.

133

Until now, her efforts to steer her charge, Camille, from danger had been successful. Guardian angels usually had a family full of angels to learn from. Each family member's guardian would draw on the other, and together the child would grow and be guided successfully to adulthood. That was the ideal. But in Camille's case, her family was torn asunder when she was very young. And that made Felice's task difficult.

When Camille was sent away to boarding school, Felice struggled to break through the rejection she felt from her papa. The demons had played on Camille day and night until Felice's voice in her mind was but a whisper.

But today, the demons were in their element. They overwhelmed Felice in number and strength. Still, she would do her best to protect Camille.

Every time the demons broke through her prayers, their fingers smeared a black substance on her. Sticky threads that clung to her skin. She had never experienced anything like it before. Not in all her time on Earth.

One of the demons sneered, "Sleep, pretty one. Satan has a special place for you."

Its words lashed her, and momentarily she forgot her place in the prayer. Another length of the thread latched onto her arm.

If it weren't for the driver in the cab's front seat, Felice feared her charge would suffer even more at the hands of the man next to her.

There was a short time, when they boarded the train for Paris, that Felice could recover from the demons' assault in the cab. Camille retired to her cabin, away from the beast of a man. It was then Felice tried to rid herself of the sticky threads, but they refused to come away from her skin.

Puzzled, she wondered whether to go up the Angels Ladder to seek assistance. It would mean leaving her charge unguarded, and only that fact kept her here.

Camille's scroll shook and quivered in her hand, and the messages appeared and disappeared erratically. Some of the threads stuck to it; where this happened, the scroll became tarnished. Unreadable. Felice sat beside her charge and prayed her heart out.

Then, as evening approached, Felice felt the presence of the demons in the passage outside Camille's cabin. Alarmed, she tried to rouse her charge, to warn her to lock her door, but she was too late. The teacher appeared and made himself at home in her cabin. The demons, with him, crowded into the small room. Felice choked on the bitterness in the air.

Camille left the room and went to the dining car. Felice held onto her as best she could, but there was no stopping the stronger demons. The teacher plied Camille with alcohol and sweet words designed to lull her warning senses. To drown out the words Felice planted in her heart.

There was worse to come. Felice had almost convinced Camille to reject his advances on her. And for a while, she thought, she had succeeded. The teacher stayed away from her cabin, and Camille went to bed. It was a brief reprieve.

The demons and the teacher came to her door before Camille reached her place in sleep where no noise could reach her. Felice had undone some of the damage done by the teacher, and then he rattled on her door, dragging her back into consciousness. Felice cried out. She had failed. And now, the sticky web encased her.

Her spirit body rose from the cabin and floated helplessly up through the realm above Earth, leaving Camille alone and at the beast's mercy.

CHAPTER 12

Paris 2000

A flurry of pigeons exploded from the path in front of Asha. A breeze teased the edge of her coat and flicked hair into her face as she hurried to her appointment. While pushing her hair back, she collided with a hulk of a man coming towards her. She landed on her behind with a thud on the pavement. Shocked, she sat for a moment to recover her senses, only to have firm hands grasp her by the arms and pull her to her feet. It was the tourist who had ploughed into her and his apologies, full of genuine remorse, broke through the pain in her derriere.

"Forgive me, miss. I am so, so sorry. Here, let me help you." Before she registered even the fall itself, he had righted her on the street and peered through her hair at her face.

She gasped for breath. Instinctively, her hand stretched out to push him from her personal space.

"I'm fine, thank you. Really." Her voice trembled. She was. Would be. She noticed the sign for Pierre Levin & Son above her head. At least she was at her destination and could regain some composure inside.

She grimaced with pain and took a step back from the stranger. He was tall. An older man with silver hair slicked back and round glasses sitting crooked on his face. Crooked because of the collision with her. He waited, genuine concern on his face. She smiled to reassure him. A fleeting moment of recognition – she had seen the same man only yesterday at Marco's café. A tourist – she didn't have time for this today.

"I should look where I'm going. I'm fine." She stepped around him and into the reception area of the solicitor's office. A few deep breaths later, she forgot the man altogether.

She was ushered into the solicitor's office by his receptionist with an apology. Mr Levin would join her shortly. An unexpected matter had arisen. Asha didn't mind. It gave her time to recover from the street incident.

The interior of Pierre Levin's inner office reminded Asha of a scene from a movie. Had she stepped back in time? Panelled walls in soft patina timber, bookcases filled with files and books. In all likelihood, these were collected and read during years of research and have not been opened for quite a few years. That was the way of things, wasn't it? No expense spared for leather binding and crisp inlay, yet once read and digested, nothing more than a display item.

It contrasted with her own life. Mama didn't have lots of books. Hadn't needed them. Asha thought hard about the ones sitting with pride of place in the flat. Next to Mama's bedside. A tatty book of poems, an old family Bible and two more modern books, one on journalism and, of all things, commerce. The last two were her father's. And all were her mother's treasures. Asha had seen her lay a soft hand on them every night she could remember. It formed part of the fabric of her childhood, a connection to Mama's past that she had never talked to her about but understood the essence that flowed from one little gesture. No, not all books were to be read. Some just had to be.

Mr Levin appeared from behind her and gently closed the door. He settled himself into his leather chair and opened a file on his desk. Furrows creased across his brow. Asha patiently sat and waited to be addressed. He peered at her from above his glasses, precariously perched on the end of his long rakish nose. Almost as if he had just noticed her presence. Asha smiled and sat up straight in her chair, eager to have the interview over with. She would rather be on the dance floor practising her exam routines. The movement prompted the solicitor to speak.

"Ms Villet. Asha. May I call you that? Or do you prefer me to be formal?" His voice was dry but kind.

She shrugged. "Asha will do, Mr Levin."

"Yes. Good. Now, I'll get straight to the point. You young things have such hectic lives these days." He sat back and smiled, his hands joined loosely in prayer under his chin, elbows balanced on the arms of his chair.

His attempt to put her at ease was mediocre at best and Asha kept her face non-committal to hide her own nervousness. It wasn't up to her to make him feel comfortable but now she wished she had brought Marco with her. What if he talked in legal jargon that she didn't understand? She knew nothing of these things. Her chest tightened.

"I've drawn up a detailed account of what you may expect. I have to say it is unusual for me to do this before"—he paused, looking for an appropriate phrase—"the event occurs that will activate my client's intents and purposes." He coughed to cover his unease. "However, it is also Madame DuPont's wish that I explain the heavy responsibility that goes with such an undertaking." He stood and looked out his window onto the street below, his back turned to her, silent for a moment.

Asha realised he was carefully choosing his words. Understandable, she reflected. How often would someone so young receive such a generous gift? Camille had hinted a bit about what she expected Mr Levin to enlighten her on. There was, of course, the scholarship program. Camille stressed she expected the program would continue as her legacy.

"There is ample there, Asha." She had waved a manicured hand at her. "Please, indulge an old woman. Keep it going. I'll give you names of people in the industry I trust will not undermine the concept or strip it of its intent."

He turned to face her. His eyes, hawk-like. "Why is it, do you suppose, Madame DuPont chose you?" Levin appeared to ask with genuine curiosity, but the question shocked Asha. Blood rushed to her face; for a moment, she was lost for words. Did he suspect she had taken advantage of Camille? Was this a trick question to prove a point? Or had Camille posed this question for her?

She shuffled in her seat, unsure of the answer. "I ask myself that exact question, Mr Levin." Her hands folded in her lap, she turned in her seat to face him as he stood at the window still. The leather of the seat creaked at her every move. "I've been the beneficiary of her scholarship for almost three years. This was to be my last term. I didn't know that Madame DuPont"—she would show him she was also on first-name terms with his client— "Camille was ill. Until yesterday. She invited me to dinner for the first time." Asha smiled as she remembered. "We talked and talked. Mr Levin, I saw a side of Camille I'd never seen in all my time under her patronage. I don't know why she chose me. She says I reminded her of herself when she started in the industry. And her love for her craft is well known, but last night I saw it in her eyes. It became as personal to me as it was to her."

She shrugged. "You tell me, Mr Levin. I'm honoured. In awe of her, to be honest. And I can only pray I can do her justice. I don't want her to die. I want more time to get to know her." Her nose tingled. She reached for a tissue in her bag.

The solicitor resumed his chair across the desk from her and sighed with resignation.

"The will itself is watertight. No need to discuss that yet." He took up his prayer pose again. "Tell me about your mother."

The question took her by surprise. What did this have to do with her mother? "My mother? Her name is Julia. She's a cleaner." Asha didn't know if it was what he wanted to hear, but it was all she would offer without knowing why it mattered.

"And your mother has never met Madame DuPont?" His brow lifted above one eye. Eyes that were riveted to her face.

"No. I don't believe so." Asha thought hard. Mama worked where she danced, so was it possible the two had met? Did Camille run into her in a hallway sometimes? She doubted it.

"Hmm. Interesting."

"How so, Mr Levin? What possible relevance is it to this matter?" Asha tried, and failed, to hide her annoyance.

"Could your mother have put you up to, shall we say, influence Madame DuPont for an inheritance? A cleaner would love to live the life of our Camille, wouldn't she?" His voice had a sharp edge. Almost nasty.

Already wary of where this conversation was headed, his assumptions offended her. What twisted imagination could come up with such rubbish? He knew neither her nor her mother. Anger spurred her into action, and she stood, pushing her chair back. Her heart pounded, and rosettes burst on her cheeks.

"Mr Levin. You know nothing of myself. Let alone my mother. You've never even met her. How can you say such a horrible thing?"

"Please, Ms Villet, sit." His tone changed back to its former dryness. Reluctantly, she sat back down, her face set like stone.

"I do apologise. I have my reasons for asking. If you don't mind, it is a great responsibility to administer such a legacy. You are right. I don't

141

know you or your mother, and I'm sorry if I came across as rude, but due diligence, my dear, due diligence."

He pushed a large document envelope across the desk at her. "This is the list of assets and interests. I suggest you keep them private until ... after Madame DuPont passes. There are clauses that stipulate any actions will be null and void should you try to take advantage prior to her death. That's standard, by the way. Nothing unusual in the world of investments."

Asha reluctantly took the envelope. It felt almost dirty in her hands. He'd made her feel dirty. She vowed that afterwards, further down this horrid road she'd been thrust upon out of no will of her own, she would change solicitors.

***

Asha made her way from the solicitor's office back towards home. The meeting could not have happened on a worse day; this afternoon were her trials for acceptance into one of the academies. The conversation with the rude Mr Levin had spoiled her mood, and only one person could change that. Marco. To do well in the exams required a level of passion only he could ignite.

When she got to the restaurant, she was relieved that the lunch crowd had thinned to a few coffee-sipping tourists. Marco stood at the servery window, waiting to pounce on the tables as they emptied. His eyes lit up at seeing her weave through the cafe furniture towards him.

Asha picked up a pile of dirty dishes and made her way to the kitchen and into his arms. She hugged him first, then kissed him quickly.

"Nice surprise, Ash. Middle of the day even. You can't get enough of me?" The corner of his mouth lifted teasingly.

"Lucky you," she quipped back. "No, I needed to see you, that's all." Her voice was strained.

Marco picked up on it immediately. "What's happened? Your dance exams, that's today, isn't it? Did they go badly?"

He lifted her chin to read her face.

"No, this afternoon, but I've lost the mood."

She slapped the envelope onto the table. Levin had said to keep it private, but she reasoned Marco didn't count. This would affect him, too. And Mama, but Asha didn't want to discuss this with her, not yet.

"What's this all about?" Marco picked up the envelope and turned it over. "A contract? Does this mean you have an acceptance already? That would be fantastic."

"Yes, and no. It is a contract, but not a dance one, not yet."

Marco looked confused.

She opened the envelope and handed him the documents, glancing at the dining room. If anyone else came, she would serve them. She didn't want him to have to walk away right now.

He skimmed the first few pages and handed them back to her. "So, you will be rich. Why is this a problem?" His eyes lit up. "We can get a place of our own. A really nice one ..."

It wasn't quite the response she'd expected.

"Marco, can you not see what this means? Rich. But someone is about to die! I feel ... sick about it."

It was true. Camille would have to die for this to mean anything to her. Just because she didn't know the woman well didn't make accepting it any easier. It wasn't like winning a lottery ticket.

He shrugged. "C'est la vie ..."

A customer walked to the counter to pay. Marco ducked past her to attend to them.

Asha stared after him, trying to undo the knots in her stomach. His reaction to the news hadn't helped.

A large group of tourists took that moment to settle in the restaurant. Marco looked up and mouthed 'sorry'.

Asha stuffed the envelope in her bag and let herself into their block of flats. There was just enough time to throw the envelope on her bed, wash her face and replenish her make-up for the exam. She would deal with the papers later.

***

The detour to see Marco had meant Asha arrived with only minutes to spare for the exam. Flushed with running up the stairs to the dance hall, she shook her limbs and closed her eyes to block out the vibes from the other students around her. Forced herself deep within, where no noise penetrated. Deep breath, tighten this group of muscles and release, repeat. From head to toe, the same process. Anton's voice floated through her head.

"Don't think about them. Dance with your heart, Asha. Become the music, just like we rehearsed. You are ready."

Them represented the three top dance companies; she was the object up for grabs. Would they want her? She hoped, yes. Would more than one? If so, her chances of a place dramatically increased.

She shook her head. Don't worry about them, she repeated as they called her name. One last deep breath in and a slow release out. She wove a path through the waiting dancers and into the main hall. A table behind which four adjudicators sat held space at one end of the floor. Anton, in control of the music, winked at her and gestured as if to pull a mask over his face – a code between themselves. Put her mask on. Yes, Anton, she would.

She took her position on the boards and waited for him to release the music to her favourite routine, soft and ethereal to begin, then building to a dramatic conclusion. Her body moved in complete sync with the music.

144

As the melody took control of her body, pictures of Camille doing the same dance routine flashed through her mind. She tried to put them aside to allow her own interpretation to guide her. Had this business of Camille and her money seeped into every part of her life already? All her work thus far had been on her strength. Yes, she'd admired her patroness' reputation, and photos abounded in every part of the studio, but this was not Camille dancing for her life. With all the effort she could muster, she focused on the music to ground herself into her own body.

A smorgasbord of her talent, Anton had once described it. As she executed her finale, she returned to the room with her mind. She stood, gave a bow and smiled at Anton. He nodded back. It was over. All that remained was to wait for the postings.

Had it been enough? Had those few moments when Camille possessed her routine taken away from her performance? She hoped not.

Asha was almost at the main door on the street when someone called her name.

"Mama?" Then she remembered. It was a cleaning day. Of course, her mother would be here. She smiled.

"How did it go?" The nerves were evident in her mother's voice. Asha hugged her, holding her hands in her own.

"I won't know until they're done with everyone. A few days at the most. I'm confident it went well."

Her mother beamed back at her. "I'm so proud of you. I have a good feeling. You will get your wish, I'm sure." Tears ran down her face.

"Shh, don't cry." She wiped her mother's face with her sleeve. "We can only pray."

"What do you think I do with my days, Asha? I clean. And I pray."

Asha hugged her and they laughed together. Despite everything, her mother was always protective and encouraging, although lately,

145

overprotective. Asha could forgive her for that. Mama had trouble letting go. She knew it was coming, Asha leaving home. All mothers were the same.

But Asha had seen something in Marco today that surprised her and left her unsettled. Marco saw only the money and not the woman, which bothered her. Indifference? Or just a different way of looking at life.

The accusation Levin made against her mother, who lived a simple life, had upset her, too. Perhaps it was Levin, not Marco. Maybe it was both.

But since the meeting, another feeling had crept in. Satisfaction. Their future was secure. If she didn't get into a company, neither of them would need to worry ever again. The envelope held that promise. No more cleaning, although the good feeling was tempered with sadness.It wasn't fair; for their security, someone she was just getting to know had to die.

CHAPTER 13

Camille wandered around her apartment in a daze. Although she'd dressed and was ready to go, the cab wouldn't arrive for another hour. She pulled back the sheer drapes separating her from the outside world.

The city lights became sharply defined. It was that moment when night gave way to the muted, soft tones of the morning. Paris never got dark. Neon overload assured that. Camille stared vacantly at the purple-infused sky. A faint star twinkled, or was it the blink of a jetliner oblivious to humanity below? No, it hadn't moved while she watched it. A star. She smiled. A long time ago, the brilliance of stars was something she'd taken for granted. In Switzerland, the nights were crisp and unspoilt by fume trails and congestion. Back then, before the war ripped open the sky and left it scarred forever. She turned away from the vista, not wanting to remember the past.

She cast her eyes around the living room. Everything was in perfect order. Pillows plumped and in place. Did it matter? Would she see any of it again? Yes, she chided herself. She wasn't about to die. Not from this procedure. God knows she'd paid enough to ensure the best surgeon would hover over her this afternoon. It was the stark realisation all would be the same when she came home that bothered her. Everything but her. Tears welled. She fought them back. She didn't want to cry. The ultimate sign of weakness.

She frowned. A carer. Would she need one yet? Perhaps a part-time nurse to deal with all the medications. She wished she'd paid more attention to the surgeon's secretary.

No point worrying, she decided. What will come, will come. She wrote Rochet a note in her diary. He'd deal with the appointments. How would she communicate her wishes? The procedure would rob her of her voice. Why hadn't she tackled the problem sooner? Because she was stubborn and refused to acknowledge it, she conceded. She added notebooks and pencils to the diary instructions. Biros would leave indelible scribblings behind. A pencil note was erasable.

She closed the diary, opened it again and ran a finger across her desk. Don't start feeling sorry for yourself. What good will it do? She cleared her throat. She told herself it wasn't so sore today, but it mattered little. Painkillers would dull the pain, but the cancer wasn't going away on its own. And leaving it allowed it to seep into God knows where else in her body. She stepped past her desk to a large mirror.

The dimmed light softened her wrinkled skin and cast shadows on her face, but she saw enough detail of her reflection. Her hair, neatly coiffed only hinted of the colour of her youth. She detested the gaudy attempts of those who kept a full body of bottled hair. Her cheeks glowed even in this dim light. Soft pillows beneath her high cheekbones. Her father's cheekbones. She raised her chin in defiance and glared at herself. She didn't need a voice to convey her wishes. One look from her was enough. It had been her major defence all her adult life, gaining her a reputation of steel.

Her voice she used when she sang. It conveyed the feelings she couldn't speak. Love, fear, anger. She used it to captivate people. Now not so much. She hadn't sung for over a decade. Like everything else, sadly, her voice eventually betrayed her. Lost its sharp edge on the high notes, wobbled, and cracked on the low. After that, her dancing kept them under her spell. Camille snapped into a ballet pose, poised on her toes, her arms gracefully raised over her head. Her lips curled with satisfaction. She could still dance, even now. She brought her arms down and relaxed her feet. The intercom buzzed, and she checked her watch. The cab had arrived. She was ready.

***

The atmosphere in the operating theatre was tense. For the second time, the theatre assistant checked all the apparatus. Everything seemed in order, but she knew this surgeon was prone to nitpicking. She wanted it to be perfect.

Satan knew it too.

The space above the operating lights gave him a splendid view of the entire room. Every time the woman counted the instruments, he whispered in her direction, "All is correct," even though it wasn't. She had overlooked the same omission every time.

Being the master of confusion that he was, this sort of thing delighted him. It was the little things that mattered. One error at a time, like dominos.

He reasoned that one instrument without the precision required, one millimetre of cancer left to grow, to spread, to kill …

A bad mood here, a moment of offence there, he could manipulate the proceedings to obtain the result he wanted. It was all too easy.

***

White. White light on white. And the noise, a constant beep of a machine. Somewhere another machine's soft air pump kept a different beat. From the depths of the fog drowning her mind, Camille heard the song. Three-four beats, she thought, in her delirium. She was back on stage just as the lights went up, waiting for her cue to dance. Only she wasn't.

The room came into focus. A plastic drip bag on a stand took shape; its tentacles stretched across her body and pierced her arm. Red lights flickered along with the occasional green and amber. Jet lights? No. Realisation came back in waves. Hospital.

A face thrust itself in front of hers. The voice echoed.

"Camille? Camille? Are you awake?" Camille wanted her to stop. It was too loud. Everything was too loud. She tried to move her head from side to side but couldn't. A weight pinned her shoulders down and tubes, like snakes on her face, crawled into her nose.

"Don't move your head, dear."

No fear of that. What then? She tried to lift a hand, but it would not respond. She frowned with frustration.

"Hush, dear. I can see you're with us. Rest now. The anaesthetic will soon wear off. Everything is fine."

Camille wanted to scream at her. It was not fine. She did not feel fine at all. She might vomit. Even that was too much effort. She closed her eyes and sank back into the blackness.

When she woke again, she was on a trolley, jostling down a hall, headed for a private room. The bag and a variety of beeping machines rode with her. First she focussed on the porter, who said nothing, then turned her eyes to the other side of the trolley where a young male nurse with a clipboard held onto the bed frame.

"Hello there," he said.

Camille closed her eyes again. She didn't feel up to such cheerfulness. At least there was no pain. Not yet.

The hospital staff lifted, heaved and patted her into her bed. They fiddled and checked all the attachments while the theatre nurse rattled off her procedure and what she could expect over the next few days. She was tired, bone tired.

"I'll check on you every twenty, dear. Rest now. The doctor will be in later after surgery." He patted her shoulder and left the room.

Peace, at last. The urge to swallow crept up on her. It was possible she'd done so a hundred times already and hadn't been aware. Why did it feel so difficult? Like someone had stuffed a sock in her throat.

She moved her fingers slowly upward over her body to her face. There were no reflective surfaces to see herself in, so she could only feel what was there: her throat and the thick plastic tube taped to her neck. It vibrated as air flowed through it, expanding her lungs. The tap, tap, of a flap as it stopped pumping and let the air release, brushing against her chin. That explained why she couldn't move; she was anchored to the machine. Another tube down her nose. She knew of that one. Meds, she guessed. And in her arm, the saline drip laced with morphine.

Relief washed over her. Battered, yes. But she was alive. A tear escaped, and she tracked its slow progress down the side of her face and into her ear. Closing her eyes, she lamented how difficult it was to be absolutely helpless. She would fight. She was not dead yet, so she would fight.

***

Camille's hospital room resembled a florist. The perfume wafted into the corridor with every person who entered and exited. She'd been here a week now, and it chafed her. Rochet had a small desk set up, and he furiously wrote at it this morning. Camille tapped on the food tray with her pencil, annoyed that he ignored her attempts at communicating with him. She gritted her teeth and drew her brows together into a deep furrow.

On her notepad, she broke the lead in her pencil with heavily scored and angry words and, in her frustration, threw the useless pencil at the back of his head. It hit the wall in front of him, and he started.

His shoulders stiffened and he turned and eyed her with a look of defeat and disbelief written all over his face.

Her eyes bore into his. This was harder than she imagined. She pushed this man to his limits but reminded herself she paid him well. She gestured to him to come to her bedside using the one hand not attached to a drip, tore the sheet from her notepad and held it up.

I want to go home. She'd underlined the words twice in heavy-lead strokes.

Rochet grimaced and nodded. "I'll tell them. In no uncertain words, Madame. I'll arrange whatever it is they say is necessary. Nurse? Medical equipment? Anything else?"

Was he mocking her? She supposed not. Camille relaxed her face. Even smiling seemed difficult, but this time she managed. She nodded and went to scribble on the pad again. In disgust, she pointed to her pencil on the floor. Rochet rolled his eyes and handed her a fresh one.

Asha Villet. Get her to come to the apartment. She held the new note up to him, and he bobbed his head in understanding. She scribbled again. *Thank you.*

Satisfied that Rochet would do as requested, she rested back on her pillow and closed her eyes, buoyed by knowing she would be asleep in her own bed by the end of the day. A promise worth every bit of the extra money it would take, even if it meant she had to endure one medical visit after the other to her room. There was a lot to consider, and she was exhausted by mid-afternoon.

A while later, Camille heard the door slide open and allowed her eyelids to lift a fraction. What did they need of her now? All her observations were done. She gritted her teeth and waited for the person to enter. A soft knock alerted her to the possibility this was not an expected visit. A heavily made-up face poked around the door.

"Bonjour. May I come in?" the person said brightly.

Camille wondered if the visitor realised she could not speak. What a foolish thing to ask of someone whose voice box had been ripped out. Where was Rochet? Out organising her release, she hoped. She waved the visitor to come in.

A well-dressed woman in her mid-thirties in a bright pink business suit, black high-heeled pumps and a patent leather shoulder bag glided into the room. Her perfume competed with the floral arrangements. Camille suddenly felt naked. She hadn't missed the daily routine of make-up until now. The perfect face reminded her of how quickly priorities changed and how vulnerable she was at this moment.

The woman dragged a chair to the edge of her bed. She held out a perfectly manicured hand and introduced herself as Petrona Orlise. Camille took the hand lightly enough to pass as suitably formal, then folded both arms across her blanket. Her eyes remained focussed on the woman's face, challenging her to look at any other part of her body. A silence grew.

Camille waved at her throat. Should she point out the obvious?

"Oh. Yes. My apologies. Well. I guess I'll state why I'm here, and then you can"—the woman looked at the notepad on Camille's tray— "let me know what you think?"

Camille nodded resignedly. A magazine puppy. Looking for a bone. She'd dealt with them before. Unfortunately, they came with the industry.

She was right. Ms Orlise was from a society magazine. Would Camille mind if they ran a piece? A photo? A blurb on her scholarship program?

There was no point denying an interview. The pink suit had come here for a story, and even if Camille declined to be 'interviewed', the paper would run one of their own design. She knew how it worked. Better to have some input and advance the scholarship's profile.

Another sobering thought took hold. This may well be her last ever interview. She hoped the pink suit appreciated that and didn't botch it up for them both.

With all the energy she could muster, Camille inclined the bed so she was sitting upright. The woman helped by adding an extra pillow behind her back.

The interview took a little over a half hour, by which time Camille had scribbled her responses and imparted as little information about her cancer diagnosis as was necessary. At the end, having declined a current photo, she agreed they could use a stock photo from a previous article if they found a recent one. When the woman left, Camille, exhausted, slid into a deep sleep.

CHAPTER 14

Julia trudged towards the studio, coffee in hand, a hard knot sitting in her gut. Two things gnawed at her mind. The first, and most immediate, was that the results for the examinations were going up on the noticeboard this morning. She'd sacrificed everything for her daughter, and today was the climax of it all. Thankfully, it was a regular cleaning day, giving her a valid excuse to be there. No other parent had that luxury.

The other thing eating her was guilt. Asha had left an envelope on her bed the other day. Clearly marked private. The fact it was from a legal firm Julia didn't know had piqued her interest enough to draw her back time and again to Asha's bed. The envelope was already open, so it didn't take much to slide the contents onto the bed and read the letter.

Nothing stood out more than the lines: Last Will and Testament of Camille DuPont. Julia had dropped the letter as though it had burnt her fingers.

So, that was what Asha's dinner meeting was about.

What burned her more was that Asha hadn't said a word. It raised another feeling for Julia, apart from the guilt for even reading the letter in the first place. Fear.

The fear came from a deeper source. It opened old wounds that Julia thought she'd healed from. Ghosts from her past now crept into her waking hours and nightmares. And she must wait for Asha to bring up the letter or be accused – rightly so – of prying into Asha's business.

A glossy cover caught her eye as she passed the newspaper stand on the corner. Julia never bought new magazines. She only borrowed the ones left on tables from the many offices she cleaned. It was months, sometimes years, after their appearance on a bookstand. Old news, by the time she saw it. It never mattered, though.

It was the photo that caught her eye. Black and white and grainy. Hardly what you'd expect for the front cover of a popular magazine. Julia slowed to a standstill and swivelled on the spot. To her annoyance, a breeze flipped the cover so she couldn't see it. The owner of the stand looked expectantly at her. Time to decide. Buy it and waste her money? Why did it matter what she'd seen? She knew the answer already, and a sick feeling wound its way into her gut. The picture – she had seen it before.

The breeze moved on, and the cover settled back in place. Julia stared. Her face drained of colour to match the picture.

"Mother of God," she muttered. The stand was close to a street crossing, and the pip-pip of a green light broke through her shock. Moments later, she was the rock in a stream of humanity, who pushed and jostled as she stood in their way. She fumbled with her purse, stepped out of the stream and thrust the coins into the bookseller's hand. She grabbed the magazine and hurried across the road against the flow of people. On the other side, she dropped onto a bench and closed her eyes to regain her composure.

With her heart in her mouth, she turned to the page the magazine promised the scandalous piece of gossip that Parisians must know about. There it was. A more recent photo of Camille DuPont took a whole page. The headline was sensational, of course. It had to be.

Darling of the dance world, Camille DuPont faces her demons

The article listed her achievements and role as a long-time benefactress of the DuPont Scholarship. Thankfully, they didn't mention who the current recipient was. The last thing she wanted was Asha's name linked to this article. She turned the page for what must explain the grainy photo on the front cover. Her heart pounded with dread. Did the gutter magazine do a thorough job and name the missing child? Or was it to be a mystery still, a mud puddle to dredge through for the sake of selling a few thousand extra copies next time? Neither, she hoped.

The photo was there. The hurt in the eyes was just as clear. Even more so, as Julia's was printed on cheap news copy and yellowed with age. The magazine's version on glossy, white paper sharpened the darkness of those eyes, accentuating the pain.

The story referred current readers back to the origin of the photo, trying to heighten the intrigue of an old story. The modern take included extra what-if scenarios. It questioned every angle of Camille's career and involvement with the scholarship. It even hinted further that her wealthy family covered up a scandal and paid her way into the coveted roles she played. And, as the magazine trumpeted, the outbreak of war buried this scandal.

They begged the question of their readers. Was there a mystery child? Would one come forward and claim a massive fortune soon to be up for grabs when Madame DuPont succumbed to her throat cancer? Julia felt sick. Sick for Camille. Imagine reading such a shocking article when you were suffering and vulnerable. Her heart ached.

An alarming thought jolted her. What would happen if this became a popular item of gossip? As the trust recipient, would it mean the paparazzi would hound her daughter? What a mess. She didn't want this spotlight on Asha.

Julia looked to the sky for answers, aware she was almost on the verge of tears, and found none. She folded the magazine, stuffed it into her coat jacket, and hurried to work.

As she jostled through the hallway full of students, she spied a copy of the magazine poking from a dancer's bag. Her worst nightmare had been realised. Rumours would spread like wildfire among Asha's peers.

Her ears rang. Every conversation she picked up, she imagined was about the article. It wasn't so, but to Julia, the pressure of knowing and not knowing exploded in a cauldron of expectation. It was only a matter of time before someone thrust it under Asha's nose.

Jealousy was a vile creature, and for all the outward appearance of these beautiful dancers, Julia understood if you wanted to dance and make a career of it, a ruthless streak was required. Something her daughter did not possess.

To make things worse, there was nothing she could do.

***

Rochet frantically stabbed the button to the elevator. He cursed the fact it was so slow. "Come on, come on. *Allez*!" Recent renovations had pared the services back. Before, this wouldn't be an issue. To him, the more modern contraptions became, the more prone they were to break down.
The wiring buzzed in the building's belly. Good, he thought. He refused to do the stairs.

Not only were there disruptions within the building, but the neighbourhood was undergoing roadworks around every corner, making him late for work. Madame wouldn't be pleased. The operation had tested her patience sorely. And his. Still, he reminded himself, better indispensable than unemployed. He doubted another position even existed that compared to his current one. Not for him, a city desk and shared facsimile. Snobbery? Perhaps so. But as personal assistants went, he considered himself top brass. He wondered how to broach the subject of a favourable referral if – he corrected himself -- when the time came and his services would no longer be required. A glum thought.

Madame sat in her study behind her desk, which was now in the centre of the room to allow for an oxygen trolley. He hoped she could discard the paraphernalia soon. The specialist had been encouraging. Her recovery was nothing short of remarkable. Tough old bird, he thought.

Rochet made a beeline for his desk and disgorged the contents of his briefcase. Bills from the operation, reports from the academy and a glossy magazine he'd picked up with apprehension. She wouldn't be happy.

It worried him that he'd made a bad move with the reporter. Orlise had overstepped. He hadn't wanted a trashy article, just one that cemented his value to Madame DuPont. Where this scandal had been dug from, he had no idea. If it were true, that was one thing, but he'd seen no evidence of what it suggested in his time with her. Still, she held most emotions to herself, so it was possible.

He'd been careful not to implicate himself as the instigator, and Orlise assured him they never divulge their sources. But it annoyed him they hadn't hinted at Asha's unsuitability as an heiress to this fortune. They'd gone completely off his angle. He'd expected more emphasis on whether she would be philanthropic with her money, thus prompting Madame to reconsider giving it to Asha's control. It was one thing to have the scholarship continue; anyone could administer that. But he knew her fortune was vast. Surely, she could do better with it. And he was well positioned to handle it if she only realised. In fact, he'd already delivered a copy to her solicitor that same morning, a step he planned to prove he could be trusted. That he cared.

"Tea, Madame?" He glanced in her direction. That was the hardest part, knowing how often to look at her in case she wanted his attention. He needed a plan. He did not want missiles thrown at his head again.

The distance between their desks caught his eye. No, she wasn't that good of a throw, still ...

She looked up from her notepad on which she scribbled furiously. More instructions. She nodded. Tea. Splendid. Should he just drop the offending magazine on her desk and leave? That would be cruel. No, he'd deliver it with the tea. He cleared a space in front of her and gave her the opened bills and the report. He decided it was best to deal with these first, as once the other matter surfaced, she'd be useless for the rest of the day. As he headed for the kitchen, she caught his arm and tapped on a note.

Have you contacted Asha Villet? Did she say when she might come?

The girl. He hadn't forgotten. She was hard to contact, but he hadn't tried too hard either. He'd left messages at the school for her. If she didn't get them, it suited him. Made her look disinterested even.

Madame wrote quickly.

Her mother. She works at the academy. A cleaner? Don't bother her teacher with it.

"Certainly. This afternoon, Madame."

A cleaner. Well, didn't that rub? She'd benefit from Asha's windfall too, no doubt. He put the kettle on. A bell. He would get her a bell. The idea made him laugh ironically. Convenient and practical, yes. But then he'd be reduced to a bellboy. Literally. He shook his head in dismay.

With the tea in her hands, Rochet retrieved the magazine. Gingerly, he placed it in front of her and set his chair on the other side of her desk. At first glance, she showed little interest. He held his breath.

As she turned the pages to the story, shock registered on her face. Her brows knitted as her eyes scanned the grainy picture, then the accompanying story. Tears filled her eyes. What they'd written was cruel. Sensationalism at its worst. She dropped the magazine onto her desk. But now he'd have to make the best of it. Remind her it was he who cared, not the absent Asha. He leant over and patted her hand protectively.

"I've given a copy to Mr Levin's office this morning. It's trash. Let him deal with it. We'll draft up a counter story if you like."

The phone rang. Rochet had been surprised it hadn't already done so. The vultures would be in full flight, looking for her response. The magazine had been on the shelves since the early morning. He kicked himself for not being quicker off the mark. To at least be given time to formulate a response to what he expected would become a barrage.

**

Asha pushed her way to the front of the crowd gathered at the noticeboard. The results were up. Her heart thumped. Every nerve tingled. As she ran her eyes down the list of names for each company, there was a derisive snort from a student behind her. Ah, there it was, her name under Paris Revue Inc., which wasn't her preferred company. Still, she'd made one at least. The second list, her name again. A thrill ran through her. Even better, a choice. The third list, nothing. The last, the one she aspired to but thought she'd have no chance, had two names listed. She gasped and gave a little bounce. She had done it. Mama would be so happy.

The snort again, closer to her. Someone was disappointed. Places were scarce. A whisper, the words too faint to discern, from one dancer to another, made the hairs on her neck rise. The comments were about her. She would ignore it. Jealousy. Nothing new in this place. Despite the scholarship, she'd earned her place on those lists.

She pushed her way past the disgruntled students and searched for her teacher. He saw her coming down the hall and called out to her.

"Ms Villet!" His face beamed, and she smiled in response. He had pushed her, yes, but in the end, her dedication and talent did it. Anton put an arm around her, and they walked the last few steps to class.

"So proud of you. You earned every bit of your place. Now, tell me, which company will you choose? I know someone at each of them. It pays,

161

you know. To have an ally." They were about to enter the classroom when her mother weaved her way past the students. Asha embraced her.

"Did you see? Mama! Did you see!"

Her mother's face told her the answer. "Yes, my love, I did. I'll cook something special tonight to celebrate."

Anton tapped her on the shoulder lightly. "Asha, before you make plans," he interrupted and apologised, "I was coming to find you. There was a call for you from Madame DuPont's secretary. She invited you this evening. It sounded urgent." He shrugged at her mother, whose face fell with disappointment.

Asha groaned inwardly. Guilt gnawed at her. If she didn't jump at the invitation to Camille, would she miss an opportunity to get an insight into the companies who vied for her? Camille knew all the companies, their good points and their bad. Would Mama understand? The disappointment on her mother's face shifted to a blank look of resignation.

The guilt increased a notch. Asha could read her feelings like an open book. This was her mother's success too. She had worked her whole life for Asha to get to this moment.

In an instant, her mind was made up. Camille might not extend the invitation again. Mama would always be there, no matter what. Asha kissed her firmly on the cheek. She would make it up to her.

"Mama. I'll have to go. We'll celebrate tomorrow night, I promise."

***

The cab drew away from the curb and left Asha in the street outside Camille's apartment block. She looked up at the strip of blue above. The sun skimmed the tops of the building, but down at street level, the shadows sat just between a dull afternoon and the moment streetlights burst into life.

The predominantly high-end business houses that traded here had closed for the day, and the emptiness in the street made her shiver. It exuded loneliness. No hustle and bustle of families heading home, unlike the narrow lanes where she lived. And it wasn't so far removed in distance; only one arrondissement away. She shivered again and slipped inside the lobby to shake the feeling. The concierge's desk was unattended.

Eager not to be alone, she hurried to the elevator and buzzed Camille's floor. The minute the door slid open, perfume from heady blooms of rose and lily hit her senses.

"Oh, Mr Ying. We must stop meeting this way," she teased.

He grinned back at her. "I hope we never stop, Ms Asha. Ying would be very sad. Up?" He pointed to the buttons.

"Yes, of course."

"Ms Camille is not well today ... I've delivered too many flowers to her already." He lowered his head and shook it sadly.

"Poor thing. I haven't seen her since the operation." Asha suffered a pang of guilt. Should she have made more of an effort?

"Flowers only make you happy for a while. Good friends, much better present."

"Well, I can cheer her up with good news today." Asha smiled. Her acceptance into the dance companies would surely do that. And she hoped Camille might help her choose the right one, having so much more experience.

"Hmm. I hope so too." As the doors opened on the top level, he added, "Tell Ms Camille, Mr Ying still prays for her – every day." His grin was the last thing she saw as she waved goodbye to the vanishing space.

Now that she was here, the coldness of the street and lobby disappeared, replaced with the scent of the Chinese florist. It made her smile.

She buzzed the apartment door, and the lock released, allowing her to enter. Music floated softly from the study and guided her to where Camille sat on a sofa, a glass of wine in her hands. Asha's first impression was, should she be drinking? Did one abstain from alcohol to give the best chance to heal from cancer or was it simply Camille choosing to drown out the shock of the diagnosis. But then, it wasn't her place to comment. Camille looked up at her with glazed eyes. Asha's heart broke seeing the tubes taped heavily around her throat and the oxygen cylinder on a trolley next to her. She looked frail. A lot smaller than she remembered.

She realised then Camille could no longer speak. A confronting fact she hadn't prepared for. It may have shown on her face because Camille patted the sofa next to her and handed her a notepad. Her eyes searched for Asha's and held them. This too was confronting. Camille took her hands and clutched them. She smiled and pointed to the pad.

Asha read the note and immediately relaxed.

I'm not deaf. Don't feel sorry for me.

"Camille, forgive me. I'm sorry I haven't been since ..." She couldn't finish the sentence.

Camille scribbled on the pad furiously.

You've been busy. I know! And you did well. Congratulations. She scribbled again, "*Which ones?*"

Asha smiled widely, her discomfort easing. "Paris Revue, The Versailles Ballet Corp and my favourite, Rudi Van Claus' Troupe." The excitement returned. "Tell me which one I should join. You know them all; which one is the best?" Her voice brimmed with happiness.

Camille raised a finger to hush her. She took Asha's hand, held it still, then placed it against Asha's breast. Her eyes filled with tears.

Asha understood. *Let her own heart decide, it was not what Camille wanted that mattered.* Good answer. What a wise person, and how lucky she was to be here. It saddened her to know their time together was short. She would make every moment count.

The music began repeating the same few beats. Camille looked crossly over to where a record player sat. Asha jumped up and rescued the needle, and the next melody floated as though nothing was amiss.

She was about to return to the sofa when she noticed the magazine open on Camille's desk. The full-page picture caught her eye. A younger Camille, but very recognisable. She picked up the magazine, and as she read the heading, she stopped and stared open-mouthed at the woman on the sofa.

One look at Camille's face told her the article had hurt. She held it up.

"Do you mind?" she said with compassion. Camille threw her hands in the air and looked away but not before Asha saw her chin quiver before she took a sip of her wine.

Asha sat quietly next to her and read the whole thing. It was horrible. Nasty even. Her heart wrenched at the gossip about a possible child. She closed the magazine and dropped it onto the low table in front of them. The sad black-and-white eyes stared up at her. She grabbed it impulsively and turned it over.

"I'm angry for you." Her voice hardened. "That was cruel. Why? Who do these people think they are?"

Camille sat as still as a statue. Tears streamed down her cheeks, but she held her head up proudly. Asha took a tissue from her bag, offered it and waited for Camille to dab the dampness from her face, before hugging her. Camille remained stiff under her embrace, and when Asha sat back, she turned to face her.

She grimaced as no sound came as she tried to speak, forcing her to fumble with the pad and pencil.

Don't pity me. I don't care what people say. I'm old. And soon I'll be gone, and they will say a lot more things I won't ever hear.

Her face set to the familiar stoic façade Asha knew well.

165

You need to grow a tough exterior. I'm giving you my estate. All of it. And I don't want these people to hurt you because of it.

The words were scratched darkly on the pad and underlined.

Asha became still.

"Was there a child?" The words were not accusing, just curious. The instant she said them, she wished she hadn't. She didn't want to upset her further.

For a moment, Camille froze.

A lump stuck in Asha's throat. "I'm sorry. I shouldn't have asked. Please, don't tell me if you can't. It's none of my business." She stumbled over the words.

Camille patted her hand and picked up the notepad.

Yes. A girl.

Asha swallowed. The lump remained.

I was only nineteen. There was war. I had no mother, and my papa had just died too.

She turned the page.

I did the only thing I could. For her, for me.

Silent tears bounced off Asha's face. Could she have done any differently? Possibly not, no. Another thought entered her mind.

"Camille, you could find her. You have time. How old would she be now, sixty? She could be here – in Paris. You must find her!" she exclaimed with excitement. The possibilities grew by the moment. Asha gripped Camille's hand. "I will help you. Really. I would love to do that for you."

Camille's head shook from side to side. She mouthed, "No."

Asha didn't understand. She sat for a moment and wondered. "Why not?"

Camille shook her head. Asha saw the emotion was too raw and worried she had stepped over the bounds.

"I'm sorry, Camille. That wasn't very thoughtful of me. Please, forgive me." She looked at the clock and remembered her mother and the look of disappointment on her face this afternoon. A pang of guilt shot through her. She couldn't know what it was like to be abandoned – not that she was accusing Camille of callously abandoning her child – but having a mother meant the world to her. To not have one ... She didn't want to even think of it.

"I must go. I promised Mama I'd be home for dinner." She took the frail hands in hers again. An inspiration came. "You two must meet. You'd like my mother. You remind me a lot of her, you know." She smiled warmly at the idea.

Camille bobbed her head in agreement.

As Asha got up to leave, she noticed an enormous bouquet on the hall table. "Oh, those flowers remind me"—she looked back at Camille on her sofa, wineglass in hand and once again in control of her emotions—"Mr Ying said to say he still prays for you every day."

Camille choked on her wine and threw her head back in a silent laugh. Asha laughed with her.

"Good night."

CHAPTER 15

Julia slowly climbed the stairs to her flat, drained by a day of roller-coasting emotion. In her bag, the weight of the magazine seemed disproportionately heavy. In the past, she would have wanted every piece for her scrapbook. Another documented chapter of the faraway woman who was, but wasn't, her mother.

"Why do you do this to yourself?" she muttered. Her chest burnt with a familiar ache.

"Because. Just because," came the same voice from deep within.

From under her bed, she retrieved an old tin trunk filled with the last remnants of her childhood. From inside it she brought out a thick, battered scrapbook, placed it on the table and opened the cover slowly. An original birth certificate glared back at her. Proof of life. But whose life?

She traced a finger over the blank line for Mother. In the beginning, before she discovered the truth, Julia had fantasised about her real parents. She'd taken what scant information existed of her own timeline and put her birth mother's indiscretion to mere months after France declared war against Hitler.

Had it been love? Was her father a soldier sent to the front, to never return? Had her mother died of a broken heart soon after and left her an orphan? These and a million other questions swirled in her head since the day she discovered she was not the person she thought she was.

This was one of two birth certificates she had. The other showed her known parents as mother and father. Julia had found the one she looked at now lodged in the spine of the family Bible after her parents' untimely death. If she hadn't dropped the book and, in doing so, dislodged the tightly folded certificate, she might never have known she was adopted.

Years later, Julia took both certificates to the Public Registrar. The woman who served her studied them for what seemed an eternity, switching focus from one to the other. She'd taken both away and had a whispered conversation with a superior, glancing at Julia with furtive looks. In the end, she handed both back and shook her head.

"I'm sorry, Ms Bruin. I can't help you. There are laws that prevent me from divulging any details of your birth mother. You could make a formal request, but ..." She shrugged. "These things are best left alone."

Julia got the impression the woman wanted to tell her more, but to do so would risk her job. She'd sat frozen for a few moments before bursting into tears.

"I have no one," she whispered.

The woman had squirmed in her seat and waited for her to regain her composure. Then she'd scribbled a name on a piece of paper and reached into her drawer for a box of tissues. These she handed to Julia; the note tucked discreetly into the protruding tissue. No words were said, but her smile was genuine, as was the message in her eyes.

Julia understood perfectly. She took the tissue, dabbed her eyes, and tucked it into her sleeve. "Thank you."

It was from then that she scoured magazines for anything to do with the name she had been given. She cleaned offices for a living. Dusted and tidied the endless waiting room tables. Magazines were everywhere. No one missed them if Julia borrowed them and, determined as she was to find answers, she'd found a free resource in their tattered pages.

She flipped to the next page of her scrapbook. A face stared back, a young girl with wide, deep eyes and a look of hurt in the outline of her lips. It was a black-and-white photo, made even starker by the obvious use of a flashbulb close to the poor girl's face.

Julia traced the contour of her chin. The pain on the face was palpable. She had almost missed the relevance of the image, but a second glance at the headline set off alarm bells. The timing was right. A few months after, Julia was born. A famous dancer and singing talent of her era. Innuendo and outrageous accusations painted a dismal picture of the subject. Had this woman earned her place in the academy in a shameful liaison, and would the resultant consequences sound the end of her career? Nothing was substantiated, nothing spoken in plain words, but the innuendo was there, and the photo supported whatever the gossip lovers would want to believe. The truth, though, did it shine through? Julia could not tell.

It fitted, she reflected. She had none of her parents' features. Not the lankiness of her father nor the thickened calves of her mother. She'd been told they'd lived originally in Versailles, but they had moved often because of the war and German incursion into French provinces. South first, but once the whole of France came under Nazi control, they'd stayed put, eking out survival as far from townships and danger as possible. For all intents, until after the war, they were poor chicken farmers, feeding whoever needed feeding, whether it be French or German. To not do so put them at risk.

But in all those early years, Julia was loved. Her parents hadn't needed the burden of a child in those years of hell on Earth. But they had taken her in. As evidenced by the polished birth certificate. The official date signed by both registrars was a matter of weeks. They had wanted her desperately.

That fact made the scrapbook even more of a dilemma. Fingers of betrayal plucked the strings of her heart. Leave it alone, she heard in her head. The next thought fought tenaciously against it. It's your right to know, rang loud and clear.

The difference now was Asha. Julia hadn't touched the scrapbook in ages. An article here or there, but as Camille's star faded, Asha's had risen, and with that, a fresh fear kept Julia's nerves taut. The fear of discovery. She wasn't ready to have the connection confirmed. Not by Camille and certainly not by the media.

This article might drag Asha into the murky past and ruin any hopes of a brilliant career forged from her own talent. She pictured the headlines: *History repeats or Family money buys Asha Villet a place on the stage. Mystery child is mother of rising protégé.*

She didn't want that to happen to Asha. Would people accuse Julia of planting her daughter into a career where she might benefit from an uncovered connection? A long shot, if even possible. No, Asha set her own course. Dance was in her veins, and yes, Julia had seen the irony. She could have forced her away from dance but resisted.

But more than anything, she didn't want to explain why to her daughter. Why hadn't she told her who her grandmother was? Why keep a scrapbook in the first place?

Could she answer her own questions honestly? She should tell her now, since their lives were becoming entangled. Did she want her daughter to find the family connection in a grubby magazine? Of course not. But when to tell her was the hardest question of all.

Julia pulled the latest magazine from her bag and dropped it next to the scrapbook, unsure if she would bother adding the new story. Above her head, the pigeons tapped on the skylight, impatient to be fed.

She filled their tin, placed it in its spot on the sill and rummaged in the fridge for her dinner. Asha was with Camille. The knowledge taunted her. Moth to a flame. Well, the flame was the problem, not the moth.

Life was cruel. She shut the fridge and reached for the bottle of wine. Bloody cruel. She took the scissors and glue from the shelf. The pieces trimmed; she carefully arranged them but gained no satisfaction. In fact, she contemplated throwing the entire project into the rubbish. It felt like a curse now.

She closed the book and glared at it. As if to taunt her, the front cover refused to stay flat, flipping open, pushed by a lifetime of snippets. Julia stared at the birth certificate that had started it all. She ran a hand over the aged paper.

"Who are you?" she whispered, tears streaming down her face.

Footsteps on the stairs interrupted her thoughts. Asha? She looked at the table covered with the cuttings, book and the magazine's remains. Before she could hide any of it, the key turned in the door, and Asha skipped up the last flight of stairs.

"Mama?" Asha picked up the remains of the magazine from the floor, where it had fallen in Julia's haste to clean up.

"You've seen it then. Please, don't keep a copy for me. I don't want it. It's a horrid piece." She threw her bag onto her bed and went to the bathroom.

Had she noticed the scrapbook? Did Asha think she kept this for her? She'd been careful not to let her see it till now. Her plan was always to leave it behind in her things as a connection to the truth but only when she was gone.

The answer to one of her questions was right there. If she told Asha what the scrapbook was for, she risked losing the closeness that she had with her. The bubble that belonged to only her and Asha as a family would burst.

Camille would make that three of them. She wasn't ready for that. Cowardice? Maybe. The scrapbook had become for her what the original birth certificate had been for her adoptive mother. A way to the truth without the revelation ever having to be made face to face. She put it back into the trunk and shoved it under her bed.

Asha emerged from the bathroom and sat at the table beside her. Julia tried to compose her emotions and look normal, which took all her strength because she didn't feel normal inside. She forced a smile.

"Hey, let's order pizza," Asha said. "Better still, let's eat out." Something they rarely did.

Julia shook her head. The wine had already affected her. She couldn't face the stairs down, let alone up again. "Order in, love. I got paid today; there's change in my purse."

Asha delved into the purse. "Mama. What's this?" She held up the shiny souvenir coin from the church.

Julia's face drained of colour. She'd forgotten it. She had not forgotten the day.

"Ah, I was at Notre-Dame the other day. A spur-of-the-moment thing, that's all." She reached out, her hand trembling. Asha handed the coin to her, and her fingers wrapped around it.

She avoided Asha's eyes. Her tears would cause suspicion. She meant to put it into the scrapbook, but for some reason, something in her wanted to keep that encounter close. That day was like a sign that God had answered her prayers, but now, with the magazine and the promise of Camille's money for Asha, Julia wondered. Was it a warning of worse things to come? The coin burned into her hand.

The moment Asha left to order their dinner, she put it in the trunk with the scrapbook.

***

A few days later, Camille was pacing her room, glancing at her watch every few minutes. Every step increased the tension in her body. The cab would be here soon enough. It would be a trying day. First, a visit to Pierre. Thinking of him made her gut clench. How she wished she could speak. She should never have agreed to him searching for her child. Never. She looked at the magazine on the desk with reproach. This was the result. Now the world knew. She shook her head. Or thought they did.

She hadn't wanted to go back there. Not at all. But the magazine had dragged her back. Nightmares. Horrid ones. That beast who had plied her with alcohol and ...

No, she would not touch the wound. She was stuck on that train, saw a hundred times every night the door to her cabin open and the shaft of light that let hell into her life. Over and over, she changed her mind about letting him in. Over and over, she failed. He found other ways and always the beast won.

The buzzer sounded. The cab had arrived.

Pierre wasn't her only appointment today. The results of the biopsy were back. The surgeon had news, whether bad or good, his clinic did not say. But today, she expected to be free of this wretched oxygen. She was tired of dragging the small cylinder with her. Against the advice, she disconnected it for longer and longer periods throughout the day. Forced her lungs to drag enough oxygen through that hole in her throat. She wouldn't let some man in a white coat thwart her years of self-control. Did he know her? No. He only saw a diminutive older woman. Apart from the obvious, that she had to breathe through a device inserted into her windpipe, nothing else had changed. That, and the nightmares, kept her awake at night.

But, she reflected, they were her demons, and no one else saw them. A little more powder under her eyes, a scarf discreetly hiding the neck wound, she'd show them all. Camille DuPont was in full control.

175

And would be until she took her last breath, she told herself adamantly as she pressed the button on the elevator.

The doors slid open and revealed the fruit cart that took up half the space. Camille's front shattered. It was one thing to bravely attest her life was the same; it was another to meet people around her that knew it was not. Instead of stepping into the elevator, she waved at Ying, who grinned his ridiculous smile. She would wait. Inconvenient, but surely, he'd finished his deliveries and was on his way down. Except Ying, being his usual obstinate self, held the door for her and motioned her to enter.

"Plenty of room, Miss Camille. Plenty of room, see?" He pushed his cart further across, making room for her small oxygen trolley.

Camille realised he would not leave without her. In fact, he looked ready to grab her trolley and drag her in. Her eyes widened in alarm, imagining it. She gave in. There was no point in dallying. The cab metre was ticking already. She stepped in and made herself small beside him.

"Miss Camille, you're still with us. Good news. Prayers do a good job ." He grinned with satisfaction.

Camille frowned with exasperation. Where was her notepad and pencil? The idea that her life hung on Mr Ying's prayers was outrageous. She noticed a small pad on his trolley with a pen attached. She pointed to it and raised her eyebrow at him. In fairness to him, she conceded, he wasn't aware her operation had rendered her speechless. She would be clear, just this once. After that, she couldn't promise to tolerate his cheerfulness.

She scribbled on the pad. Did he read in French? Surely he must. The last stroke she did with a flourish and firmly dotted the sentence. She wrote: *Doctors, not God.* and watched out the side of her eyes as he read it to himself. He laughed. One of his close-the-eyes, tears-out-the-side laughs. She shook her head as he wiped his face with his apron.

"Miss Camille, I prayed you got a good doctor. See, God still loves you. Sent a good doctor."

The doors to the elevator slid open, and Camille marched away from Ying and his God. As much as she wanted to be annoyed with him, she found herself smiling. How was it possible? How could God still love her after all this time? Hadn't she just a few days ago spewed her hatred at him? Wasn't it his fault this happened in the first place? Hadn't he allowed her past to be dredged from the sewers and thrown at her face? Every image that surfaced replaced a brick in the wall around her heart. A wall she hid behind against the world. Her smile faded. She just had to stop it from crumbling again.

***

Pierre Levin wondered how to tackle his next client. He knew she would be, at worst, furious or, if his luck held, only seriously annoyed. The offending magazine on his desk stared back. He'd gone over every scenario to explain how a breach in his impeccable privacy procedure happened. Of course, he'd warned her this sort of muck existed. It wasn't entirely implausible; his original fear had, in fact, been justified. It could be totally coincidental, couldn't it?

He sighed. But he was a realist. Someone somewhere smelt a story and money with it. He'd contacted the magazine immediately.

"We'll sue you for damages," he'd said, knowing their legal team knew the ropes well enough to pull the 'protect the source' card on him.

"Prove it," the editor responded. Blunt, no pausing to think things over. He knew his game. Unless Levin proved they gained knowledge by deception from his company, they argued plausibly. "It's all out there, and we bothered to look."

Levin knew from the tone of his voice the editor was enjoying his discomfort. It didn't matter to him if an old lady got offended. She was public property, wasn't she?

And the fact Levin was offended on her behalf gave him the impression there was more to it than they already had. He heard the greed in the editor's voice on the other end of the phone. Levin's only chance of nipping this in the bud was to convince Camille to take the front foot.

When Jacques had gotten back to him within hours of giving him the file, Pierre had been shocked. One, it had been that easy to find Camille's daughter. Two, she lived right here under Camille's nose. And three, perhaps the most shocking element, was that Camille's own granddaughter would inherit everything, anyway. He shook his head in disbelief. It was too impossible to be true. Things like this did not happen unless in the movies.

At first, he suspected a rat. There had to be some plot to this. His questions to the girl, Asha, produced no clues. She seemed innocent enough. He'd upset her by asking, though. The mother. It had to be. But how and why? He put himself into her shoes. Abandoned at birth? Angry that she was robbed of a lifetime of comfort and ended up living in hardship? Possibly. Hardly probable. The mother was sixty. If you wanted to pursue inheritance rights, would you wait that long? And he reminded himself this story broke after Asha learnt of her inheritance. So, no, the mother already stood to gain from that windfall by proxy. Muckraking put that in jeopardy. Was it just coincidence, after all?

The intercom buzzed. "Madame DuPont is here to see you."

Pierre jumped from his seat and opened the door for her. The sick feeling in his stomach clawed its way up and sat behind his Adam's apple. This would not be easy. He held his breath as his client and her trolley brushed by him and took a seat.

The conversation was difficult, even though he was the only one able to speak.

"You're angry. And rightly so." He tapped on his desk nervously. "But can you see it this way, Camille? Your life was never private. It's an old magazine, not even in circulation now. But it was out there. It's no stretch to believe someone had a copy. I did warn you."

Camille scribbled on her pad.

Did you find the one you were looking for?

Pierre avoided her eyes.

"No. Dead end there." The lie rolled off his tongue. Had his heart just missed a beat? Whatever possessed him to say that? He drew his hand over his mouth to hide the guilt on his face.

Jacques' file was too fresh; he wanted time to digest it. To understand the ramifications. It occurred to him Julia might be unaware that Camille was her mother. She may not have ever tried to find her. If that were so, Asha's response to him made more sense.

It was hard to miss the droop of her shoulders. He wondered if, despite her initial reluctance, Camille had warmed to the idea of finding her child after all.

"Let's focus on minimising the damage, shall we?"

Camille agreed with that. She wanted Asha shielded from the paparazzi.

"I think they will leave her alone. She wasn't mentioned in the story. Maybe they don't care about the scholarship recipients that much." He thought this might be true, at least while Camille lived. He'd pressed on Ms Villet about the importance of the terms not being discussed before her death. If she talked to the media, it sealed her own destruction. He guessed she wouldn't want the attention either.

When he thought about it, the article didn't have all the facts. Only he did. They had no idea who the mystery child might be. That was never mentioned in public. This realisation made him confident that at least Asha would not be linked to the scandal. Not yet. On the bright side, he now had the means to legally support the connection and deny other false claimants.

179

His lie would buy him more time, ironic considering his client lacked exactly that.

He would find the source of this leak and dismiss that person immediately if it was someone from within his practice. The last thing he wanted was for his reputation to be tarnished. Camille's death, and the execution of her will and all that entailed, would place Levin & Son into the spotlight, and he'd be damned if one tiny slip-up would mar his family's good name.

***

Camille left Pierre Levin's office deflated. Having to write everything she wanted to say was exhausting. She hadn't bargained for the impossibility of getting her point across. Her bravado suffered a brutal blow. Now, to add salt to the wound, walking took all her effort. The old Camille would have marched into and out of that office without a backward glance.

If she'd been able to talk, she would've been much more forceful with Pierre. He shut down her intentions to sue that magazine. To extract an apology from the pink suit.

"Why would you want to feed their story, Camille? It's all gossip. They haven't mentioned a name other than yours." Levin kept the excuses coming. "Look, you know what they want from you. A reaction. Give them nothing. The story blows over in a week."

Typical male view of the world. What did he know of the pain this caused her? What if they kept looking anyway? What if more than one person stepped forward, claiming to be her child? A disaster. She'd be fending off money chasers till she took her last breath.

And what if ... *he* was still out there? Was it possible? Her heart surged with a burst of anxiety. She chided herself immediately. Don't be ridiculous. She was eighty, so she guessed, thinking back, he would be at least eighty-five. Or younger, perhaps? It was so hard to know. His age

hadn't mattered. What did a young girl know of these things? He was sir.
A teacher and teachers were respected.

Her heart squeezed in anger. Pity the respect wasn't reciprocated.
She hoped he was dead. Hoped he'd gone to war and died young in
the mud.

The vehemence of her feelings shocked her. It had been so long
since she'd wasted time thinking of him, and it shocked her to realise none
of the enmity had gone. He was still unforgiven. She forced him from
her mind.

Then, of course, there was Asha. If they discovered she was her sole
beneficiary, they would hound her too, and she didn't want that.
She personally understood what the paparazzi could do. Had experienced
it herself. The evidence was there in that blasted magazine. A photo telling
one side of a many-sided story. She felt old.

It was in this mood she found herself seated in the specialist's office,
attempting to read the medical report. She was conscious he talked, yet his
words flowing around her did not register. What she held did. As feared, it
had spread. She had more decisions to make.

"Soon," he impressed upon her.

Now she wished someone else was here with her. The doctor
talked too fast. Made plans she struggled to comprehend the outcomes of.
Dizziness made her ears ring as she struggled to get enough oxygen into her
tightening chest. She held up her hand to interrupt him, but it was too late.
The floor greeted her and then blessed darkness.

CHAPTER 16

The conference was a success. Armed with new insights and just as many questions, Alfredo's skin prickled with excitement. The scroll quivered in its case against his shoulder, and the urgency of it heightened every sense in his body. But the urge to eat remained. One glance at Felice reminded him she needed to build her strength. Sixty years is a long time between feasts.

Though the dining room was crowded, they found a table in the back corner, affording them some privacy. Felice munched on fresh fruits as Alfredo took the scroll from the leather case. It quivered in his hands. He took a deep breath and unrolled it between them.

Felice gasped and pointed. "Look, Alfredo! The Angels Ladder." She beamed at him and clapped her hands with glee. "We're going!"

The enormity of it hit Alfredo squarely on his chest. This was it. His first assignment. The moment he'd dreamed of for so long was here. Was he ready? He looked at Felice, who, realising his awe, sat in silence opposite him. She smiled her encouragement.

"Alfredo, you can do this. We can do this. I'm here with you, remember."

He smiled back. Adrenaline pulsed to dispel the doubt. "You've been before. I remember you said the first time was the hardest. Tell me about 'them.'"

Felice shivered. "You'll be alright. Don't forget, I also told you they can't defeat us because Jesus already destroyed their power." She grinned. "And the Father's Grace is with us as well."

He had to believe her.

She leapt from her seat and grabbed his hand. "Come on! I can't wait to be with Camille again. Let's go!"

He hastily rolled the scroll and followed Felice.

Outside in the village street, Felice led him through the flow of angels towards a large avenue. Here, the crowds increased to where it was impossible not to be carried along. She held his hand and forced a space for them both. They fell in step with those around them. Alfredo's heart quickened.

It didn't take long for the entrance to the ladder to appear before them; a large stone gateway, pillars standing sentinel on each side. Two or three steps were visible, leading downwards, but an immense cloud from which angels emerged or disappeared hid the rest of the ladder. Suddenly, Alfredo stopped, forcing Felice to stop with him. The crowd flowed around them.

"Remember, don't engage with the eyes. Your armour is enough to protect you. Keep moving down and pray in the Spirit the whole time. That way, they won't touch you." She stepped through the gates and into the cloud. He followed.

Alfredo kept one foot in front of the other. The steps were set, so each foot fell onto the next one, and only an even pace allowed him the confidence to go forward. The cloud was so thick he couldn't see anything, not even Felice beside him. She sang out loud in the Spirit tongue, and he joined in.

Suddenly, hands were upon him, clawing at his tunic, and a horrid voice hidden in the cloud spoke his name. His heart raced faster. Who would know his name in this realm? Alarmed, he sang louder to drown the voice out. Shadows loomed beside him; faces contorted in anger taunting him. He remembered Felice's warning. Avoid their eyes. They cannot touch you or see you. But they could recognise you for who you were; a warning to be ever on guard.

The thick cloud disappeared, and Alfredo gasped at what lay below him. Felice laughed with joy. Spread below was a city, not anything like the village. It was night, and while the sky above was black and sprinkled with stars, below, the city hummed with noise and colour.

"Welcome to Paris, Alfredo."

***

Satan's ears pricked up, and his nose itched. In the distance, he watched a dark form materialise as it came closer. He already knew what message the minor demon bore for him. He'd placed a sentinel at the edge of the Angels Ladder to wait for the angel Felice, and now it had brought the news. The missing angel had arrived.

Smirking, he noted with satisfaction that she'd left it too late. He'd already sealed an early death for Camille DuPont. Wasn't she in hospital at this very moment because of him?

Yet the news was cause for concern. Enough to consider leaving what entertainment was splayed in front of it – a room full of hopeless drug-addicted mortals in the last throes of consuming a lethal concoction he had arranged delivery of. Part of him wanted to stay and see the group leave the room for good. Wanted to greet them himself and show each of them the miserable lives they had led with his help. Ah, well. He would have an eternity to deal with them.

The sentinel was posted on the Angels Ladder for a reason. Satan had been in the earthly realm long enough to trust his instincts, and when he realised a Sleeping Angel had been granted a reprieve, he knew something larger than usual was afoot. Just because the angel hadn't appeared at the time of the initial release didn't mean nothing had happened up there.

"She's not alone, Master." The demon reported. "Another angel with a strange aura attached."

Satan seethed with anger. A guardian for an angel? This was even more unusual.

One of the drugged mortals left their body. He sat stunned, looking at his own feet, wondering what crazy trip the drug had taken him on.

Satan couldn't resist. He wrapped his arms around the soul and, laughing evilly, looked heavenward, hissing, "This one's mine."

The lesser demon sniggered.

Satan growled. Enough sport. He needed to discern what this additional angel – with an aura, no less – meant.

"Where did the arrivals go? Paris?"

The demon nodded, and Satan's eyes narrowed to two red slits.

"It's her then? Felice? And the other one? Does it have a name?"

"Alfredo, Master."

"Hmm. Welcome to my Paris, Alfredo." He threw back his head and laughed.

***

High above Paris, the two angels took some time to get their bearings. Felice struggled to recognise her old city. The old landmarks were there, but a modern Paris had sprung up around them. She took Alfredo on tour, pointing out the places she'd visited when Camille was a child, including

Notre-Dame, before the scroll led them to Camille's apartment building. It was empty.

After a moment of confusion, a vision of Camille in the hospital appeared on the scroll. Instructions to remain at the apartment were clearly marked, so the angels waited in anticipation of her return.

"It's odd we don't have to go to her immediately, isn't it?" Alfredo commented. Nothing seemed straightforward to him. Felice shrugged. "Ours is not to question why ..."

Morning arrived and, along with it, Rochet. His entry to the apartment brought with it a black haze. Alfredo and Felice warily watched as he moved from his desk to Camille's. He opened the drawers and rifled through them, looking for something.

The hairs on Alfredo's arms were charged with energy. Felice whispered prayers of protection under her breath. They retreated to a corner of the room, observing him. The haze that swarmed around him, looked and sounded like a million flies.

Rochet didn't stay long. It looked as if his search of Camille's desk had been in vain. The moment the door clicked shut behind him, both angels came to the centre of the room.

"Whatever is he up to?" Alfredo said out loud. He remembered the holy water vials in his armour pouch and had an idea. He handed one to Felice.

"Wherever he touched, sprinkle this. We don't want whatever that black haze was to hang around." They busied themselves, clearing it from the room.

CHAPTER 17

Camille woke to find herself in a hospital bed, attached to multiple machines. Confused, she first assumed she might be dead. So, this was Heaven? White walls and soft lights? As the fuzz cleared from her mind, she scoffed. God wasn't on her list of appointments today.

Her head hurt. She tried to remember what happened that resulted in her ending up here. In frustration, she groped about the bed for a buzzer. Someone would know. The nurse on duty swished into her room with an efficiency that pleased Camille. She tried to sit up, but the nurse frowned and shook her head. Camille signed for a pen. She needed to communicate somehow.

The nurse nodded. "I'll be back soon, dear."

Camille lay back and closed her eyes. The thump behind them, unrelenting. Her head was heavy and hot, and raising a hand, she was confronted by bandages. Had she hit her head? It seemed so. Alarmed, she tried desperately to remember the morning. She'd seen Pierre and then, afterwards, the specialist. After that, a blur. She must have fallen. Well, she grumbled, whatever painkiller she'd been given had worn off.

The sound of soft shoes approached her bed. Her eyes opened a crack to investigate. To do so took effort. It was the nurse again, armed with an IV drip and a pad for Camille to write on. Camille smiled. As tired as her body felt, she lifted an arm and touched her other wrist. Time?

"Two o'clock," came the answer. No, that wasn't possible. Hers were wretched morning appointments.

"The doctor will be here any minute to discuss your treatment." The nurse patted her wrist and took her pulse. Her fingers were hot on Camille's skin.

Treatment? What treatment did she need? She hadn't consented to anything, had she? In desperation, she waded through the fog, threatening to close all thought. Tried, but failed. Even the sharp bursts of sound from somewhere beside her barely pierced it.

Whatever transpired, Camille woke again feeling decidedly groggy. Had she dreamt it? Her mother had been here.

"Pray, Cammie, don't forget to pray ..." her words, over and over.

As her conscious mind resurfaced, her own prayers echoed. She hadn't forgotten how to pray. A tear slid down Camille's cheek. Maman's voice sounded so real. No, she decided, she must be ill. Very ill.

The room came into focus. It was not the same room as before. Camille turned her head with great difficulty to face a wall full of machines. Lights flickered and devices beeped. They'd hooked her up to a ventilator through her neck opening. She pushed the buzzer again and again.

Was she going to die? She couldn't. She wasn't ready. She refused to entertain the idea. Camille wondered if she'd dreamt it, but she was sure she'd heard a baby cry. Her baby. An overwhelming urge to find her daughter surged through her. She couldn't die. Not yet.

***

Julia closed the doors to the academy, turned the key in the lock and started down the steps towards home. She didn't like being alone in the building, but she was the last to leave on a Thursday. The street was quiet, past business hours, and while the rest of Paris settled into its usual touristy groove, here became an empty void, bypassed by foot traffic. Julia would meet the flow of hungry sightseers at the end of this street. She would blend in and allow them to carry her along. On the western side of the Île de la Cité, she would step out of the crowd and into her locale.

The man bounded into her path, startling her. Dressed in an immaculate business suit, he brushed past and rattled at the door she'd just locked. He cursed in frustration. Julia kept walking. It didn't matter to her if he missed an appointment there. He didn't look like the usual visitors, though. He'd see the opening hours on the door. Not her problem. So, she wasn't prepared when he called after her.

"Miss. Excuse me."

Julia turned and stared at him. She pointed a finger at herself as a question. The man rushed to her and she took a step back.

"Yes. Please. Did you just come from there? I'm after a student."

Julia shrugged. "I'm not a student, and it's closed. Come back tomorrow." She walked away from him.

He cursed again. "Do you know where I'd find Asha Villet? Does she live around here?"

Julia froze. Asha? She whirled and faced the stranger, raking over his face and suit. Had she seen him before? She thought not.

"What business do you have with her?"

His face lit up with hope. "Do you know her? How can I find her? It's important."

"Asha is my daughter," she said coldly. "What do you want from her? I'll give her a message."

He visibly relaxed and reached for her hand. Julia shrank back, alarmed.

The man's eyes widened as he realised he'd frightened her. He held his hands up to apologise. "Oh. Sorry, I haven't told you who I am. Please let me explain. I'm Madame DuPont's secretary, Mr Rochet. You've heard of Madame DuPont, yes?"

Julia nodded. Camille's demands on her daughter made her uncomfortable. It irked her they'd become so close in such a short amount of time. Why would Camille need to contact her daughter this late in the day? Hadn't she only been over there last night?

"What does Madame DuPont want of her now?" Julia was annoyed. Did she think giving her all her money meant she owned her time?

The man's face grew serious. "Madame is in hospital. The hospital rang; as she is listed as next of kin, only Asha can give consent." His voice betrayed his annoyance.

Asha was the next of kin? It was one thing to give her money, but did Camille really have no one else to take on this important role? What about her secretary?

"Please, Madame. Time is short. Can I drive you to your daughter and explain more in the car?" He pointed to a Renault parked nearby.

Julia's pulse quickened. It sounded serious. Enough for her to overcome her fear of travelling in cars? The palms of her hands sweated, and she rubbed them on her sleeves. Could she trust him? He didn't appear dangerous. She sighed. "As you wish." She climbed into the passenger seat, and Rochet, leaning over the wheel, anxiously eyed breaks in the traffic. He accelerated, the tyres squealing their protest

Alarmed, Julia gripped the seatbelt and stared straight ahead.

"Camille fainted at the specialist's clinic and is in hospital." He glanced at her sideways.

She wished he would look at the traffic, not her. Julia hated being in cars. Her parents had died in a road accident, and for her whole life, she had avoided being a passenger or even driving herself.

After a moment's pause, as though wondering how much to tell her, he continued, "Treatment is required, and because Camille's papers have Asha as her next of kin ..."

"Surely Asha needn't be involved in this treatment. Why can't Camille just sign whatever papers she needs to? That's a heavy burden to place on a young girl, don't you think?"

"I agree, Mrs Villet. But Camille is not well enough."
She heard the scorn in his voice. It was a sore point. She was not the only one then who questioned Madame DuPont's decisions.

As they approached her street, she tapped on the dash. "Drop me here." He didn't need to see where she lived.

Hurrying down the street towards home, she thought how Camille's intrusion into her life was peeling back the layers between them, and with each step closer she got to Julia, the more exposed and vulnerable Julia felt.

She found Asha in the cafeteria with Marco.

"Do you realise she made you next of kin?" Julia kept her voice neutral. It wasn't easy.

Marco gasped.

They had obviously discussed Camille, the two of them. A pang of jealousy and hurt shot through Julia. She was losing her daughter. If not to Camille, then to Marco. It added another layer to her despair.

"Mama?" Asha asked quizzically.

"DuPont. You're her next of kin." Julia's eyes stayed on her daughter's face. "I've got her secretary waiting around the corner." She waved to the end of the street. "She's in hospital, and they want you to sign papers?"

The shock registered on Asha's face. "Hospital?"

"I'm coming with you," Julia said.

Her heart thumped in her chest as she realised what it meant for her to go with Asha. A dull pain flared in her breastbone. Another layer lifted away.

What if Camille died? Was it wrong to keep Asha from knowing who Camille really was? Her grandmother. She saw how attached her daughter had become to Camille. Asha might never forgive her. But was there time to make it right? And how?

As Rochet raced to their destination, Julia had one other thought. She wanted Camille to know who she was. Her daughter. All those prayers to keep them apart, she regretted them now. She never wanted it to be like this. Unless she revealed the truth, it was a meeting of strangers. Not family.

***

Rochet's car wove through the evening traffic as fast as possible. Difficult in peak hour when homeward-bound workers and early diners on their way out melded together. Asha sat in the back seat and twisted her hair nervously.

"Madame Camille drew up the details of her personal affairs. That was not my privilege," Rochet announced.

Asha noted the affront in his voice. Had he felt pushed aside by Camille's preference? It sounded very much like it. Yet here he was, acting as a cab driver for them, after working hours, at his employer's behest. He must have some fondness for her.

At the hospital, he muttered about having one more thing to do. When their doors closed, he sped into the dusk, leaving Asha and Julia facing each other. Arms linked, they entered the hospital together.

"I'm glad you're here, Mama," she whispered. "I don't know if I can do this by myself."

Given directions to follow to get through the labyrinth of passages, floors and elevators to the hospital's private section, they arrived just as Camille's doctor started his patient rounds. The desk nurse ushered them into a small waiting area, assuring them that the moment his rounds were over, the doctor would update them on Madame DuPont's condition and after that they could sign all the necessary paperwork.

"Coffee machine there, vending machine for anything else down the next hallway to the left." The nurse's arms waved in general directions as she said all this, giving the impression that she had no time to spare for any questions. She was much too busy. As she bustled off to her station, Asha stood with her hands clenching and unclenching. They had come in such a hurry but now nothing seemed urgent and the adrenaline surging in her body had nowhere to go. She paced the waiting room, agitated and increasingly fearful.

Her mother took a seat, crossed her legs and leant her elbows on them. She bit her nails to hide her unease.

After ten minutes of nervous pacing, Asha plonked herself in the chair beside her mother. "Mama, what am I going to do? They don't expect me to make big decisions, surely. What if Camille can't tell me what she wants to happen? That would be the most awful thing." Her hands shook involuntarily.

She reached for her mother's arms for comfort. It had been a long time since her mother had been the strong one of the two.

An hour passed before the doctor finally came to find them. He looked at Julia. "Asha Villet?"

Julia shook her head and pointed to her daughter.

"Oh. I ... Never mind." He covered his surprise and turned to Asha. "We have consent forms here. Madame has late-stage cancer; you do know this? No one would want her to suffer unnecessarily." He opened a file and held a pen out for Asha.

She shook her head, her eyes wide with fear. "No. I won't sign anything without first seeing Camille. I don't even know what happened to her." Asha stood her ground and glared at him.

The doctor was quiet for a moment. He hadn't expected to be questioned. A voice down the hallway called out.

"Excuse me. Wait! Ms Villet, do not sign a thing." It was Pierre Levin.

Asha still hadn't forgiven him for his accusation. She did not like him, but she must tolerate him for now. Even so, he was a welcome sight at this moment.

"Mr Levin. I'm glad you're here. I've refused to sign anything. We haven't seen Camille and know nothing of her condition." She turned back to the doctor. "We could do that now?"

The doctor sighed resignedly and led the way to where Camille lay attached to a bank of machines. Asha's heart broke to see her like that. She gently took her hand in her own.

"Camille, I'm here. It's Asha. You're going to be fine, I promise you."

Levin and Julia had remained near the open door, giving her space beside Camille's bed, but Asha stiffened when Pierre spoke to her mother. "May I ask who you are, madame?"

She heard the drag of his breath when her mother replied. Not that again, and not now. Asha turned to her mother and beckoned her to come closer. She wouldn't let this man belittle her. As Julia reluctantly stepped forward, Asha met Levin's eye with her warning stare. He didn't hold it for long.

She turned back to Camille.

"I'll go and check what the actual diagnosis is, shall I?" he said.

"Yes, thank you," Asha responded frigidly. She would not be bullied.

Camille stirred and opened her eyes. She smiled weakly and feebly pressed Asha's hand in recognition.

"I'm here. You will be fine. Rest. I won't leave," she whispered and wiped a tear from Camille's face. "Look. I've even brought my mama." She smiled and moved so Camille could see Julia. "We'll stay as long as we have to."

Asha saw the look of shock on her mother's face. For a moment, Asha wondered if this reminded her of when her papa died. Perhaps it was too much. Julia's face had drained of all colour. Asha squeezed her hand. It was enough to release the look of fear, allowing Julia to smile at Camille.

Levin returned to the room and the moment passed. Julia stepped aside to allow him closer to Camille. He leant over and patted her knee.

"Camille, I've sorted that rogue of a doctor out for you. No need for forms tonight." He stood tall and addressed Asha. "Infection. Nothing too serious. Antibiotics intravenously and in two days she will be sent home." His voice showed he did indeed care for his client. In fairness, it was probably that he didn't approve of her, that was all.

"I'll have Rochet employ a nurse. No more of this singular stubbornness, Camille." He gave her a friendly stare. Camille closed her eyes.

Asha had an idea.

"No, I'll do it." Her mother's surprised look prompted her to say emphatically, "I can. Classes are almost done." She smiled with satisfaction. Camille wriggled her fingers still clasped in Asha's hand to show her agreement.

A nurse arrived and waved at them all to leave. It was time to go.

CHAPTER 18

Rochet met the cab that brought Camille and Asha home. The doctor insisted Camille use a wheelchair for the next few days as a precaution. He unloaded it and, with Camille seated, pushed it through the lobby into the elevator.

Asha squashed in beside them and breathed deeply. "Lilies. Smell that! Mr Ying was here." It gave her a warm buzz. Like she was coming home.

Camille looked at her with a strange expression. She scribbled on her pad.

Has my greengrocer taken to selling flowers?

Asha shrugged. She didn't understand Camille's comment. Mr Ying was a florist, not a greengrocer. Perhaps the medication dulled her senses. Rochet made no comment, his face a stone wall.

At the apartment, Camille immediately abandoned the chair, her stubbornness evident in her slow but steady stride. She pointed to the shelf where her records lived and motioned for Asha to choose something.

She slid Pavarotti from its cover and Nessun dorma floated throughout the apartment. Rochet settled at his desk and busied himself with his usual duties.

The hospital had listed Camille's medications, what must be taken and when, along with a list of dos and don'ts. Camille and Asha sat on the sofa and read through them. Camille crossed one or two off the list. She scribbled on her pad.

I am not a child!!!!

Asha laughed.

Consider this as you would your own home. Come and go as you like. I insist.

Asha nodded. If it made Camille comfortable to have her here, then that suited her.

A short while later Rochet closed his computer down and with measured attention, tidied his desk. Asha watched as he crossed the apartment, his back straight and shoulders stiff and wondered if he was trying to convey his disapproval of Camille's arrangement. He hadn't stated it outright, but Asha suspected he preferred the nurse option for Camille.

Camille took Asha through the apartment, tapping on a bedroom door and pointing back to Asha. This was to be her bedroom.

Asha hugged her. Camille had made it perfectly clear she didn't think she needed a nurse, and as far as she was concerned, Asha was not one. On her notepad, she had written the word nurse, crossed it out and wrote 'companion'.

Asha's plan was to cook Camille a lovely dinner and spend the evening watching movies. She'd asked Mama to join them, but she'd declined. Maybe another time, but just not yet. Her mother understood why she wanted to do this for Camille, but Asha had picked up the undercurrent of tension.

"Mama, I want to stay the night so she is safe, but I don't want to leave you alone either." She felt torn. She knew how her mother got when she wasn't around. Saw her lip quiver and the struggle to put on a brave face. Then she had rallied and smiled back.

"I'm a big girl, Asha. You were always going to leave home one day. I will be fine."

Asha wasn't convinced. But this was important. Camille needed her too, and Mama was right. She would leave, had been planning it. This might be the test her mother needed.

Later that night, with Camille in bed, Asha sat on the sofa, her feet tucked under her, resting her chin on her knee as she stared out at the night sky. She had time to reflect on life. And where she saw herself in the future. Would she be as successful as Camille? Was this where success led? To an empty apartment and a lonely old age? She hoped not. She thought of how her mama still missed her papa. They must have been so in love. Would she, Asha, find that love in someone? Marco? Poor Mama. To have that and lose it. Was that worse than Camille's life? Camille didn't talk of any great love from her past.

Asha sighed. Her mind swam in circles around the questions. She didn't have the answers. Perhaps they would come, but not tonight. Both women she loved. And their loneliness made her own heart ache. If only she could wave a magic wand and fix it.

On her way to bed, she heard a noise from Camille's room. Her heart rose to her mouth. Quietly, she opened her door and peered in. Light from the room behind her fell across the bed. Camille's form tossed restlessly. Asha sat on the edge of the bed in the darkness and took her hand. She stroked it gently. She touched her forehead – cool, so not a new fever. Nightmares then.

"You and Mama both," she whispered. How often had she done the same thing for her mother. Had crawled onto her bed and held her hand while she fought the demons in her sleep. She smiled sadly. This is what she knew. It was why she wanted to be there for Camille. The dreams were the worst illness of all.

***

Camille sank back into her pillow. How wonderful to be in her bed. No buzz or murmur of the heartbeat of the hospital. And yet, even here, there was change. A presence. She pondered what it was for a moment, then clicked. Asha. That darling girl was here, in her apartment, a few metres away.

Camille tried to reflect on the last time she slept with another person in her home. The answer shocked her. She hadn't thought about it before. Hadn't needed to. Hot tears welled behind her eyes, and she closed them tight to deny them. An answer crawled through the wall erected around her heart. The last time she'd been in a home – she didn't count Switzerland as a home – was the night before Papa sent her away.

As the thoughts burst into her mind, tears flowed. Like a dam bursting. With it, agonising pain stabbed her heart. The power in it jolted her. She leant over to a box of tissues beside her bed. This would not do. Had she taken the wrong medication? She checked the packet. No. This pain, as real as the bump on her head, was self-inflicted. She rolled onto her side, the tissue crumpled in one hand, the other clinging to her blanket. Go away. Why must she be tormented? She dragged her mind to her ballet routines, where discipline was king, and called forth the beats, willing the body to respond to them. Exhaustion overtook her, and she fell into a deep sleep.

Her teacher clapped. Slowly. She remembered. He came out of the darkness into the hall, and she felt his energy. Huskiness in his voice. Was it then she'd sensed a change in him? She searched her mind. Perhaps. Yes. She remembered the hair on her arms rising. A warning. The next moment, they were on the train. Alcohol. Sweet and bubbly. And his laugh as she hiccupped. The mouth, too large, too near. Her body shrinking, wanting to be away from him.

A voice slipped between her and the horrid man.

"Cammie, always pray."

"Maman. Maman! Stay with me. Don't leave me with him."
The darkness overwhelmed her, thick and solid. Darkness, followed by a piercing light. She gasped for air but couldn't breathe, drowning.
The weight of him holding her down.

She began to pray, but the words faltered. She had forgotten how. Maman pressed her. "Remember, Cammie, you know the words, you do." One by one, they came back to her, slowly at first, then in a rush.

And somewhere from a distant part of her, another soft voice – not her maman – telling her they loved her. Over and over. Someone took hold of her hand and dragged her away from the heaviness. Warmth spread through her fingers and veins, comforting her. She shivered and surrendered. Safe. She was safe.

***

When Camille came through the door in a wheelchair pushed by the man Rochet, Felice had danced and sung around the room with delight. It gladdened Alfredo to see her joy, but that joy was tempered with wariness as the cloud that surrounded Rochet touched everything, including Camille.

"Soot. It reminds me of soot," he grumbled, removing traces of it from the door handles.

And as much as he wanted to sit and talk to Camille's heart so that she could learn his voice, he spent the time removing and undoing the mess Rochet left behind. He left it to Felice to try to penetrate the solid casing of rejection around her heart. He breathed a sigh of relief when Rochet finally left. The mood in the apartment lifted.

One thing they both noticed immediately was the girl. Where the aura around Rochet was black, hers was green. And she smelt of lilies. Alfredo recognised the smell. It was the same one that had filled his apartment in the village the night of his graduation.

"Alfredo, have you noticed when the girl Asha is with Camille how calm she is? I sense a presence but can't see it. It's very odd."

Night fell, and Camille went to bed. Asha remained on the sofa in quiet contemplation. The angels retired to be with Camille. This was the first chance they'd had to be alone with her.

Camille slept fitfully below them. Alfredo frowned, wondering what they could do to reach her. Felice came up with the idea.

"Read from her book, Alfredo," she exclaimed.

"We don't have it," he reminded her. He tried to remember what the pages had shown him.

"No, but I am going back to get it," she said, leaving without a further moment passing.

No sooner had she left than the room turned cold. Colder than Alfredo ever imagined possible. Frost dripped from the air into tiny crystal shards, and black shadows emerged from every corner of the room. They circled him, hissing and baring their teeth. Alfredo sat quietly, watching their every move. He knew they studied him, trying to find a weakness in his armour. His heart slowed, and he prayed. Earnest prayer for strength.

Then, as suddenly as they arrived, they vanished.

Asha entered the bedroom. She had heard Camille toss and turn. The moment she entered, the room warmed again, and Alfredo let himself breathe. He watched with interest as the girl sat on the bed and held

Camille's hand. The sleeping woman relaxed and slipped into a less troubled sleep. The girl left the room and went to bed herself.

Alfredo was left to wonder at what had just happened when, a few moments later, Felice arrived back. She settled beside him, giving him a strange look. She shivered.

"They came, didn't they?" she whispered.

He nodded and smiled. She had felt the chill.

"Shall we go back to the beginning, Felice? You read; she will know your voice."

CHAPTER 19

Julia climbed the stairs to the flat, every step a chore. Asha would not come home tonight. For the first time since before she met Asha's father, Josef, she'd be alone. And it hurt. She'd known it was coming; a time she'd be in that place but knowing where Asha went hurt more.

Why did she feel so threatened by Camille? Wasn't it good for Asha to get close to her natural grandmother? It'd be perfect if the world was perfect. But it wasn't. Camille had no connection other than what she forged through her scholarship program. That wasn't enough. In that world, it might've been anyone.

Inside her, a war waged. Part of her craved the truth to come out. To confront it all head-on. She'd tell Camille to her face who they really were. And Camille would accept and embrace them. They could be a family.

Yet the other part of her beat that yearning down. Be realistic, it screamed. She didn't want you! Did she look for you? No! You are nothing to her. It's Asha she wants, not you. Right now, this side was winning that war.

Julia went through the motions automatically. Fed the birds, ate dinner and dressed for bed. She looked at Asha's side of the room; a few clothes were hastily pulled from her drawers when she packed a bag to take to Camille's, then discarded. She sat on Asha's bed, folded and put them away. The ache in her chest grew. From where she sat, she saw her wine glass, still half drunk on the table. Is this what Asha saw of her?

Shame added to the ache. What had she become? A drunk. Did she drive her daughter away?

She pulled herself off the bed and defiantly drank the last dregs from the glass.

"So? This is Camille's fault, yes?"

The words bounced back. "No."

"Why?" she screamed at the voice in her head. "Why is it my fault? I'm a good mother. Not like her."

The voice had no answer.

She switched off the kitchen light and sat on her bed. In the dark, her toe connected with the metal trunk protruding from under the bed. Pain shot up through her leg, and she felt the moist surge of blood.

She cursed her clumsiness and turned the light on again. It needed a plaster. Attending to the toe dispelled her fatigue but not her self-pity.

She dragged the trunk out and put the scrapbook on the table. No longer tired and without Asha to disturb her, she took time to turn each page. It was all here. Her mother's career. The only link to herself was the birth certificate. And the coin. She flipped it again and again in her palm, the shiny disc a gaudy false gold colour.

What would things have been like? Supposing her mother chose to care for her rather than give her up. A single mother in a war. She remembered how hard life was for her adoptive parents, all the moving around, the fear. Not an easy life. Camille's family had wealth, though. She might have fled with her. Gone to the Americas.

Why had Camille never married? There was no hint of romance in any of the articles. Was she as intensely private as she was now?

Or something else? That first photo showed such vulnerability in the eyes and around her mouth. An icy chill ran up Julia's spine. Why had she not understood before? She was no love child. Dear God, no. Was Camille raped, and she, Julia, the result?

Julia's heart broke. She tried to stem the tears, but waves of anguish crashed over her and shook her body. She curled herself onto the bed and sobbed until exhaustion claimed her.

***

It was still dark when Asha quietly dressed and let herself out of Camille's apartment. The sun had barely risen above the parklands along the Seine, and Asha revelled in the fresh air. The scarcity of tourists made the walk even more enjoyable. It gave her time to assess how she might juggle her mother and Camille. And then there was Marco.

Her mother worried her of late; her anxiety had reached another level. Especially since she read Asha's letter from the lawyer, Pierre Levin. The whole thing with Camille had enormously pressured her, and Asha blamed herself. That wasn't rational, but whenever she mentioned Camille, her mother flinched. A mask, always a moment too late, descended on her face. When her mother struggled, she drank more. Last night would've been difficult.

Marco was a work in progress. Gone was the familiar boy of her childhood, replaced with a musky tinderbox of passion. It was fresh and delicious, but underneath that spice was another flavour. One she still wasn't sure of.

They had different values. Which wasn't such a bad thing, but she was still working out what she wanted from life, and now she had to contend with someone else's dreams. She wondered if she should step back a little or dive right in and swim out to meet him halfway. Both prospects were daunting.

Marco grew up with a family – a complete family. Asha hadn't. There was just her and Mama. It gave her a different slant on things, and yet, she appreciated that Marco wouldn't understand. She was even keen to ensure that in the future, her version of a family would have the complete deal. Mama and Papa. It wasn't that she didn't value her mother's choice – no one chooses to have a partner die – but had mother remarried, would things have been different? Would her mother be so ... vulnerable to the change coming? Asha would leave, nothing was surer.

And now that Marco knew she was inheriting money, he had escalated his dreams to be even grander. Before, they had talked about a studio apartment. Somewhere close to his family's restaurant so he could walk to work, and she would be close to Mama. They'd joked about how they would be poor like sparrows, but so in love it wouldn't matter. Now he talked of owning his own restaurant in the arrondissement next to where they lived. More foot traffic and tourists, he'd said.

Talk like that crushed Asha. She hadn't asked for this 'gift', and now it was becoming tainted. Or so she thought. Was she being overreactive?

She reached the flat before the restaurant showed any sign of life. Why did she feel relieved? Another sign things were changing beyond her control. She didn't want to feel this way. She loved Marco, but she didn't want Camille's money to influence his feelings towards her. At this point in time, there was no way of knowing the truth.

Asha crept up the stairs and let herself into the flat. Silence met her. She took in the empty glass and inwardly sighed. It was as she suspected. She peeked around the corner at her mother lying on her bedclothes, looking altogether dishevelled.

"Oh, Mama."

Then her eyes fell on the scrapbook. The front page was open, as the thickness meant it would not lay flat. She turned it to get a better look. The page held a birth certificate – her mother's. She flipped to the next page. Another birth certificate. That made little sense. Why would Mama put in two copies of her birth certificate? She flipped back and forth between the two, the differences easy to see. It aroused her curiosity.

The next page made her cry out in shock. That photo. But old. A newspaper clipping, not the one from the magazine. Her heart pounded, and she looked at her mother, who moved when Asha gasped but stayed asleep. Asha quietly picked up the scrapbook and sat on her bed. Cross-legged, she flicked through each page. Every article about Camille. Every step of her career, from that photo onward, was meticulously cut and pasted in order.

Asha was numb. Why did her mother have this? She closed it and reopened to the first page. Now she pored over each line. Saw the blanked-out details. The missing information – father unknown. The birthdates, a few days different, but so what? Did Mama believe she was Camille's daughter? Was she? Asha had to admit the evidence was compelling. It explained her behaviour. But could it be true? Beyond doubt? Awareness dawned on her. If true, that meant she was Camille's granddaughter.

Tears streamed down her face. She didn't know what to feel. This was something her mother kept from her. Had known for a very long time. She understood now all those magazines she had brought home. Her obsession with Camille DuPont. Asha hadn't taken much notice of it. A ballet memento, encouragement for Asha to aspire to her dream. It had meant nothing to Asha, something her mother did as a hobby.

Her mother stirred. Asha wiped her tears onto her sleeve and waited. Her mother leant on the partition between their beds, her face unreadable.

"Why, Mama?" Asha whispered. "Why didn't you tell me?" She sniffed.

Her mother's voice held no bitterness. Just defeat. "When? When you were little, so you could dream of happy families and face the same disappointment I did?" She sat on the end of Asha's bed and laid a hand on the scrapbook. Her face contorted with pain.

"Can you appreciate how hard it was for me when you came home and told me you won that scholarship? First, I wanted to ban you from accepting. I was scared you might discover this." She waved at the book. "Then I changed my mind. You won it from your strength and talent. Dance has always been in you. From her. You didn't have to know." She sighed and rubbed her face.

Asha wanted to hold her but sensed her mother needed more time.

A tear splashed from Julia's eyes, and she blinked it away. "I was always going to give you this. When I was ready. When you were ready. But ... then she involved you in her affairs." She gave a wry laugh. "Never saw that coming. Not in a million years."

Asha patted the bed next to her. Her mother crawled into the space, and Asha held her tight in an embrace. Her own tears slipped silently in two rivers on her face. The ache in her chest intensified.

"What now?" Julia whispered.

Asha thought back to when she and Camille discussed the mystery child. How much it grieved Camille.

"Don't judge her too harshly, Mama," she said. "I saw the magazine article at her place. She had a copy. It was such a painful thing to read. She said she didn't have a choice. She had no mother, and her father had just died too." Her fingers intertwined with her mother's. Julia smiled knowingly.

Asha continued. What she had to tell her mother would hurt, but a little more pain now was better than another wound later. "I offered to help her find you." She paused. "But she said no."

Her mother's eyes closed. "Asha, I wasn't born out of love. I think Camille might have been ..." She didn't finish but hung her head.

Asha gasped. It made sense now. Camille's aloof persona. Before any of the business with the cancer and Camille approaching her, Camille presented as a force to be respected and Asha only assumed it came with being famous and an icon of the industry. Not a defence against everyone over her whole life. How ghastly.

Then it dawned on her, Camille wasn't the only one damaged. An innocent baby. Her Mama. Her heart wrenched.

"Oh, Mama, I'm so sorry," Asha said through tears. "How sad."

They huddled together for a few more minutes before her mother looked questioningly at her.

"Why did you come home? Won't she need you?"

Asha smiled. "You needed me too." She swept her mother's tears away with her thumbs. "Agh! What am I to do with the pair of you?" The sombre mood lifted.

"Breakfast. Then you'd best go back. I'm fine. And now you have the truth, I feel a lot lighter." She smiled happily. "I love you, baby. And whatever, however you want to deal with this, I will accept. It is your birthright.

Even if she never knows that. And if you tell her the whole truth, well, we can't be accountable for how she reacts, can we?" She kissed Asha on the cheek.

Mama was right. Either way, it was up to Asha to decide.

***

Back in Camille's apartment, Alfredo and Felice sat in Camille's bedroom while she slept. Cross-legged on the end of the bed, Felice read Camille's life story to her, and Alfredo saw her restlessness cease. A small smile tugged at the corner of his mouth.

Felice's words, softly spoken and full of love, reminded Camille how she'd seen Felice in the Notre-Dame that night. Had seen the other angels

213

with her. Cajoled her about how her papa made her walk the following Christmas instead of riding his shoulders.

"Did you know, Cammie, he had a sore back that Christmas? That's why he made you walk. Not because he didn't want to carry you."

Page by page unfolded until Camille lay still.

"Enough. She is beyond the dream state," Alfredo said, stretching.

She closed the book, propping it on the pillow next to Camille. "While she sleeps, we must meditate for a clearer understanding."

The morning came sooner than they thought possible. Their charge was an early riser. The moment her eyes opened, a steady stream of thoughts had them busy.

Alfredo delighted that Camille formed intentions to find her daughter and make amends, but the battle constantly raged as Camille wavered between fear and fearlessness. Felice wrote furiously, noting the people Camille intended to meet. She studied how their angels might influence her plans, sending message after message to them.

Meanwhile, Alfredo stood over Camille's shoulder on constant alert for the dark shadows that crept into the apartment. And this morning, the first few rose with a vengeance when Camille discovered that Asha was not in her room. She had gone. It had been a reality check of sorts that the girl still had a life apart from her.

They came with whispers of doubt intended for Camille, but Alfredo held his hands over her ears blocking as many as he could. He constantly prayed to the Spirit to dispel the words. To jumble them into meaningless jargon. His arms ached, but he refused to remove them.

Felice looked up expectantly, alerted to a new presence. "Alfredo, do you smell that?"

Alfredo sniffed the air. At first, he detected only the foul whiff of demon. Then a familiar aroma wafted through the air. Lilies.

"Asha must be back. Whoever guards her surrounds her with that scent. It's her protection. And thankfully, it's powerful enough to quell the demons." His smile widened.

They heard the key engage at the door. Both Alfredo and Felice held their breath. Asha, dressed in a long flowing black cardigan, creamy silk shirt and loose black pants entered and, on finding Camille in her bedroom, kissed her on the cheek. Instantly, the shadowy figures lurking in the apartment retreated. Alfredo released his hands from Camille's ears, stretched with relief and joined Felice near the patio window where she sat studying the scroll.

She looked up. "Camille plans to speak with Callo and Orpheus' charge soon. Remember the angels who came to the conference and talked of Camille's solicitor?" Felice frowned. "They sent a message just now. There might be a slight problem where he is concerned. I can run ahead and speak with them if you like?"

He nodded, wanting to check Camille's life book again. Reading it last night, they hadn't gotten to where the pages were sealed. He hoped more revelations had come and, with the lily bearer present, he felt safe leaving Camille.

***

This morning Camille rose to an empty apartment. She had softly tapped the spare room door, but Asha didn't answer. It left her disappointed. A tiny voice barked in her ear.

"Did you expect any different, Camille? What are you to her? An old lady who bought her favour. Foolish woman."

She had dressed and tackled some make-up. How easy to slip into old age, she lamented. Her hair looked thin. It badly needed a treatment. She sat staring at her reflection in the mirror. The negative train of thought flowed and gathered speed. So much so that she missed hearing the apartment door open and close behind Asha. She jumped at the knock on her bedroom door. Her face reddened with guilt at her bad mood. Her hair looked even more jaded against the crimson hue.

Asha's face looked strained as she came in and kissed Camille on the cheek. Either she had bad news or hadn't slept well.

"Good morning. I'm sorry I left early before you woke." She smiled at Camille's reflection in the mirror. "I had breakfast with Mama."

Camille scratched on her pad.

You don't need to explain. How is she? She reminded herself she'd told her to come and go as she pleased.

Asha's face blanched as though the question troubled her. Her answer hinted at a cover-up. She was a terrible liar.

"Mama's fine. It's her day off today. I forgot and woke her up." Asha picked up a brush from the dressing table and stood behind her. She gently teased the flattened hair into shape.

Camille smiled gratefully. Perhaps she was too ready to judge. She should be more trusting, though she admitted it didn't come easily.

"You didn't sleep well last night, Camille. Nightmares?"

The question surprised Camille, and she caught her breath sharply. She raised her palms and shoulders in defeat. This girl was astute. She liked her even more because of it. It reminded her of herself. But Asha was an innocent. Please, God, she should not suffer the same fate because of it.

Camille stopped her thoughts in midstream. Had she just prayed? She was losing her grip. What happened to her steel will?

Their eyes met in the mirror, and she noted the rising blush on the girl's neck.

"Mama has them too. The nightmares," Asha offered. Her face said there was more. "I hope you don't mind. I sat with you for a while last night. I do it for Mama, have done for as long as I can remember."

Camille reached for Asha's hand over her shoulder and held it still. She turned, pointed to her bed and exaggerated her lip movement whilst slowly mouthing her words so that Asha might understand what she was saying, "Sit. Tell me about your mother."

Asha's eyes watered.

"She reminds me of you. Only softer." She grinned. "She hasn't had to deal with difficult people like you have." She fiddled with the brush in her hands. "She's worked hard all her life." The girl struggled and took a deep breath. "She was adopted as a baby. And her parents moved a bit during the war. They died in a car accident when she was in her early twenties. Mama got cleaning jobs till she had me."

A moment of silence ensued. Camille willed her to continue. This was the first time she'd gotten a glimpse of Asha's family history, and hearing it resonated, even if only to learn that someone else had suffered as she had. Lost parents too soon, just as she had.

Asha sighed and continued. "She met my papa, and they had me. He died in a riot when I was two. Just in the wrong place, at the wrong time." She looked down at the carpet.

Camille rose and sat on the bed next to her. Her heart was heavy. Asha looked so sad. How could she have begrudged her leaving to see her mother this morning? How selfish of her.

"I don't remember him. Only from the photo Mama keeps." She shook her head as if to remove the memory and rose from the bed. "Enough. We are too sad today. Why don't we go out for a bit of fresh air? I want to take that wheelchair for a spin." Her eyes sparkled. "I dare you. Let's find a hair salon. I can't work miracles." Asha left the bedroom and Camille followed her to show her where to find the addresses of reputable salons who might fit her into their schedule at such short notice.

The moment was over. Camille wanted more, but she hoped, with what time she had left, the girl would tell her. It had prised open a window on her own memories. Yet Camille wasn't certain she wanted it left open or slammed shut. Whatever her heart decided, she could only go along for the ride.

***

As Alfredo stepped back into the bedroom where the women had just come from and where Camille's book lay in the centre of her bed, a force pushed him flat onto the floor. A heel pressed into his back, and the stench of burning flesh threatened to overpower him. Ash rained on the floor around him. It was all he could do not to breathe it in. He had no pain, just the heaviness on his back.

The dark forces were closing in.

"In Jesus' name, I command you to desist!" Alfredo shouted. That was one thing Yaseem drummed into them.

Expect attacks. They will come, never to your face. Be on your guard always.

Alfredo hadn't been on his guard.

The foot came off his back and the presence, a man in a dapper suit, swaggered in front of him.

Alfredo leapt to his feet and crossed his arms, pulling himself to his fullest height.

The man laughed a nasty chuckle. "She is ours, angel. What business do you have here?" With that, the man split into two men, both identical.

"Silence! You speak with no authority over Camille or me," Alfredo fired back.

"We have her, don't we?" they sneered.

Alfredo shook his head. "She belongs to Jesus and the Father. I tell you, you have lost. Begone, in Jesus' name, demons."

They laughed an ugly laugh. "Name us then. Unless you do that, we will stay." They grasped at him, but their fingers failed to connect.

Alfredo closed his eyes and prayed for their names to be revealed. When he faced them again, he had a glint in his eye. "I bind you, Greed and Suspicion. Leave."

Instantly, both demons vanished. Alfredo breathed a deep sigh of relief. He retrieved Camille's book and returned to the living room, where the lily fragrance was strongest.

The two women sat on the sofa, hand in hand. Alfredo perched on the back of the sofa and watched with interest. Asha's face creased with concern as she read the latest note Camille had written.

Camille wanted them to go together to the solicitor this week. She'd agreed, but Alfredo sensed reluctance on Asha's part. It wasn't possible to read her thoughts; it left him puzzled. It was obvious she cared for Camille. Was she finding this too difficult to do? He hoped it wouldn't be an issue, this free-will gift. What if she refused, and it meant Camille did not reconcile with her daughter? He wished Felice was here. She knew so much more than he.

Distracted, he flipped the pages to where he had last opened the book. Where Felice had said she'd seen the train coming. And the war. He found the next page loose and smiled expectantly as he turned it.

His eyes widened with horror and his mouth fell agape; he had to look away. White hot pain seared his heart. Now he understood. He gently closed the book. Felice would feel this more than he did.

At that moment, she returned. "I would feel what, Alfredo?" He looked at her with sad eyes. "The train." He glanced over at Camille. "I understand the grief on your face now."

Felice nodded. Her eyes glistened, but she did not cry.

"Alfredo, I found Callo and Orpheus. They're working on a plan for the solicitor as we speak. Tell me, what else happened here? I sense turbulence ..." She looked around the room as if something amiss might prove her right.

Alfredo grinned and recounted the battle with the demons.

"Oh, well done." She clapped. "The first ones you deal with, you will always remember." She shrugged. "Then it becomes second nature, and they all merge into 'them.'" She looked at Camille and Asha. "And these two? Anything?"

"Yes, Asha is going with her to the solicitor's office, but I sense reluctance, and I don't know why."

Felice flitted about the room, dancing and singing a praise song.

"I do. I found out why. And it's glorious news!" Her laugh tinkled around the room. "Alfredo, check the scroll."

CHAPTER 20

Camille looked on as Asha dove into the wardrobe and picked out a pair of soft knit fawn trousers, vowing to lift Camille's spirits. The blush pink cashmere top was one she hadn't worn for years. And that fur coat. Camille ran her hands over the fur and smiled. It was no longer possible to wear the coat without thinking of Notre-Dame and the Chinese tourists. She would be outrageously overdressed for a hair salon, but her heart floated in a warm sea of happiness. She was young again. And that's all that mattered. Grabbing her favourite red lipstick she confidently applied it to her lips.

The wheelchair bounced across the pavement at a cracking speed. Too fast for Camille, but she wasn't willing to slow Asha down. Not yet. This was an adventure, she told herself over and over. More to the point, Camille realised if she wanted to feel alive, she must force herself past her usual aloof nature. Her apartment wasn't the haven she imagined; it was a prison, keeping her away from everything and everyone.

They found a salon – one Camille knew well enough to trust their treatments – and she insisted that Asha take a chair for a wash and head massage as well. They were not doing this just for Camille, she argued.

Asha must accept her wishes too. Afterwards they sat at a café in the sunshine, hair glossy and immaculately in place, enjoying coffee and pastries.

Asha flicked through a newspaper for shows or exhibitions they might go to later in the day while Camille savoured the moment she was in right now. It had been decades since she had enjoyed such a casual outing. Decades. That thought mollified her. She had spent so long living like a hermit she had forgotten such simple pleasures.

An idea came to her. She dug her hand into the coat pocket. It was still there, round and solid. She clenched it and let the memory return.

She hadn't planned to be in the church that day. It just happened. Like today wasn't planned. What if, she wondered, staring at the head bent over the paper in front of her, she hadn't planned her life, had let things happen? Would she have survived? The way Asha and her mother survived their tragedy?

Asha looked up to catch her watching; a smile played on her lips. "You okay?"

Camille nodded back.

"We could do the Louvre if you like."

Camille shook her head. Instead, she pulled the coin out and placed it on the table. It clacked loudly.

Don't plan, Camille repeated in her mind.

Asha picked up the souvenir while Camille intently scrutinised her face. The girl's reaction surprised her.

Her eyes widened, and the colour drained from her cheeks, then flooded back. She looked questioningly at Camille. "Notre-Dame? You want to go there?"

Camille nodded once, firmly, determined.

Asha turned the coin to study the date punched on it. "I saw one of these only the other day. I'm sure of it."

Camille tapped the table, impatient to go, in case she changed her mind. She held out her hand for the disc and slid it back into her coat pocket.

It wasn't far, and even as the breeze was fresh, an unseasonable winter sun warmed Camille's cheeks. They waited at the lights like she'd waited behind the Chinese tourists that day. She looked about nervously in case they materialised. Now she was being silly. Of course, they wouldn't still be here. Mr Ying? Her heart pounded faster. A million to one chance.

The traffic lights changed, and they scooted across to the forecourt packed with tourists. From the vantage point of her wheelchair, the familiar sidewalk and tourist stalls that lined the square took on a new perspective. Nothing had changed, she knew that, and yet it was different. Blood rushed to her head. She was seven again, the first time she'd walked here with her papa and maman.

Once inside the cathedral and her eyes adjusted, Camille directed Asha to where she'd sat before. She scribbled a note and held it up for Asha.

Thank you. Give me a few moments here. If you haven't been before, the stained-glass windows are a must-see. She smiled apologetically at her.

Asha patted her hand and retreated.

Camille eased out of the wheelchair and settled herself in the pew and closed her eyes. And waited. She let the clacking of shoes on the tiles and the murmur of whispering tourists that echoed in the cathedral fade. Her breathing slowed, the tap-tap of the air vent in her throat the only noise she allowed. That, and the sound of a baby crying somewhere. The one she'd heard from her hospital bed, echoing in the fog of painkillers.

"God? I'm here." Tears pricked the back of her eyelids, and she fought them back. "I'm sorry I didn't take the child you gave me." There, she said it. Her nose tingled. "I was scared and alone. He hurt me. Back then, I thought it was my fault. I let him believe I was ..."

"Was what?" the voice in her head cut in. "Deserving of that? No. You're an adult now; you know what happened."

She stifled a sob.

The voice said, "I was there with you. I heard you. I suffered the pain with you."

"You did? Then why didn't you stop him?" she cried back.

"Why? Because he had free will. He could have stopped. His choice. He paid the price, Camille."

Her head lowered. The tears fell onto her coat. "And my choice? Did I pay a price?"

"You know the answer to that already."

A sob escaped. "I'm sorry. I really am. I'll make it up to her if I can." She fumbled for her tissues.

Above her, the pigeon flapped from its nest and landed in the aisle near her. The sheen on its neck shimmered in the dim light from the chandelier.

She looked up to see Asha approaching. What would the girl think of her? She blew her nose and patted her eyes dry. By the time Asha reached her, she was back in the wheelchair, ready to go.

As they reached the exit, Camille held up her hand. Asha stopped, and Camille pointed to the side alcove and the souvenir machines. She fossicked in her purse, found a euro, and gave it to Asha, pointing to the machine. Together they watched the gears grind and the blank disc transform into the familiar image of the cathedral's front façade. Asha retrieved the token and handed it to Camille. Camille shook her head and pushed it away. She pointed to Asha. It was for her.

The minute they got into the sun, Camille put her dark glasses on and smiled contentedly. She scribbled on her pad.

Home.

A flotilla of fluffy clouds marched across the afternoon sky driven by high winds. The sun was covered and uncovered; its warmth was snatched away and restored. It left those who ventured out wondering whether to bother shedding coats for the sake of five minutes of discomfort. Julia weathered the fractious conditions in the safety of a small café.

Her stomach was knotted by her anxiety, and she hid her eyes with large sunglasses while her feet tapped with a life of their own under the table. Now and then, she grasped her knees to still the restlessness as she waited for her daughter and Camille to arrive. Every fibre of her body resisted the temptation to get up and leave.

Asha begged her to come. There was no way to refuse. It would only prolong the agony, knowing at any moment, Camille might discover her identity. Far better to just lay it out. Be done with it. The fallout, well, it wasn't for her to decide how Camille would react. In the end, Julia reasoned, the closer Asha became to Camille, the more difficult for Asha if Camille wiped them.

She checked her watch for the hundredth time. They were late. She'd already drunk two cups of coffee, and now the caffeine surged through her. Five more minutes, and she'd go. She knew she wouldn't, but stating it gave her some notion of control.

A commotion at the door alerted her. They were here. There was no escape now. Julia's heart went to her mouth. She stood, kissed her daughter on the cheek, and greeted Camille, who regally sat in her wheelchair. Her face was unreadable. Julia hoped hers was too.

Asha said Camille wanted to talk, to ask her a few questions. Personal ones. Julia first thought Asha had told her everything, but her daughter said no. Only the bare facts: she'd been adopted as a baby, grew up with a family until their deaths and had raised Asha on her own. Camille hadn't realised the connection between them. Not yet.

While Asha ordered more coffee and a plate of sweet cakes, Camille, discarding the wheelchair, arranged herself next to Julia, then reached over and grasped her hand. It took strength for Julia not to flinch. She reminded herself this woman's search was no different from her search for her mother. It's just that she had waited until now to begin.

Julia tried to put herself in Camille's shoes, knowing in all probability she'd been assaulted, and the memory would have to be exposed to take this next step. Thank God that had not been her own experience. Still, it didn't make it easier for Julia. Ever since Camille came out of hospital, her own conscience had grappled with her dilemma. To tell or not to tell.

Asha took her seat on the other side of Julia. "Mama, Camille has written some questions. I can read them out if you like, but it's okay if you want to read them yourself."

Julia took the list from her daughter. It was easier to mask her reactions if she read it herself. She removed her glasses and began.

How old were you when you discovered your adoption? And how did you feel about it?

That was easy enough. The truth. "I found the second – first – birth certificate hidden in the family Bible. I didn't have time to process what it meant until later." She paused. "How did I feel? A range of emotions, honestly. I loved my adoptive parents. To take me in, and keep me safe through a war, showed the depth of their love for me. I missed them dearly." To state it brought back the warmth in her heart for them. "But I felt lost, too. Suddenly, I wasn't who I thought I was. I guess I was orphaned twice over."

She glanced at Camille's face for any reaction, who showed nothing but attentiveness. Julia continued cautiously.

"About my birth mother? Curiosity mostly. What circumstances led to the adoption, the usual what-ifs?"

Would that offend? She sipped her third coffee. Her hands trembled. Was that the coffee or her vulnerability? It's one thing to make a scrapbook at home with hours of self-talk, but this brought a whole new level of discomfort. How would Camille react? Being the only one to speak had become uncomfortable and she shifted in her chair.

Her heart rose in her throat, and she mustered the courage she needed to speak directly to Camille. "Why do you want to hear all this? Is it because of that awful magazine article?"

The spotlight turned on Camille. Her cheeks flinched, and she hesitantly scratched on her pad.

Yes. And no. I have years of anger to erase. Stupid anger. At my family, at one man especially. And myself.

She showed them the words, then continued to write.

There was a child. Not from a happy – she scrubbed happy out – *man, who loved me.* Her face became drawn.

From that place I found myself in, I rejected that child. Wanted nothing of it. Unfair to the child. It's taken me until now to see that.

Julia could not stop herself. She stifled a gasp, coughing into her hand to cover it.

Camille continued, the pencil flying across the pad.

I am a selfish old fool. I'd take all those years back if possible. But I can't, can I?

Asha put a hand over Camille's, stopping her from writing any more.

"You're not a fool. What you did, any of us may have done under the circumstances. Right, Mama?" There was pleading in her daughter's eyes.

"Asha's right, Camille. What's done is done." Julia's voice was firm, unlike her heart.

What now? Did Asha want her to confess? She couldn't. It was too hard. What if either of them broke down in public? No, this wasn't the time, and she couldn't say when that would be.

Camille smiled at them both. A tear tracked down her cheek. She scribbled again.

Thank you for sharing. It's helped me to make up my mind. I will look for my daughter. If she wants to know me, good. If not... She shrugged.

When Julia read the note, she closed her eyes. The blood pulsed in her ears. Tears burst from under her eyelids, and she bit her lip. She took a deep breath, then stopped. She had an idea, delving into her bag in a frantic search. What she wanted wasn't there. Disappointment hit her. But the idea still gave her hope.

"I'm sure, Camille, your daughter will want to know you."

***

In the crowded and noisy café, Alfredo scanned the room for the angel they were to meet. A woman seated near the back of the café nervously fiddled with her serviette. At the table with her, two angels waited patiently. Asha and Camille greeted the woman, kissing her on the cheek. The angels stood and greeted Alfredo and Felice.

"We are Orlando and Perise." The larger angel spoke for them both.

Alfredo introduced himself and Felice, then asked, "There are two of you? For Julia?"

It surprised him that Asha's mother had two angels, given that Asha herself had none.

Orlando put an arm over Perise's shoulder.

"We never saw it as strange, ourselves," Orlando replied. "I was Josef's angel until he passed. I wasn't recalled to the village, and Perise needed me. So, I stayed."

"Asha never had an angel," Perise said, looking up at Orlando "so we assumed she was given over to Orlando by proxy, and it wasn't until she grew older and more independent that we realised we weren't her actual guides." She straightened the folds of her tunic. "We didn't question it. God does things His way, does He not?"

Orlando pointed out Alfredo's situation. "There are two of you for Camille."

Alfredo nodded in agreement. He thought his situation was different. A baby not having an angel assigned seemed at odds with everything he had learned in class. Still, as Orlando said, God's design was not to be questioned, and he had more pressing matters than the technicalities of guardianship.

Meanwhile, Felice focussed on the conversation at the table and made an observation. "Julia looks upset. Even fearful. What troubles her here?"

"She fears rejection. A natural reaction, given the circumstances," Orlando offered.

Perise chimed in. "Yes, fear. It's been with her from the very beginning. Those first hours when her mother rejected her. So sad. I had my work cut out finding parents to fill that hole. It was difficult; I can attest to that."

Orlando added, "When Josef died, we thought we might lose her. She was so grief-stricken. It was Asha who kept her with us. With God. A prayerful woman, our Julia."

Alfredo regarded the women. Something didn't sit right. Camille's defences wavered. One moment she shut the words from Julia out; the next, they flooded her soul like a tide crashing over a rock wall.

Julia's discomfort was obvious, too. Her nerves were so on edge that had she been seated near the door, Alfredo suspected she might have bolted. Some of the questions undoubtedly caused her pain.

He glanced sideways at Perise and Orlando, who were whispering encouragement to her. The expressions on their faces told Alfredo this was a common dilemma where their charge was concerned.

How difficult it was for the earth souls to act on their heart's wishes. Being an angel, he had no such problem. An angel heart could only fall into whatever God's wishes were for them. Out of pure love for their creator.

The enigma of free will brought with it reminiscences of Yaseem's view of it all. How did it go? A curse, a gift, a flaw ... or perfection. Alfredo failed to see the perfection here, not just yet. If Julia didn't say something, then Levin was their only hope.

Felice frowned and cut through his thoughts. "But things are progressing. We sensed good things would come from today, did we not?"

Alfredo stroked his chin thoughtfully. "Indeed. But the great reveal was to be at the solicitor's office. According to the scroll." Or so he thought.

He unrolled it to check. The words swam in front of his eyes. Was it just him or were things getting tangled? There was no time to verify the swirling mess in front of him; he might miss something vital in the present.

"The scroll hinted at a reunion. But didn't divulge everything, only that it was imminent. I expected she'd discover the truth at the solicitor's office this afternoon. Callo said his charge knew who the mystery child was ..."

With one eye on Camille and her scribbling, Alfredo continued to address the others.

"So, Perise," he asked, "Julia looks about to divulge the truth. What say you? Is she willing?" Free Will could complicate things.

"Not quite, Alfredo, but I've given her a suggestion. We'll see if she listens."

They all watched Julia rummage in her bag.

"Oh, Perise," Orlando interjected with dismay, "you remember she put the coin in her trunk. It's still there." They let out a collective groan.

The women rose to leave and Asha helped Camille back into her wheelchair. Had the moment passed? Alfredo hoped not.

***

After they left the café, Asha wheeled Camille into Pierre Levin's office. Alfredo paced the room behind them while Felice stationed herself at the door to block any unwanted demonic interference. Dust motes swirled, their passage highlighted by the midmorning light streaming from the window, blown about the room by the nervous movements of every human present. Camille folded and unfolded her hands in her lap, picking at the edges of her jacket. Asha, in a businesslike fashion, took her place next to Camille and settled herself, back erect and with a stony look on her face.

A manila folder lay closed on the table. Levin's fingers strummed a nervous beat on the cover.

Alfredo studied the man with hazel eyes set in a narrow face. When Alfredo peered into them, he saw traces of the young boy he must have been. Well-meaning, a fire for justice. Perhaps inherited from his father before him. A hint of righteousness, even.

But his skin had the pallor of a person who spent too much time indoors. Regardless, he had aged well, even though the pores around his nose resembled tiny craters on the moon. Smooth cheeks, a well-formed mouth, and no hint of morning stubble. A man who took pride in his appearance. His skin folded under his chin and rested on the collar of his crisp shirtfront, his tie in perfect symmetry, holding everything in place.

The aura around him was not entirely clear, but Alfredo was satisfied he was a good man at heart. This relieved him considerably. There was hope then that today Camille might have her prayers answered and the truth revealed. It was good that Asha was present as well, as she could then be the advocate for her mother and herself.

Alfredo looked up at Callo and Orpheus standing behind their charge, whispering prayers of encouragement to Pierre. It wasn't achieving a thing.

Alfredo knew the contents of the file on Levin's desk contained everything Camille needed to know about Julia. Camille's scroll said Pierre Levin had the truth. Callo had shown him.

Yet, the man sat there without blinking an eye and told Camille there was no news.

"Camille, we have come to a dead end," he said. "The records for that period are destroyed, I am told." He shrugged. "There was a war, you remember. A difficult time for everyone. So much confusion ..." He let the words trail.

Callo and Orpheus groaned in unison.

"He chooses to lie," Callo said. "Pierre will not change his mind when he makes such a decision."

"And he believes he has Camille's best interest at heart," Orpheus added. "He worries the reunion will not be amicable. Unfortunately, there is not much we can do to sway his conscious decision."

"Callo, get the file to fall again," Alfredo pleaded, knowing that was not possible. It sat in the middle of the desk and no window opened to allow even a puff of air to dislodge it. No one received directions for an out-of-the-ordinary intervention on either Pierre or Camille's scrolls.

Alfredo's brow creased. The other angels came to his side, and together they pored over Camille's scroll.

Orpheus laid a hand on his shoulder and said, "I know this is hard for you. Your task is one of greatness, and even I, with all the experience of two lifetimes here, am worried for you."

Nothing he said made Alfredo feel better. Failure was the worst outcome. How could he ever go back to the village? Face Yaseem. Another thought occurred. What if he, like Felice, ends up in the Garden of the Sleeping Ones? And Felice – would she end up back there with him? Or worse, be lost forever if Camille should go to … the other place.

Every hair on his body stood in alarm. He looked at his charge and Felice, who now had come to Camille and wrapped her arms around her to shield her from the hurt of the news.

Alfredo registered Camille's disappointment in her dropped shoulders. The air around her darkened. He recognised the signs and immediately flew to stand behind her. With one hand on her shoulder, he prayed. The air cleared instantly, encouraging Alfredo. All was not lost. While she still breathed the air in this realm, Alfredo would not give up on her soul. And neither would Felice. They had to get her out of there, away from the influences pulling her back to the dark emotions of the past.

But Camille wasn't ready to leave. She produced some documents and a letter she had written from her bag. She gave a copy to Asha.

From where he stood, Alfredo read over Asha's head, then looked up with dismay at Felice.

The documents visibly upset both Pierre and Asha. Asha pushed them back, shaking her head, but Camille refused to be swayed. She signed the papers and made Pierre sign them as well. The deed done, she hugged Asha and signalled she was ready to leave.

Even though the peaceful aura remained around his charge, Alfredo knew the battle lines were drawn.

"He's denied her wish for reconnection to her long-lost daughter," he said gravely, "and a chance to make amends. And because she's accepted death to be inevitable, the dogs of Satan will hound her."

***

The mood back at the apartment was sombre. The contents of the documents that Camille sprung had numbed Asha, but there was nothing either angel could do to comfort her. Camille asked to be left to rest on her bed, and Asha retreated to the kitchen to make a coffee, taking it out to the patio to drink.

The scroll quivered in its case.

"An intervention? Let's pray it is so." A wave of relief flooded Alfredo.

Felice wasn't as sure.

"You realise this may not be the case, Alfredo. As much as we are praying, Camille has been in the grips of the Dark One for such a long time ..." She flitted to his side.

"I can't give up on her. I won't," he said firmly.

She responded softly, "And neither will I." She gazed fondly at Camille. "But will she?"

Alfredo sat on the end of the bed to decipher the scroll's new messages while Felice stood guard over Camille.

What had been a difficult day had just become more so.

"We've been recalled to the village. Both of us." Alfredo couldn't understand the reason. He wanted to stay to protect Camille. "And look, Felice. Three more Chinese markers."

"Alfredo, we must go. God has Camille's full plan laid out, so even though I worry, we must do as bid."

He thought for a moment. "We should ask for revelation. In any case, we must pray over her and leave. The scroll commands."

He rolled it up and strapped the cylinder to his back.

Together, they laid their hands over Camille and prayed for protection.

The ladder beckoned them, its steps bathed in the light of a full moon and clear sky. Alfredo stepped onto it and ran as fast as he could upwards. He thought nothing of the shadows awaiting him in the thick cloud ahead, only those lurking below around his charge.

CHAPTER 21

Night descended over the city. The skyline changed from crimson red to the purple-green, neon greyness that constituted Paris' version of darkness. It left Camille with no sense of peace. She wanted total darkness to match her mood.

The day had been charged with emotion. First at the café with Julia and Asha, then later at Mr Levin's office. Camille pulled a favourite record from her collection, a sad melody, to reflect the turmoil within.

She'd upset Julia. Who was she to stir up the past for someone else – a stranger? Grateful, yes, for the insight she received, but terribly guilty it came at that woman's expense. And what had she achieved? For a while, hope that her daughter's experience might be like Julia's. A hope dashed when Levin said the trail ran cold. Still, she'd tried, hadn't she? Was it enough? No. Like a fool, she'd left things too late. Time had run out.

It wasn't the only reason she'd gone to Levin's. Or why she'd insisted Asha come with her. It tired her, having to explain things more than once. Better to do it with the two people entrusted with her affairs at the same time. That had been difficult, too.

Her medical reports had come back. Not as good news as she expected. The cancer had spread and was aggressive. Months were reduced to weeks if she understood it correctly. After her last trip to the hospital, she realised how unfair it was to put Asha in a position of making decisions about treatment. That wouldn't happen again.

Camille walked through her darkened apartment to the kitchen. There was enough light from the balcony, and she knew by habit where the glasses and whiskey were. She pulled the oxygen tubes from the trolley. She would breathe on her own, with no one fussing over her.

Her thoughts returned to Levin's office. She'd splayed the medical forms on the desk before both Levin and Asha. Made Levin read them out so Asha understood what Camille intended. Do not resuscitate. Clear and concise. In her handwriting, she painstakingly wrote the sentence on one of Levin's fine linen sheets of paper. No medical treatment is to be undertaken. None. No medication besides pain relief; she was still a coward, after all. She'd have no arguments. Her actions ruled out Levin's citing coercion and Asha's protests.

Camille regretted the shock on Asha's face. She did. But honesty was better. She'd come to love the girl, and it hurt her deeply to say goodbye too soon. How she would have delighted to see her grow into her talent. To see her fall in love. She would miss seeing her have a family of her own. But most of all she wanted Asha to not waste her life as she had.

These thoughts opened a flood of tears. Camille crossly wiped them with her palm as she poured a generous amount of whiskey into her glass. How dare you! She scolded herself. Don't cry tears of pity; that won't help you. Nothing will help you, Camille, she told herself.

"Nothing?"

The voice startled her. Searing pain burnt in the space around her heart. How could he haunt her this way?

"I did try. I did," she sniffed through tears. "And I said I'm sorry. Is that not enough?"

"Can you forgive yourself?"

Camille had not expected that. Could she? She held both hands on the bench and leant forward, trying to ease the heartburn. Tears dripped onto the floor.

"Yes," she said back to the voice. The pain eased marginally.

"Can you forgive me?"

She gave a half laugh, half cry. Without sound from her voice box, it came out as a croak from deep within her chest.

"Yes." There she'd said it. It wasn't God's fault. It wasn't her fault. It just was how it was.

"Asha."

Camille's awareness sharpened. The pain in her chest vanished. What did Asha have to do with it?

"I gave you Asha."

Camille reeled as if a bolt of lightning had struck her. She jerked back from the bench and, in the process, dropped the tumbler onto the tiles. It smashed, sending shards of glass everywhere. The whiskey sprayed over her clothes and hand. Camille couldn't drag enough air through her wound opening. She gasped like a fish out of water, and as her lungs struggled, she fell upon the glass on the floor.

***

The apartment was dark. Satan cautiously sniffed the air. No trace of lingering floral scent from the young one. No smell of angel either. An evil grin spread over his face, and he rubbed his hands in glee. A sense of despair pervaded the room. Perfect.

Today was surprisingly easy, despite the proliferation of angels surrounding the women. The solicitor's ego didn't need much stroking to be fooled into hiding the truth about her daughter.

He had almost convinced Julia to leave the café early. Perhaps he could have arranged something else to achieve that. A stronger coffee, perhaps? One that would have sent her stomach churning. Never mind. She was no match for his wiliness, and neither were those two guardians with her. He had worked out their plan to use the coin. Of course the coin wasn't in the woman's bag because he put fear in play. Fear of discovery. He sneered with a mix of satisfaction and anger at the angels' audacity. Did they believe their power would outwit him, Satan?

Thoughts of the coin brought with it another memory. He had seethed with rage when Camille gave the girl one of her own.

But in the end, he had won. Now, because of Pierre's lie and Camille's self-loathing, she was here on her own. For a moment, he wondered where the two angels had gone. He dismissed this absence as unimportant. He had to be opportunistic – every moment would count.

Satan searched for his quarry in the darkened apartment. He sniffed the trail of despair and found her in the kitchen. Why she lay on the floor mattered little. The circumstance might bring more confusion, to increase scattered thoughts in her head. To deepen the fear of loss.

Camille lay surrounded by glass and spilt whiskey. Satan sat on the counter and watched her. She hadn't fallen on any shards of glass. Pity, he thought; a slow bleed was always a welcome sight. Had she drunk any whiskey? He lay on the floor beside her and drew in a deep breath through her open mouth. No. What a shame.

"Let's see. What lie can I give you? Oh, yes." Satan put his lips to her ears. "Your daughter hates you. Asha will hate you. She'll take your money and laugh at what a fool you are. You've missed your chance, Camille.

God hates you for that. He's angry with you because you didn't listen, and now you're too late."

He sat back and studied Camille's face. Usually, their eyelids fluttered; something to show the words sunk in, but nothing. He scratched his chin and flew back to his perch on the bench. Had he underestimated that green angel? Or did something else protect her? He flared his nostrils with rage and his eyes burned red.

He leant down, putting a clawed hand on her side. Where was the cancer in her body? Had it spread to a place he could play with? Nothing. Even cancer needed time to grow. He growled. Satan poked Camille's body roughly until he found what he wanted. An evil laugh exploded. There it was. Now, if he could just …

Satan looked up suddenly. A perfume wafted past his nose and he shivered in disgust. He had to hurry. She was coming. One final twist against this spot would be enough.

CHAPTER 22

Asha ambled down the narrow street to her flat. The streetlights flickered on. Tourists bustled past her to catch up with friends – out for dinner, then on to a bar somewhere. Living life. Usually, she ignored them, but tonight she was on edge. Someone called out from behind her. She cringed. A man ahead answered and waved in her direction. She felt rather than heard the brisk steps that danced past her and clumped further down the street.

She felt old. She envisaged herself still climbing the stairs to the flat when she was thirty or forty. Isn't that what happened to Mama? And when she got to the flat, would anyone be waiting for her? Don't, she told herself. She was not her mother. Besides, she had Marco, didn't she? A flicker of doubt flashed in her mind, and she made a conscious effort to address it.

She did have Marco. And if what was between them wasn't strong enough to ride through this, it wasn't meant to be.

At least she was not as reclusive as Camille in her isolated tower and all the money in the world but no one to share it with. She shook her head. Plenty of time for a full life. Camille made choices Asha wouldn't be faced with. At least she hoped not. She sighed.

Her steps ground to a halt at the chocolate shop next to their street door. Chocolate. That would solve everything. After today, her mother needed a tonic. Asha appreciated how difficult it must've been discussing her past with, of all people, Camille. She'd been so sure Mama would tell her. But she froze. It was too much. Asha understood. It was a lot to ask. But Camille didn't have much time. Even less time than Asha had first realised. The letter at Levin's office showed her that.

Secretly, she was glad Levin didn't know the full story. She desperately wanted the truth to come from her mother. But it hadn't, not yet. And now Camille insisted Asha not stay the night. She wasn't comfortable leaving her there alone, but Camille was stubborn.

Her mother was already home, and dinner awaited her. Two places set, and a posy of flowers poorly arranged in a water jar. Her mother's way of saying sorry. Asha hugged her and sat down to eat. The conversation was stilted, both skirting around the café discussion until Julia finally brought it up.

"How was she after I left?" she said, swirling the remnants of a chicken stir-fry with her fork.

"Oh, Mama. What you said made her so determined she was doing the right thing. The search, I mean." She reached over and took her mother's hand. "I'm so proud of you, by the way. I know that was hard."

Her mother smiled sadly. "No, I let you down. I just couldn't say it was me." After a moment of silence, Julia continued, "I was going to give her the coin, but I put it in the trunk after you found it in my purse." She paused. "I thought, if she remembered that day, she might ... I could explain how much I'd prayed for it to happen. And was glad she'd been there that day, like a sign from God my prayers were answered."

Julia broke down and cried, her head in her hands.

"Aww, shh." Asha came around and hugged her until she regained control.

"You know what," Asha exclaimed, "why don't we go over there? Take her some dessert. Let's eat ice cream together. And cry. And tell her we're so glad we found her ourselves." The plan took shape as she spoke. "It's early. She won't go to bed. She'll be sitting in her study listening to music. It's what she does."

Her mother blinked through her tears.

"Mama, get your scrapbook. And the coin. Come on, let's do it. We'll catch a cab."

Asha grabbed their coats and waited with the door held open, listening to the scrape of the trunk on the floor and her mother's hesitant footsteps.

The cab journey seemed to take forever with the evening traffic at its peak. Asha fretted her mother might lose her nerve and tell it to turn around.

At last, they arrived at Camille's quiet street and stood in the darkened foyer, waiting for the elevator. Asha linked her arm in her mother's to bolster her morale. They followed the progress downward on the monitor.

The moment the doors slid open, Asha exclaimed, "Can you smell that? Flowers. Every time I come here, it smells beautiful."

Her mother smiled vacantly, her mind obviously elsewhere, probably stuck between fear and trepidation. Asha wanted to move her past it, move her forward.

At Camille's door, she stopped, turned to her mother and held her closely. "Whatever happens, it's the right thing to do. For you and for her."

Her mother grinned nervously, but her brow was lined with fear.

"If she rejects you, Mama, it will break this." She put a hand on the book. "You won't have to live with the not knowing."

It was true. One way or the other, the scrapbook was doomed for the rubbish bin.

She kissed her mother's face. "And if she doesn't, which I am sure will be the case, you can move forward and make up for lost time."

***

Asha let herself in with her key to find the apartment in darkness. The only sound was a soft tapping coming from the lounge. It only took a moment to realise what made the noise. Asha headed to where the record player ticked over and over; the needle bar stuck in the centre track. Her heart leapt to her throat. Something was not right.

"Camille?" How silly of her. She couldn't answer.

She turned the main lights on and rescued the vinyl record from its relentless spin. Julia had followed her and stood looking around the apartment.

Asha pointed to the closed bedroom door. "Check the bedroom for me. I'll check the bathroom. She may have fallen." Worry crept up her spine.

Her mother didn't move. She was sniffing the air. "Is that whiskey?"

Asha tried to discern the scent her mother had picked up but couldn't.

The empty apartment alarmed her. She ran all the possible scenarios over in her mind, trying to find a plausible explanation. Had Rochet been after she left? Had something happened while he was here, and he'd failed to alert them?

She checked both his desk and Camille's. There may have been a note left. She hoped. And hoped not. The menace of the do-not-resuscitate letter hung in her mind. There was no note. Her heart hammered in her chest.

Her mother's voice broke her train of thought. "Where does she keep the drinks?"

"The kitchen ..."

The sound of moving glass greeted them. Broken glass.

246

Both rushed to the sound.

Luckily, when Camille fell, she hadn't landed on any shards. A scratch here and there, but nothing serious. Their voices had roused her.

"Camille, oh you poor thing. How did this happen?" Asha said, squatting next to Camille.

They picked her up and carried her to the sofa to assess her properly. Julia found a cloth, wiped what whiskey remained on her face and arms, and then cleaned the mess in the kitchen.

Camille cried and held her hands to Asha's face. Her lips mouthed the words, "I'm sorry," again and again.

Asha cradled her hands in hers. "You have nothing to be sorry for. We love you. Where does it hurt? Did you faint?" Asha kept the questions to something she could nod yes or no, but already she saw the colour come back into her cheeks. She breathed a sigh of relief. No harm done.

"You came." Camille mouthed the words.

Asha nodded. "Yes, we did."

Julia came back to the sofa. She had a glass of water and the scrapbook in her hands and looked at Asha with questioning eyes.

Asha nodded. Camille looked more like herself now.

"Camille, we came for a reason. Both of us." She warmly smiled as her mother sat on the sofa with them.

Camille's eyes were drawn to the scrapbook and Julia's face.

There was still confusion on Camille's face, but now they had started, and unsure another opportunity would arise, she continued. "You don't have to look for your daughter anymore," she whispered. She put a hand on her mother's knee. Her heart throbbed in her chest and her eyes never left Camille's face. "She found you!"

***

Camille woke to voices calling her name. She tried to call out, then remembered her inability to do so. The frustration still hit her hard. Her eyes refocused. She saw the fluff under her fridge, a few centimetres away. Why? What happened? A fall? She tried to pull the threads of the past few moments back together. The voices persisted.

Camille moved her hands, but the sound of glass frightened her. She dared not. A light switched on in the other room, reflecting shards of glass littering the floor. Ah yes. She remembered now. She'd poured a whiskey – the honeycomb smell returned, but something had happened, and she ended up on the floor. Her chest burned. A heart attack?

"Asha! In here!"

It was Julia's voice. And Asha was with her. A wave of relief washed over Camille.

Thank God. She may have been here all night otherwise.

They cleaned the whiskey from her and settled her on the sofa.

"I'm sorry," she mouthed. She was. What happened to her, this health crisis, was unfair to Asha. What right did she have to put such a strain on her young shoulders? She was glad Asha had her mother to support her. Glad they had come. But what had made them? Worry over her? She told Asha this afternoon she had wanted to be alone.

Julia joined them on the sofa. She held a battered scrapbook in her hands. Camille saw a nervous look pass between mother and daughter.

Julia placed her scrapbook in front of Camille. Did this concern her? Was this why they had come? Asha's words broke the questioning thoughts.

"You don't have to look for your daughter anymore. She found you."

Those words sent a shock through her body. Had she heard right? She stared at the scrapbook as Julia opened the first page. A birth certificate. Whose? Julia's voice, full of emotion, explained.

"Camille, I found this hidden in the seams of my parents' family Bible. It's my original birth certificate."

Camille listened in a daze. The words connected, but it was the document holding her attention. She traced the lines on it, willing herself to read each line slowly. Could it possibly be her daughters?

Julia flipped the page to the next certificate. They were almost identical. Almost. The date differed by a few days. And there, different names for Julia's parents. Her adoptive ones?

"I didn't find out the connection to you until years later. And the woman who told me risked losing her job." Julia's voice cracked. Difficult words, not easy to say.

The next page turned, and that photo – the one from the old gossip papers – stared back at her. It jolted her, and she drew back from the book. Julia flipped it quickly and on through the bulk of the scrapbook. It was all there, every article ever written of her. Her life, glued into a cheap scrapbook by this woman, who happened to be Asha's mother.

"I prayed every day I would find you," Julia whispered. "That you'd look for me. Either way, I wanted to exist for you."

Camille's chest burned. What was she to believe? A miracle? Julia herself said she had sometimes not believed, hadn't wanted it to be the truth. But why now? Why didn't she come out and say it at the café? It might've saved her the agony at Pierre's.

She looked at Julia's distressed face. It was too much to process. She needed time. Julia had opened a floodgate and, overwhelmed as she was, Camille was powerless to stop her.

"And Asha, she had your talent for dance even when she was little. When I looked at her, I saw you." Julia sniffed and wiped a tear. "I toyed with the idea of not letting Asha dance. I admit, at times, I was angry you didn't know me. Couldn't know me. But in the end, Asha was drawn to you. Was it fate? Was it God's way of making it up to me? I don't know the answer."

She watched as Julia closed her eyes, tears running unabated down her face. Asha beside her cried as well. Camille realised the two of them must have known. How long had they hidden this from her? Was their compassion towards her genuine, or based on believing Julia was her daughter, a fact yet to be proven?

She wanted them to leave. She was grateful they had rescued her from the floor, but this, this was too much.

Julia reached into her pocket and placed something in Camille's hands. "Do you remember this?"

The coin had a familiar warmth about it. Camille knew what it was the moment Julia placed it there. Her eyes glazed as she was taken back to that day. Julia's words were the only thing holding her in the present.

"I went to Notre-Dame. I poured my heart out to God. What did he want from me? From Asha. Was I being punished? Or was I receiving a sign from Him that I might finally meet you through Asha? In the end, I asked that you never find out the truth – that Asha was your granddaughter." She sobbed.

Camille refocused on Julia's face. Her conversation with God that day resonated. It seemed they both sought the same answers.

"Can you believe how God answered me? I looked up that day and saw you walk towards me. Right there, at that very moment." Julia said. "I got up and left, and you followed me."

Camille flipped the coin over to see the date stamped on it. She knew instinctively already and shook her head in disbelief. She did remember the day. All of it. The Chinese tourists with the imitation fur coat. The pigeon. And the woman who gave her the euro.

Camille stared at Julia. How had she not recognised her before? It was her. She clenched her fist around the coin. Fresh tears ran down her cheeks.

Asha spoke excitedly beside her. "I've seen yours, Camille. Remember, you showed it to me. And when I took you there, you got one for me." Asha dug into her own pocket and pulled out the fresh token, placing it in Camille's hand.

Camille looked down at the coins and laughed through her tears. She knew. Hadn't the voice told her?

"I gave you a child." Isn't that what the voice said that day? And tonight. "I gave you Asha." She gasped for breath. Her whole body shook despite every effort she made to stop. There was so much she wanted to say. Words she couldn't speak, even if she hadn't lost her voice.

Camille rose slowly from the sofa, using Asha's shoulder for support, and reached out to hug Julia. There would be time. God willing, He would give them time.

Julia embraced her, and Asha wrapped her arms around them both.

Camille stiffened as a sudden pain stabbed her in the side. She pushed away from the embrace; her face contorted. Her grip on Asha's shoulder tightened, and she gasped for breath in sharp, quick intakes. The attack was excruciating and relentless, and the blackness closed in on her again.

***

Alfredo bounded up the ladder. He sensed Felice at his side. None of the grey shadows mattered. There was nothing to quench the urgency that propelled him upward. The clouds parted, and they were at the gate, racing into the avenue along with the tide of returning angels. Alfredo's face was flushed, and his breath came in large gulps.

"That was exhilarating!" He laughed and slowed to allow Felice to catch up.

They stepped from the traffic and fell in a heap onto the grassy verge. The scroll quivered; it hadn't stopped since they left Camille's apartment. Alfredo unrolled it and studied the changes eagerly.

A picture appeared of Camille standing in darkness in her apartment. Alfredo experienced a piercing stab in his heart. Sorrow, immense sorrow. It was palpable. He touched the image on the scroll.

"It's her heart breaking, Felice." It brought him to tears.

Felice's face told him she understood.

"She so wanted to find the truth. To have a chance to make amends." A sense of failure overtook him.

Felice put a hand on his arm. "Alfredo, that's what you must take to the Father. That's her prayer. It's from her heart and now we are called back, you must convey it with conviction."

"You're right." He couldn't give up, not yet. "And we do that, where?" He looked at her questioningly.

"Oh, Alfredo. You are so green." Felice laughed. "The chapel, of course."

He grinned at her. "I'm a quick learner, though." He leapt to his feet and offered his hand to her. "Race you."

He set off at high speed to the chapel near the centre of the village.

"You do know, don't you, that if you'd followed the crowd, we'd have got there sooner?" She teased him as they joined the queue at the entrance.

"Next time, I'll know."

The beauty of the Grand Chapel captivated him. Like the library, huge pillars held up the edifice. Beautiful carvings laced the pillars, and every curve and whorl were lined with gold. The steps gleamed in pink and grey marble, polished to a sheen from the feet of the angels. They moved in awe through the giant door and came to a soft billowing curtain that hid the interior from the street.

As they passed through this, the sound of prayers in all languages surrounded them, whispered from the lips of angels who knelt facing the altar with heads bent.

Alfredo looked around at the worshippers and suddenly came to a halt, startled by who was staring back at him. Yaseem. His heart lurched and he bowed at his old teacher.

Yaseem bowed in return, the tiniest of smiles on his face. He leant his head in the direction of the altar, keeping his eyes on Alfredo. Encouragement Alfredo found comforting at such a moment as this.

He stood taller, acknowledged the gesture given by Yaseem and continued down the aisle with less trepidation. He hoped Yaseem would be proud of him.

Felice found a spot at the end of one of the seats, but Alfredo walked further towards the altar. His was a prayer with no words. How could he convey it?

No sooner had the thought occurred than a brilliant light shone in his eyes and forced him to stop and cover them with his hands. He fell to his knees, hit by a force he could not see. He bent his head and prayed he might convey the message from Camille.

A dove, white as fresh-washed linen, flew to him from the light and he stretched out his hands to give it a perch. It settled in his hands and Alfredo closed his fingers around it, gently encompassing its body. He brought the image of Camille to mind. The pain flowed from his heart into his veins. He watched his veins glow as the sensation travelled through them. The bird changed from white to grey as the pain drained from him. The bird flew back into the light, which faded in intensity.

Alfredo rose and walked back to the entrance. Yaseem was no longer there. Had Alfredo imagined it? No, his teacher had been there.

Alfredo was happy to have noticed his presence. He had not disappointed his teacher after all. A calmness descended on him, and he held his body erect. Felice fell in beside him and glanced up at him.

"Well?" she said.

"Well, what?" Alfredo asked. Was there something he missed?

"Oh, nothing, like did He say anything to you?"

He shook his head.

Angels didn't lie. The Father hadn't said anything. He had, however, shown him something. Something he couldn't bear to share with Felice. Not yet. There was no need. It didn't concern her, just him.

"Hmm. You look different." She frowned. "Taller."

Alfredo laughed. He felt different, but taller? No, he didn't think so.

"We have to go back. Camille needs us."

He did feel something. A buzzing in his head and pain in the side of his body. The scroll quivered. He unrolled it as they walked, and what he saw confirmed why. He grabbed Felice's hand and ran.

CHAPTER 23

Asha sat with her mother in the waiting room and nervously picked at a thread in her coat. They'd been here for two hours, and no one had updated Camille's condition.

She wondered if Camille's earlier blackout had played a part. She seemed recovered from that initial fall.

A tiny smidgen of guilt blamed the shock of their news. It had been so sudden. One moment she was well, and the next, she collapsed on them.

They'd made frantic calls for an ambulance, but the minutes ticked too slowly. While Julia held Camille's hand as she lay on her sofa, Asha rifled through her desk for Rochet and Levin's numbers.

The document Camille forced her to witness with Pierre Levin gnawed at her. She toyed with the idea of not calling him, but Mama said not to be foolish. Camille had made her choice. She wanted no treatment other than pain relief.

She hoped Levin hadn't done anything with the forms. If that were so, at least they'd keep Camille alive until, well, she didn't know the answer to that. All she wanted was a chance for Camille and her mother to speak.

It would be so unfair if, after all that happened, they never got time to talk. Asha stole a glance at her mother. Her heart ached. Julia sat hunched forward, staring into thin air, her eyes sunken and underscored with dark shadows. All traces of make-up were gone. In her hands, an empty disposable coffee cup pirouetted through her fingers, its edges slowly being crushed.

Asha stood, stretched her shoulders, and rechecked the corridor for action. Futile, as the double doors to the emergency wing remained closed. Somewhere in there, Camille was fighting to stay or letting herself go.

"Mama," she whispered, "please pray she makes it."

Praying was something her mother did. Constantly. Asha never really believed any of that. But she respected her mother's dependence on it. Was it laziness? Did she deep down believe in prayer but was happy for her mother to do the heavy lifting to God?

The sound of squeaking rubber-soled shoes from the other side of the doors made her jump. With the click of a lock, a gowned doctor emerged. His mask hung from one ear. Weary-eyed, his face spoke of a long shift about to finish.

Her mother leapt from her chair and stood beside her, an arm sliding around her waist. Together, they held their breath and waited.

"You here for Madam DuPont?" He squinted tired eyes at them. They nodded. "She's resting comfortably now. Appendicitis. We've dosed her with pain relief and antibiotics for now and will discuss removing them in the morning. You've done the right thing bringing her in."

He removed his mask. "Go home, get a good sleep, and we'll talk more in the morning. Yes?"

Asha closed her eyes and breathed a sigh of relief. Appendicitis. Not the cancer. "Thank God!"

***

Alfredo and Felice raced as fast as possible down the Angels Ladder and found themselves beside Camille in a hospital bed. The moment they burst into her room, the heat from the demons engulfed them. Fine pin-prick needles stung their bare arms and legs. Alfredo drew to his full height.

"I command you to leave!" One or two skulked away, but some of the strong shadows retreated to the corners of the room. They refused to leave.

Felice took Camille's hand and whispered into her ear in Spirit language. Soothing prayers.

Alfredo faced the demons. They sneered at him. He watched their countenance but refused to make eye contact – for that was where they had their power.

Nurses came and went, and Alfredo spoke in Spirit language to the angels they brought in and out with them. Every time he did this, the demons in the corners hissed and cowered.

Yaseem said demons could not understand Spirit language.

"If you want to foil demon plans, angels, take note. They cannot speak our language and cannot make up plans of their own. They must use age-old methods to destroy human souls."

Alfredo could still see his teacher pacing the lecture hall, hands behind his back. "Make your plans and petitions only in Spirit language, and you will confuse them. They will run from you."

At the time, Alfredo hadn't realised what he meant, having never met a demon and therefore had no prior reference to guide him. The textbooks were full of examples, but to him, one textbook was the same as another. Words. He needed experience. And now, here it was.

By night's end, the nurses' angels provided the reason Camille was here and not at home in her own bed. She had collapsed. Julia and Asha had brought her in. The doctors thought appendicitis. That heartened Alfredo. Not the cancer. He knew the document existed that would stop intervention. But so did the demons. Were they here in such numbers because they smelled death?

In Spirit, Alfredo and Felice conversed, discussing what Camille might fear. Pierre's refusal to tell her what he knew had dashed Camille's hope of finding her daughter. Julia almost revealed herself but lost courage at the last moment. They could not know what had transpired in her apartment while they were gone because it hadn't shown on her scroll. They had no way of knowing until Julia arrived with the angels Orlando and Perise.

"I'm going to call one of these demons out, Felice. We both agree it would be Fear, yes?" She nodded in agreement.

"Felice, I want you to lie full length over Camille, face down, to avoid their eyes. When I call it out, it may try to go back into her and hide. Hold tight, pray in Spirit with all your might." He waited until Felice covered Camille from head to toe.

Taking an almighty breath, he released it onto one of the demons.

"I see you, Fear. Reveal yourself in Jesus' name. I command you to flee, now!"

A demon screamed. An ugly, terrifying sound that blasted the room with heat. Alfredo's heartbeat quickened, then steadied. It took the form of a dragon that morphed into a beautiful woman draped in a green robe. The woman shape sneered and tried to embrace Alfredo. He pushed her back to arms-length.

"You have no power, Fear. Flee in God's name." His voice drowned out the sound it made. Suddenly, the door to the hospital room swung open and banged against the wall. A cold rush of air filled the room, wrapped around the demon, and dragged it out. The door slammed shut again.

Alfredo's ears rang with the sound the second demon made. What started as a low hum increased in power until each boom was a hammer in his head. He prayed aloud in Spirit for it to cease.

Instantly, his ears were blocked. The noise vibrations pulsed against his body, but he could not hear it. This allowed him to concentrate on what was in front of him.

The other demon rushed from the corner of the room, leaping on the end of the bed and clawing at Felice's legs to get her off Camille. Alfredo wasn't going to let that happen.

The pain interrupted Felice's prayers. She whimpered but kept the words flowing.

Alfredo grabbed the beast and rammed it into the far wall of the room. He pushed with all his might as it clawed at him. Its strength waned. From behind him, Felice gasped.

"Alfredo! You have wings. Use them!"

Wings? He thought of the great angels. He remembered the power in Gabriel's on his graduation day. Is that why he felt different? A surge of pure joy flooded from his chest into his arms and legs. With it, an extraordinary pulse of strength allowed him to overcome the demon's grasp. He took hold of it by its arms and shook it with such force it broke into tiny pieces. The pieces tried to reform into one body, but Alfredo raised his new wings and brought them together to create wind, flinging the pieces in all directions.

He looked about for more demons. The air had cleared of them, the heat gone from the room. They were alone.

Felice jumped from the bed and walked around him.

"Oh wow! They're beautiful." She stroked one. Her face wore a wide smile.

He had wings. Though he couldn't see them, their weight was evident. He arched his back. The wings spread wide. Now he could see part of them. Not huge, like Gabriel's or even Yaseem's. But they were there. A thrill ran up his spine. He had wings!

A ray of sunshine peeped under the curtain and fell on Camille's face. Both angels turned to watch her eyelids flutter in her sleep. She dreamed. They stood beside her, laying their hands on her head and body.

Alfredo unrolled the scroll across her chest and spoke the words written upon it as they appeared. God's promises to her. And while she slept, she would hear them in her dreams.

***

Julia and Asha sat in the waiting room and watched the hours pass. Camille had a restful night, and the surgeon cleared his schedule for an emergency operation this morning. In a matter of hours, it would be over.

Julia sighed, stretched and rose to drop more coins into the vending machine. She'd slept little. Her eyes were puffy. One look at Asha told the same story.

She repeatedly played the moments in which she revealed their truth to Camille. Had she imagined her response? Had she really accepted her as her missing daughter? It was hard to be sure without hearing the words spoken. The embrace was real, she told herself. Asha witnessed it, but the tiny voice in her head saying she'd got it wrong would not leave.

Levin arrived.

Julia gasped, as did Asha beside her. Both had hoped he would not arrive before the operation, but here he was. They'd left messages on his business phone last night. A quick call to say Camille had collapsed.

Now he strode into the waiting room, briefcase in hand. Asha jumped from her seat and intercepted him before he could hand over to the nurse the instructions agreed upon the day before.

They took their conversation down the hall, out of earshot of anyone else. Asha's body language showed a new strength in her daughter.

Something she suspected she had. Shades of her father, perhaps. Or her grandmother. That thought pleased her.

Levin's arrival worried her. She prayed he was too late to stop the operation. Then again, her prayers were already answered. Camille knew who she was. That could not be undone, but she wanted Camille to live and be well enough to share some time together.

The missed time could not be recovered; this was the price paid by them both. But what time was left might be enough to fill the void in her heart. To melt away the resentment built over a lifetime and give her daughter an anchor for the future.

Julia watched Levin's raised arms drop to his sides in defeat. Asha stood tall and folded her arms, staring at him defiantly. He raised the documents to her one last time, then turned and left her standing there. Once he disappeared into the lift, Asha returned, a victory grin plastered on her face.

"There is still time, Mama, there is still time."

**

Asha waited for the elevator doors to close on Levin before she took her next breath. Adrenaline surged, leaving her weak at the knees. She slowly unfolded her arms and swivelled on her heel to face her mother. She could not believe what she had just done.

"Mr Levin, please, it isn't cancer this time. It's something fixable. Surely the do-not-resuscitate order can be ignored in such an instance?"

Camille had already gone up to the surgical ward. Did he think it right to stop it now? Something as mundane an operation as appendicitis. She'd held her breath as he rubbed his chin.

"Technically, I should lodge it today." He looked away to avoid her steely eyes. "All documents take time. Shall we agree this document will

261

be lodged the next time I'm in the office? I might take today off work, so perhaps tomorrow?"

Asha's face lit up. A reprieve.

"But the moment Camille is lucid, you will confirm her wishes. As will I," he warned.

CHAPTER 24

Camille sat with her pillows plumped up high behind her. The room overflowed with flowers; the cards were neatly placed within reach of her on the hospital trolley. Visiting hours started soon, not that she expected many. Asha, Julia, and of course, Rochet.

Poor Rochet. She wondered why the man stayed. His need to be orderly and organised had been tested over the past months. Perhaps she would see him more appropriately rewarded. Part of her instructions for Asha was for him to continue – if he chose to, of course – to administer the scholarship. Had she overestimated her importance? Would any of it matter? She'd be gone soon, and her reach from the grave depended on the continued goodwill of Asha.

A warmth rose in her chest. Asha would do her utmost to fulfil her wishes, she knew that. Her intuition was vindicated. There was something about Asha she had immediately connected to. No one imagined the outcome. To have bestowed her fortune on a stranger, only to find she was flesh and blood. Family. Knowing she had a family at all gave her a thrill. Yet the sense it was almost too late tempered the delight with regret.

Thoughts of Asha couldn't be separated from Julia. Her heart ached just that bit more. Here was someone who'd lived so close to her, followed her like a shadow for a lifetime, yet couldn't reach out. Wanted to, but the sting of rejection had been branded indelibly on her.

How ironic. Didn't rejection stunt her own life, rejection by her papa? She would tell Julia she was deeply sorry for everything. She owed her that much.

A knock on the door heralded their arrival. Both faces held genuine smiles of relief when they saw her sitting up. She felt well, but the wound stabbed at her if she moved suddenly. Appendicitis. How ridiculous to get to this age and be brought undone by that.

After she came round from her faint at home and found herself again in the hospital, all she could think of was that the ink wasn't dry on the documents to stop medical intervention from happening.

Asha had been with her, fortunately. When the doctor mentioned surgery again, Asha had grabbed her hand and held onto it tight. No words, just pleading eyes.

The moment she knew she needed surgery, Camille regretted her decision. She fretted; if someone knew, the operation would be cancelled. Had that happened, she wouldn't have time to speak to Julia first. But here she was, and now she'd been given the moment, she would make the most of it.

Julia and Asha kissed her cheek and pulled chairs close to the bed. Julia brought a basket of fruit and Asha a bouquet of fresh lilies. Both saw the overabundance of flowers already in the room and laughed.

This was the first time Camille had heard Julia laugh, and the sound jolted her senses. It was the same lilting laugh of her own dear maman. If she closed her eyes, it was her. The ache grabbed at her heart. There was no doubt. None whatsoever. This was her daughter.

Camille pushed the table trolley out of the way. She reached for their hands and squeezed them tightly in her own. How she longed to speak. Just one more time. It seemed cruel. She held on a moment longer, then reached for the pad.

Julia, what you told me last night made my heart sing. She scribbled.

Julia smiled through her tears. "Mine too."

When I'm gone, remember me kindly. It agonises me that I didn't search for you.

Julia shook her head. "It doesn't matter. You can fight this – if you want to. We'll be here for you. Both of us."

Asha nodded silently beside her.

Camille shook her head and wrote furiously.

No. This is my punishment, and I will accept it. I am old. It won't be a pretty death. I've decided no more surgeries. Just pain relief. She gripped Julia's hand again.

You will be here for me. I know. Please move in with me, both of you. I want to die at home. Her tears splashed on the pad. *With my family around me.*

***

The angels – Alfredo, Felice, Orlando and Perise – stood at the end of Camille's bed with huge smiles. They watched the three women. Despite everything, it looked like they would succeed with Camille. The family was whole again, and Alfredo's heart burst with joy. His first assignment – a success.

It was Orlando who pointed out the perfume. He turned to Perise and commented on the sweetness and its strength. "I wonder if we'll ever meet her – or him?" he said casually.

Alfredo had to ask. It intrigued him, the smell. It had something to do with Asha – the perfume was always present when she was – other than that one time in his room at the village.

"Lilies?" He pointed to the bouquet Asha had brought. "So, it's not from real flowers, then?"

"No," exclaimed Perise. "From when Asha was born"—she smiled knowingly— " we've asked many times in the village what it meant. That and the lack of a guardian."

Orlando took over the discussion. "The only answer we got was Asha had an Appointed One."

Felice clapped with glee. "How wonderful."

"You know of them, Felice?"

All eyes turned to her.

"I've heard of it. Asha can see her angel. Oh, she doesn't recognise him or her as an angel. And they're not revealed even to us, other than with perfume or in some other cryptic way."

Her eyes widened, and she turned to Alfredo. He had the same revelation. Together they said, "The Chinese Motifs."

Alfredo's cheeks flushed with heat. Why had it not occurred to him before?

"Felice, do you think that's why the Father made us come back together? He had it covered. When Asha was with Camille ..."

She nodded in agreement.

Orlando turned to Alfredo and stared at him. "By the way, awesome wings, my friend. May I?" He reached out and touched them.

Alfredo's face was hot now. He was still self-conscious of them.

"Thank you, Orlando; they came in handy against the demons the other night."

"Perhaps you will have need again, Alfredo." Perise's voice was serious. "There is still a war over Camille. I feel it."

"But there are all of us, yes? With Julia, Asha and Camille all together, we will keep the worst at bay," Alfredo said confidently.

In truth, he hadn't thought past this first victory. His assignment could still fail, and that was sobering.

Orlando stretched and said, "Perise is right. Satan won't give up easily. Yes, we'll all be here as long as the battle comes when they're together."

Alfredo stood to his full height; the wings arched behind him.

"Then we will petition for just that," he stated firmly. "God willing."

***

In the hospital's basement, the doors in the morgue slammed open and shut with a fury not seen before. Satan threw an empty trolley into the wall, scattering the instrument trays stacked neatly on top of it. The next time an attendant entered the room, they would scratch their head at how such mayhem occurred, but that mattered little to him.

He had waited here for too long. Waited for her body to be sent here for his pleasure. Nothing excited him more than seeing the knife cut away to the blackened heart of a dead person. To force the soul of the deceased to look on and see its earthly demise and gloat at his victory over them and God.

Morphing into black vapour, Satan slunk into the air conditioning system in search of Camille's room. Finding the room was easy, though not pleasant. One look through the vent revealed the source of his displeasure. The room was full of them. And the problem angel had become larger since he last observed him. Satan hissed in disgust.

The angel had wings. This meant his status was elevated. A more difficult opponent. A development that required a higher degree of skill to undermine. But there were still things Satan hadn't tried yet.

He noticed Rochet and his swarm of black dust in the corner of the room. Rochet wore a knitted frown.

Satan stroked his chin thoughtfully. There was still some use for him. And Satan had another ace up his sleeve. His eyes glinted with momentary satisfaction.

These women celebrated their connection. But there were others connected to them. They didn't exist in a vacuum. It would only take one brittle memory to destroy her. It wasn't much, but Satan, seething with anger, thought it might be enough.

CHAPTER 25

Julia fumbled for the key to her old apartment. Every day of the last few weeks, she'd climbed the stairs and fed the pigeons. If she didn't, then who would? Truth be told, she longed for the privacy of her little flat. She wasn't accustomed to living in a modern townhouse like Camille's.

It was hard work emotionally. Camille was sick. Very sick. The cancer had spread throughout her body. She lost so much weight; it was easy to pick her up and carry her from her bedroom to a borrowed hospital bed in the living room. She spent her days there, staring out at the clouds.

Her hands were too frail to write much these days. Asha made cards with common sentences, and they shuffled through them, holding them up to find the right one for the moment. It broke Julia's heart to watch.

"Julia, Julia!" a voice from behind called out. She turned to see Marco waving at her.

"Hello, Marco." She waved back and opened the street door. She missed the banter with Marco and his family. He was also suffering. Asha had barely any time to devote to him of late, and whenever Julia mentioned him, Asha turned sullen.

"This is what I must do for now," she'd said. "Marco will have to understand. It's not forever, is it ..."

Coming to check on the flat and feed the birds made Julia realise that this was where she felt most at home. Here, where the street barely had room for two cars to pass. Where the shop owners were her friends and neighbours.

"Is it true?" he said over the noise of a car passing between them. He took his apron off and bounded over to her.

"Is what true, Marco?" She had no idea what he was referring to.

"This." He thrust a newspaper a customer left behind at her.

She took and read it. There, splashed on the front page, were pictures of herself, Asha, and Camille.

Julia's throat closed over, and her heart pulsed in shock. It took a moment before she could focus on the words.

Exposed! A miracle or manipulation?

Julia frowned. The initial shock gave way to annoyance. She skimmed the bulk of it. At the bottom, it promised more insight on the inner pages.

She didn't have time for this, not here in the street. Marco's eager face wanted an answer, but she couldn't give him one. Well, she could, but wouldn't. Not till she had studied the innuendo and what the paper considered facts.

"Marco, I don't know where they got all this. It's rubbish journalism."

"But Julia, is it true? Are you really the missing daughter?" His question held no malice. He had a good heart, and Julia worried Asha was too hard on him. In his shoes, she would've felt the same about coming into a significant windfall.

Afterwards, she hoped they would work things out. He was good for Asha.

Julia nodded. "Without reading it, Marco, I will say only this. Camille is my birth mother. That makes her Asha's grandmother. Anything else is garbage."

She watched as he processed her affirmation. His smile told her he was pleased for them.

"Can I keep this?" She shoved it into her bag. She would read it with Asha. They had always expected media attention once the truth emerged because Camille's fortune naturally brought public scrutiny. Something she hoped wouldn't ruin their lives.

"Sure." Marco dove into his apron pocket. "Can you give this to Asha for me?" He held out a card covered in hand-drawn love hearts and grinned sheepishly.

Julia accepted it with a grin. Yes, she liked this boy.

***

Asha paced the floor in Camille's apartment. Rochet brought the morning papers with him. A new article about Camille, Julia and herself was even worse than the previous one. Someone had done a lot of digging to find such private things and the media picked up on it. Even the morning television ran a few lines on it. The phone rang continually, so much so that Rochet took it off the hook.

Camille floated in and out of sleep, stirring at every sound, the volume of phone calls bothering her.

She tapped on the 'who is it?' card, but Asha couldn't tell her; instead, she made excuses but knew Camille wasn't fooled.

The door buzzer rang. Media representatives were looking for the story.

"Go away." Asha pleaded into the intercom. "Madame DuPont cannot speak to you." They kept buzzing. Later that afternoon, an older man's voice came on the intercom asking after Camille.

Asha had had enough and snapped, "She is not speaking to anyone. Not now, not tomorrow. Her lawyer will give a statement when he sees fit. Go away."

"I'm not a reporter." The voice was low and husky. "My name is Howard. Howard Roach."

"I don't care who you are. Madame will not see you. Go away." Asha spoke rudely to discourage him. She released the intercom button and walked away. After a momentary silence, more static crackled through the intercom. Asha accepted the call intending to explode at the audacity of this caller.

Before she could speak, the man said, "I'm Julia's father."

Asha released the button as if it had given her an electric shock. She put her head on the wall above the intercom. Her heart pounded, and blood rushed to her ears. She looked across at Camille in bed, hoping she hadn't heard the voice.

How dare he! Bile rose in her throat, remembering her mother's thoughts on how she was conceived. Not a love child. No indeed. Camille had never said it but both Asha and Julia knew something awful had happened between them. She retracted that thought. If it was rape, it wasn't something *between them* at all. It was something done *to* Camille.

Mr Rochet had seen her reaction, heard the name. His face resembled a ghost, drained of all colour. Asha wondered if he knew of Roach. His eyes quickly averted when Asha looked directly at him. He never said a word to her. For Asha, this amounted to guilt on his part. He did know him. Or at least, knew of him.

With her heart hammering in her mouth, she pressed the intercom. "You are not welcome. Not ever. If you don't leave, I will call the police." She spoke as quietly as possible.

The intercom was silent. Asha closed her eyes and leant on the wall for a few more minutes, wishing her mother would return from work, the job she insisted on keeping. Her eyes snapped open as a thought occurred. No. Mama don't come now. She might meet him downstairs, and if he says who he is ... That would be a disaster.

She slipped out of the apartment. If Roach was still there, she would make sure he didn't come back. Ever.

***

When Julia was up in her flat, she read the entire article in silence. Whoever had provided the information had either guessed a lot or had overheard conversations they were not supposed to repeat. There was no point trying to narrow down a suspect. It was a waste of energy she didn't have. And what good would it do?

They were all comfortable with each other. She would support Asha through any media storm that might arise. Camille would be gone soon, anyway. As it was, Asha and Julia shielded her from the outside world. And Levin and Rochet were the only other people who had any time with Camille these days.

Levin. Rochet. Was it one of them? A sick feeling in the pit of her stomach erupted. It was possible. Even probable. But again, it didn't matter. Either could be cut loose from them in the end. She owed, they owed, no allegiance to them. She liked Levin. Had come to like him, despite her daughter's aloofness towards him.

Asha had explained her first meeting with him. How he'd accused her of orchestrating Asha into Camille's life. It was laughable, and Julia knew he'd changed his opinion once he got to know her. He was decent.

That left Rochet. Snippets of her interactions with him returned to her memory. Little things. His fluster when he met her for the first time outside the studio. His disgruntled manner at the hospital.

Julia folded the paper and threw it in the bin. In a quiet moment, she would question the man. If it were his doing, he would be the one to

273

suffer, not them. She couldn't imagine he would find another position with such a shadow of distrust hanging over him. She gathered her bag and left for Camille's apartment.

In the foyer, a man stood speaking into the intercom. Julia walked past him without a second glance. She was preoccupied with the new exposé, wondering how Asha would react.

As she watched the elevator arrow descend, a voice came over the intercom. Rochet.

"She's coming down. You had better leave." His voice crackled.

The man responded. "I'm not leaving until I speak to her myself."

Julia turned to face the man. The intercom was a few metres away, and she had a clear view of him. He was intent on his conversation with Rochet and ignored her.

She studied him. Stocky build. White hair greased into shape. His back bowed, but in his youth, he would've been quite tall. Athletic even. His coat was of fine quality but dated. Shoes, leather, and again, not a new style. His clean-shaven cheeks sagged with age. He wore thick gold-rimmed glasses.

"Speak to who?" Julia's voice had a hard edge.

Surprised at someone addressing him, the man stood taller and stared at her. She didn't recognise him. At least he wasn't someone from the academy.

"Do I know you?" he asked curtly.

For a moment, Julia's boldness left her. Perhaps she had been mistaken, and this was not her business. Her cheeks tingled.

"Was that a Mr Rochet you spoke to just then?"

"And if it was, what business is it of yours?" His lips curled derisively.

Julia's anger roiled. He could only be here for one reason. Was he a reporter?

"It is my business if you are trying to get to Camille DuPont. I suggest you leave. Now."

The man's surprise altered. A knowing look spread across his face.

"Would you be Julia?" Incredulity crept into his voice.

He knew her name. He'd read the article then. Julia had already decided he was too old to be a reporter.

"Who are you?" she said frostily.

The elevator doors opened. Asha burst out into the foyer next to her.

"Mama!"

Her face was flushed, and she locked her eyes immediately onto the man at the intercom.

"And this would be my granddaughter." He smirked at his cleverness.

"I said. Who. Are. You?" Julia clenched her fists at her sides.

"Your father," he stated flatly.

The words struck Julia like a lightning bolt. It took her breath away, and she gasped for air. Asha grabbed her arm to steady her.

"Mama! I'll call the police." Asha screamed at the man. "Leave!"

Julia's ears rang.

"My name is Howard. Howard Roach. I'm your father, for what it's worth. I came to see Camille before ..."

"Before what? She dies? You filthy cockroach!" Asha spat the words at him. "Just as your name suggests."

He was still alive.

Asha was right. His name fits perfectly, and just like a cockroach, he'd crawled from whatever hole he lived in, intending to suck the remaining life from Camille. Well, she wouldn't have it. Camille deserved better. She had better. She had her daughter and granddaughter, and there was no chance she would stand by and see her hurt again.

"Leave. If you don't, I may just kill you." Her voice sounded remote to her ears.

The blood rushed to her head, pulsing behind her eyes and the room spun. Asha's voice echoed in a tinny way. Please don't faint, she whispered to herself in her head.

The last thing she remembered as the floor came up to meet her was Asha bending over her and the man stepping into the elevator.

***

Alfredo looked up from the end of Camille's bed as Asha slipped out of the apartment. He sensed her leaving. The air had a distinct taste of ash to it now. Gritty.

Camille was restless. She lay on her bed, alert and listening, too weak to get out of bed on her own. Her hearing wasn't dulled. The buzzer rang repeatedly.

Rochet paced near the door, wringing his sweaty palms with angst, and the black haze around him sprayed in every direction. It had become even thicker.

Alfredo motioned to Felice and handed her the last vial of water from the cleansing pool. "Sparingly," he said. "Use it only if you must."

Felice nodded and tucked it into her armour pocket. She held Camille's hand and whispered a fervent prayer into her ear.

"Don't listen, Camille. He can't hurt you."

Alfredo met Felice's eyes and gently said, "And he cannot hurt you again, either, Felice. Remember that."

Rochet held his finger on the intercom button. They all heard his voice.

"Camille? Are you listening?" It carved through the silence left in Asha's wake. "It's me, Howard Roach. You remember. Your teacher."

The intercom crackled. "I was in town and read about you. About the daughter you had. She's mine. I know it."

Camille's face contorted. The swarm of shadows seeped from the intercom.

"The time has come," Alfredo said to Felice in Spirit.

For a moment, the intercom was silent. Tears streamed down Camille's face. Alfredo saw her memories return and crystalise. Someone knocked on the door. Urgent rapping. It could only be Roach.

Alfredo watched in trepidation as Rochet inched the door open. It made sense. These two knew each other; else, how would Roach know where to come? They should've worked harder on Rochet. If they'd done so, this connection might have been foiled. He had let Camille and Felice down. But there was no time to hash over his failings. A bigger battle was about to unfold before his eyes.

None of his companion angels were in the room. He and Felice had been ambushed. This was to be their battle. He puffed up his chest and prayed for divine assistance.

The moment Roach barged the door open and stepped into the room, a swarm of demons came with him. They flitted into the apartment in as great a number as the angels Alfredo had seen on the ladder on their way back. Hundreds of them. Felice gasped in horror.

Alfredo spread his wings and stood between Camille and the men.

"Now is not the time," Rochet said, stepping in front to stop Roach from proceeding further.

"Where is she?" Roach demanded.

Rochet waved to the bed where Camille lay staring at the open door and the man who caused her so much pain.

Alfredo vibrated his wings in slow but powerful arcs. No one had told him what he could or couldn't do with his new wings, but he instinctively knew what was needed for this moment.

By vibrating them just so, Roach could not see Camille, but she could see him. Rochet could see Camille, but the man could not.

Confused, Roach became agitated. "Camille?"

"She can't speak. I told you that. You are a fool to come here. I would have ensured you got a share if you just listened to me, Roach." Rochet's anger became desperation. "I told you I'd introduce you to your daughter when Camille died. You were supposed to wait ."

Rochet took hold of Roach's arm, trying to herd him back out the door. "Get out of here before they come back. If they put two and two together, that you know me even, neither of us will get a cent."

Roach shrugged him off. "I wanted to see her *before* she dies."

"Is that so?" Asha stood behind them, hands on hips. "Thank you, Rochet, for your confession. Now, here's some information for you both. The police are in the foyer waiting for you."

Alfredo stopped moving his wings.

Roach saw Camille for the first time, staring directly at him. His face paled. The cancer had drained Camille of any features that would make her recognisable. All Roach would see was a bony frame covered in paper-thin skin and patches of blood bruises. His eyes were riveted to her.

Asha stepped between Roach and the bed; his eyes turned to her.

The cloud of demons attached to Roach crouched behind his aging frame. The heat from Asha was too intense for them to bear.

Alfredo grinned. The balance of power in the room had shifted their way. Still, a darkness was filling the room, and neither he nor Felice could change that until Orlando and Perise returned.

At that moment, Julia entered with two police officers.

Roach stepped towards Camille, but Asha was too quick. Stronger too. She blocked his path.

"Camille, I can explain. I just wanted to see you again. That's all." Roach's voice choked. "I'm sorry." The apology was almost a whisper.

A police officer grasped him roughly by his arms and pulled him away.

Camille turned her head to look out the window. Anywhere but at him.

Julia rushed to her side, one hand clasping Camille's and the other smoothing stray hairs from her forehead. She leant close, whispering reassurances.

Alfredo's attention returned to Rochet. After a brief scuffle, the second officer cuffed his hands behind his back.

"I have done nothing wrong," he protested. The officer escorted him from the apartment, and with him, the black cloud followed. Alfredo's grin widened.

The moment the door closed, the angels prepared for battle.

CHAPTER 26

The howling began. Above their heads, the air seethed with black haze. The noise of it thrummed in Alfredo's ears, and adrenaline quickened his body. The air became so dense and hot that it glowed red. He beckoned to the other angels to join him at Camille's bed.

Julia was there, at Camille's head, stroking her forehead, assuring her that both Rochet and the intruder were gone. Arrested. Their wicked plans were thwarted.

Asha had gone down the elevator with the police to deal with what would come next for Rochet and Roach. Without the power of the mysterious guardian, Alfredo wondered if he could take control of the demons himself. Even with the help of Felice, Orlando and Perise, he knew this battle would be an almighty one.

The other angels formed a ring around Camille's bed. They prayed in Spirit, their hands linked, heads bowed in concentration. The bed vibrated as though it may lift off the floor at any moment.

Camille's skin drained of colour. Remnants of the black web appeared on her head. Some of Roach's words had filtered into her soul.

They were whispering. Memories of his deed surfaced, threatening to drag her backwards towards desolation.

"Felice. Anoint Camille with the holy water."

As she carried out this deed, the colour returned and the black web melted away. Alfredo's courage grew. Each minor victory mattered.

Julia kissed Camille's forehead. Alfredo felt it on his own. Camille's heart responded with a cry of sadness for Julia. A mother's broken heart, crying for a long-lost child. The agony of it clawed at his own heart.

"Orlando, whisper to Julia. She cannot hold on to Camille's spirit with any regrets. Comfort her. Tell her God has given her a mother, even if only for the shortest of days."

A hysterical scream from the cloud of demons diverted his attention away from Camille. Alfredo called out in a loud voice, addressing the one who had screamed.

"Show yourself. We are not afraid. God has claimed these souls. Come, show yourself."

The heat intensified. Sweat broke out on the other angels' faces. A haze materialised in front of them. The demon, taller than any of them, took shape. Its red eyes sprayed fire in all directions. Wherever it looked, the air melted.

"Be afraid. I am stronger than all of you." It laughed mockingly.

Alfredo stepped forward and spread his wings to shield the others from the heat.

"Your might is an illusion, Dark One. Victory is ours already. Begone!"

The demon breathed in deeply, sucking the life from the air itself. Alfredo stood firm, which angered it even more. It rushed at him and wrapped its hands around his neck. Alfredo gritted his teeth, remaining anchored to the spot.

He prayed for the strength to overcome the beast. In an instant, his wings quivered, and energy flowed into them. The demon let him go and retreated to the cloud.

At that moment, Asha opened the door. Behind her stood a small figure wearing an apron. In his hand, he carried a bunch of lilies, and on his face, a wide smile.

Alfredo's eyes lit up with excitement. "Greetings," he shouted over the noise of the demons.

The lily bearer bowed in return. "Allow me to introduce myself." He waved the lilies and dropped them on Camille's sofa. "Mr Ying. At your service."

As the pair approached Camille's bed, the air cleared in their wake. The black haze became a less oppressive grey mist. Alfredo allowed himself to breathe normally.

"Welcome, Mr Ying. Well received."

Camille's eyes brightened at the sight of Asha. She was calling her name. Once again, his heart constricted in agony, but for only a moment. Camille's love for this girl overwhelmed the pain, and for Alfredo, that burst of love sent strength into his being.

The calm in the room was short-lived. The demon with the red slit eyes appeared again, this time with a troupe of smaller demons clinging to its back. The small demons' heads were shaped like dragons and had horrid festering sores on every surface of their bodies. Their breath stunk of sulphur and rotting flesh.

Alfredo spread his wings again and flapped them menacingly at the creature and its progeny. It stepped back once, then advanced on Alfredo collectively. Their claws swiped at him, some touching, others not. Alfredo spoke his prayers out loud in strong Spirit language.

This angered the demon, and it screamed and hissed at him, spitting foul liquid in his direction. Alfredo's armour protected his body from the worst of it, but he felt the sting on his arms and legs. It did not deter him. He prayed even louder.

The demon leapt onto Alfredo and sunk its teeth into his neck. Alfredo shrugged it off and threw it against the far wall, where it bounced back onto its feet and growled.

On the bed, Camille's heart monitor wavered and missed a beat. Alfredo knew he was running out of time.

He surged forward, encasing the demon in his wings. With a mighty leap, he dragged it through the walls and into the atmosphere outside where there was no danger to anyone else.

The demon continued to claw at him, but Alfredo's wings were like steel. The heat against his body grew in intensity. Alfredo prayed for protection, and an icy blast of wind encased him. He remained rigid; the demon caught firmly in his grasp. The beast's heartbeat wavered, and Alfredo realised his own had also missed a beat.

So, what the Father had said, that he too might perish along with Camille and the beast, was real.

This thought galvanised him into action. He must deal with the beast before Camille's death. It wasn't enough to remove it from near her; he had to destroy it. Nothing must stand between God and Camille.

Alfredo crushed the beast in his wings. He concentrated on every fibre of his body and wings and drew them tighter and tighter. His breath became shallow, and he called on the Father to bring the battle to a conclusion.

The beast struggled for space to expand its lungs against his strength. Alfredo brought the wings tighter again. The beast stopped struggling and went limp for a moment. Alfredo dared not release it in case it was a desperate ruse. The seconds ticked by.

A flurry of wings burst around the side of the high-rise building where Camille lived. A flock of pigeons raced past him, headed for a faraway roosting spot. Alfredo threw the demon in their path and, surprised at being released from his grip, it sprang into life again. But it wasn't quick enough. It became entangled in the flapping wings of a hundred pigeons who carried it away.

Alfredo watched as the angry demon tried in vain to disentangle itself from the flock of birds. Its form disappeared behind the high-rise buildings, and its screams of indignation faded with it.

Alfredo let out a joyous whoop. His heart filled with the rush of victory. He stretched his wings and breathed deeply to remove all traces of the demon and its scent.

At that moment, the sun emerged from behind a cloud and cast a golden glow over the window to the apartment. It reflected into his eyes, and he squinted at the brilliance. He blinked and brought one of his wings overhead to shield his eyes, then realised Felice was next to him.

"Alfredo, we did it! You did it," she whispered.

He smiled and draped an arm over her shoulder. "The victory came from God, Felice. We just played the part He asked of us. But I say, well done!"

Peace descended on them both, and they floated back towards the balcony.

"What do you think of Asha's guide, Felice? He had us guessing. Didn't he?"

She laughed. "Mr Ying is certainly special. He has funny stories to tell of our Camille, as well." She looked through the window at the women and other angels, including Ying.

"Did you know Camille could see him as a person too? Only to her, he was a Chinese greengrocer. To Asha, he was always a Chinese florist!"

Frowning, he asked, "Wait. Can Asha see him now? And Camille?" He looked sharply at Asha through the glass.

Felice laughed. "No. Neither can see him now. He said his job is done and his cover blown." Her laughter echoed and was snatched away by the wind.

Alfredo's brow creased even deeper. "And if that's so, will Asha require a new angel?"

Felice nodded and stood in front of him, her chest puffed out. "Me! The scroll just told me so!" She grinned. "I get another chance."

Alfredo bowed. "Congratulations."

Sobbing from within the apartment alerted them. Alfredo's heart stopped beating. He knew what it meant. He turned and waited for Camille to join him on the balcony. Through the window, Camille's body lay limp in Julia's arms. Orlando and Perise each had a hand on Julia's shoulders, comforting her.

Asha stood beside her mother, staring out the window at the setting sun. She had a beautiful smile on her face. Sorrow, love and acceptance emanated from her. To Alfredo, she looked as though she saw Camille and himself looking back at her. He knew this wasn't so. Perhaps she felt Camille's spirit let go.

Camille stared directly at Alfredo. He held out a hand to her, and she took hold. Together they turned to look at her form, still on the bed. Camille smiled widely and waved at her daughter and granddaughter.

Alfredo spoke gently to her. "Come."

And together, they walked into the light.

The End.

ACKNOWLEDGEMENTS

Many thanks must go to my family and friends, especially my husband John, for their patience and understanding while I took the time to follow my life-long dream of writing and publishing a novel – or two. Despite all the eye rolling, the intakes of breaths when I tortured you, I treasure each of you. It is a hard thing to live with a writer and without your support I could not have achieved any of this.

Thank you to my spirit-filled sister and friend, Kat Phillips for your support, long chats, and interesting points of view. All of us need that one person who 'gets it', just as Alfredo needed Felice.

All credit to our mother Aileen Curran for her inspirational example of resilience against all odds and her never failing faith. You are the light on my hill for when I lose the plot – literally. You famously said to me before I started Alfredo, "Well, it's time you wrote something else, isn't it?"

To the editors who worked with me on Alfredo, you are both wonderful humans.

Kelly Rigby can be found at *writewithkelly.com* . Thank you for tearing my first draft to pieces and giving me the whole summer holidays to rebuild it into something special.

Jo Speirs, from *www.nurturingwords.com.au* , your insights and thoughtful nudges and craftwork of my clumsy manuscript were much appreciated.

Chris Nardo, I am in awe of your talents. The cover is amazing and without your fabulous publishing skills, Alfredo would still be sitting on my PC gathering dust. I can never thank you enough.

To my readers, thank you for getting this far on the journey with me. I hope you enjoyed reading Alfredo as much as I loved bringing him to life. If you did enjoy my novel, could you please take a minute to leave a kind word or two on Goodreads or over on my Insta and FB pages *@a_pocket_full_of_Prosemary*. I would appreciate the effort and I will read them all.

ABOUT THE AUTHOR

Rosemary Garreffa is an Australian author and a member of Australian Society of Authors. Originally from the Mallee, she lived for a short time in South Australia before settling and raising her family in Euston on the Murray River in New South Wales.

The family owned and run second-generation vineyard, and her marriage into an extensive Italian-Australian family, her numerous children and grandchildren give her endless material and character traits for her work.

Her short story titled Mack won first place in a competition run by The Creatives Journal in July 2020 and brings back the days of living on a farm with dams.

Rosemary, fuelled by her love of all things genealogy, travelled through Europe, England, and Ireland in 2016 & 2019 investigating the family roots, soaking up atmosphere and settings to feed her other great loves of writing and art.

Her first novel Alfredo explores what it might be like to be a Guardian Angel and how having one such creature assigned to us as humans, might influence our lives for the better – or worse. Walking the streets of Paris, visiting the cathedral, and the little five-hundred-year- old flat behind the door next to the chocolate shop – home for five glorious days – was all it took to cement the scenes for her. A second novel, an historical fiction, is her work in progress. Based on her own great-great grandmother's life, Rosemary hopes all the skills learnt from researching missing family members will bring Annie to life for the reader.

Rosemary's writing calls her readers to see how the past connects to the things of the moment and how our lives are influenced by the actions of others we can never know.

www.ingramcontent.com/pod-product-compliance
Lightning Source LLC
Chambersburg PA
CBHW020910130726
47904CB00006BA/1797